Volinette's Song

By
Martin F. Hengst

A Magic of Solendrea Novel

Martin F. Hengst
PO Box 86
Windsor, PA 17366
www.martinfhengst.com

Ordering Information & Quantity Sales: Special discounts are available on quantity purchases by corporations, associations, and others. For details, contact the author at the address above.

Printed in the United States of America

ISBN: 978-0692201084

First Edition

14 15 16 17 18 / 10 9 8 7 6 5 4 3 2 1

DEDICATION

This book is lovingly dedicated to my Mother, whose love and support has always been unwavering.

OTHER TITLES IN
THE SOLENDREA SERIES

TABLE OF CONTENTS

Chapter One

"I said NO!"

Volinette pushed the lute back into her mother's arms with more force than she had intended. There was a dissonant twang and snap as the neck of the heirloom instrument broke free of the body.

"Now look what you've done," Reanna said, her lips set in a thin white line. "Your grandfather's lute, ruined."

"I'm sorry." Volinette *was* sorry. She remembered sitting on Poppy's knee, watching his fingers dance across the strings while his rich baritone rolled along with tales of battles long past and loves lost. The memory of those evenings by the fire, listening to him sing and play, were some of the best of her childhood.

Poppy was a famous minstrel, just as her mother was, and her father, and her sisters and brother. In fact, as the youngest child in a family known throughout the Human Imperium for their beautiful music and fine performances, she had been expected to know every word of every verse and every note in every score. That hadn't been much of a feat for Volinette. She seemed to have a head for music. She could almost see the notes as they were being played and hear the poignant words of a ballad in her head a moment before she had to sing them. Her mother said it was a family gift.

Even so, she hadn't wanted to follow in Poppy's footsteps. Music didn't speak to her like it did to them.

The screaming adoration of throngs of fans quickened their blood and pushed them further in pursuit of their art. It just made Volinette nauseous. The first time she'd been up on stage in front of a thousand people, she'd burst into tears and fled to the dark comfort of the trees at the edge of the village.

"I'm sorry," Volinette repeated after a moment's hesitation. "But I'm not Poppy, I'm not Father, and I'm not you. I'm not a bard or a minstrel. I don't want that. I don't want to 'carry on the line.' I want…no, I NEED to do this!"

"Don't be ridiculous." Reanna's voice was sharp but low. Her eyes darted around the courtyard where they stood, checking to ensure that no one had overheard their heated conversation. Her mouth snapped shut as she watched a young man pass by them. He nodded to them, and Reanna offered him a curt bob of her head. "What you NEED to do is stop this foolishness and come home. It isn't too late to fix this mess you've made. Father will help if you'd just go to him and beg forgiveness…"

Volinette stared at her mother in stunned silence. She felt the first prickles of tears behind her jade green eyes and forced them back. She refused to stand here in the shadow of the Great Tower of High Magic and blubber like a little girl with a skinned knee. She'd passed her fourteenth nameday not too long ago. She wasn't a child any longer. It wouldn't be too many more years before she was expected to settle down with a husband and turn her thoughts to adult matters. Even so, the insinuation that she should go crawling back to her father and ask his forgiveness, when he was the one that cast her out in the first place, was appalling.

"Beg forgiveness?" Volinette's voice cracked as the question squeezed from between her lips. "For what? For being a…what did he call it? Oh, yes, I remember. A carnival monstrosity. Please, Father, won't you forgive me for something I can't control and you couldn't beat out of me?"

Reanna's hand moved so fast that Volinette didn't realize she'd been slapped until her cheek began to burn with painful intensity. She raised a hand, her fingers stroking the lightly tanned skin with its almost imperceptible smattering of freckles across her nose and high cheekbones. The flesh was hot, a reminder of the sudden and unexpected assault. The tears that she'd been holding at bay seemed very close now and Volinette fought with every ounce of control she had to keep them from slipping from the corners of her eyes. She was afraid that if even a single tear stole past her guard, she might not be able to stop the deluge that would follow.

Volinette closed her eyes, humming the chorus to her favorite song to herself. The song flowed through her, helping her clear her mind. She could feel the vibration of the song in her throat, and it helped center her in a way that few things did. Once she'd finished the chorus, the threat of tears had retreated, thwarted by the music that steadied her. The music she loved was something private. Something inside her that responded to the melody and the rhythm. Not the flowery, cloying stuff that her family belted out to the wild applause of their fans.

Looking up at the great obsidian tower glistening in the summer sunlight, Volinette smiled. She could feel the power of the place humming just below the surface of the physical realm. The Quintessential Sphere infused all things, flowing outward from the Ethereal Realm and passing through everything. Every blade of grass, every person, every leaf on the trees. The Sphere influenced everything and left an imprint on the world that existed beyond what mortal eyes could see. There was no way she could be sure of winning a place in the Academy of Arcane Arts and Sciences, but she had to try. She was a vessel for the power of the Quintessential Sphere, and the thought of exploring that power, the power that had been forbidden to talk about, quickened her pulse in a way that music never had.

For years she had been forced to keep her communion with the Sphere a secret. Her father was terrified that if people found out about the freakish skills his daughter commanded, it would impact their bookings and the life to which they'd become accustomed. The family coffers were packed with gold coins earned by their musical talents. Though she was expected to contribute, Volinette would sneak away as often as she could, haring off into the wilderness on her own. She was more at home among a quiet copse of trees than a concert.

During the last Spring Festival, they had been blessed with a free night. Volinette's father normally had the family working every night, so the open time was an unexpected pleasure. Sitting around the fire with the other performers who traveled with her family, she'd entertained a few of the children with a couple simple spells. They were no more than cantrips, really. Easy spells that anyone with innate magical talent could master. A tiny firebug that danced to a tune she whistled. A colorful shower of harmless sparks.

Nothing that could have hurt anyone. At least, not anyone other than Volinette. She would never forget the savage beating her father had rained down on her under the pretense of her own safety. No one could know, he'd said. They wouldn't understand. They'd be afraid of her.

After that night, Volinette had realized that her father wasn't afraid *for* her. He was afraid *of* her. She'd also realized that there was no place for her in a family that was more concerned about their reputation than the wellbeing of the people who made the music possible.

Through clandestine meetings with friends and acquaintances made through years of traveling performances, she'd kept an ear out for the news that the Academy of Arcane Arts and Sciences had opened a Trial of Admission. As soon as she'd heard that the School of Sorcery was open to new apprentices, she had gathered her belongings and approached her mother, all but demanding that she accompany Volinette to the Great Tower. All she needed was her mother's mark on the registration chit that would allow her to participate in admission proceedings. Then they could be done with each other.

"You'll be rid of your little problem soon enough, Mother." Volinette was still looking at the tower that pointed up into the heavens, but she spoke to the woman shifting from foot to foot in front of her.

Almost as if Volinette's words had touched off the action, the great silver bell at the top of the tower began to peal, calling those who would compete for a place in the Academy to assemble. Volinette ripped her gaze away from the tower and tried to smooth down the unruly shock of golden-brown hair that seemed to stick out every which way no matter what she did with it. Not that she spent that much time bothering with it in the first place. She hefted the small sack that contained her meager belongings and slung it over one shoulder. Without looking back, she strode toward the entrance to the tower.

"That's my cue, Mother. Time for a performance of my own."

Volinette walked across the courtyard, her head held high, her chin thrust belligerently forward. *Don't show any fear.* The mantra of her family seemed particularly apt in this case, so she grabbed it and rolled with it.

A page met them at the wide doors that led into the massive entry hall of the Great Tower of High Magic. Once inside, he led them through a labyrinth of smoky glass corridors, commenting on various displays, pieces of art, and artifacts as they went. The page was obviously bored with his rote recitation of facts and dates, but Volinette was nothing less than fascinated by the wonders they passed.

The bored young man ushered them into an immense subterranean chamber. Volinette recognized it from descriptions she'd read in books. One advantage to traveling all over the Imperium was that every sizable city had a library where she could lose herself for hours while avoiding her family. Her hours in those libraries were often spent studying all manner of trivia pertaining to the Orders and their trappings, including the room in which she found herself.

This was the High Council's Concordance. She gazed around the room in rapt awe, trying to take it all in at once. Never in her life had she seen such ornate furnishings and decorations. The walls were draped with brightly colored tapestries depicting scenes from the Orders' varied pasts. Each was expertly woven, with meticulous attention paid to every detail. Each hanging that Volinette looked at was more captivating than the last. It was almost as if she were there, inside that moment in time that the artist had chosen to represent.

An exquisite obsidian throne dominated the head of the room. Its intricate detail was the life's work of a dozen master craftsmen and mages, by the look of it. She took a step forward and faltered as she felt its latent power wash over her. She gasped and stumbled backward, finding surer footing where the strange power of the throne didn't affect her as much.

The tables, where the Masters would sit when the Concordance was in session, were arranged in wide semi-circles in front of the throne. There was a hint of roses in the air, but Volinette saw no evidence of fresh-cut flowers anywhere in the room. Large oil lanterns hung from stout brass chains anchored in the glass ceiling, casting circles of pale orange light on the floor and helping to warm the vast chamber.

Volinette ran her hand along one of the tables. They were ancient and worn smooth, almost soft to the touch. She'd often imagined what it would be like to be a Master in one of the Orders. Being in the room where the most important business of the Quintessentialists was conducted only intensified that curiosity.

Becoming a Master in one of the Orders was her heart's true desire. To harness and control the power of the Quintessential Sphere and travel the Imperium to right wrongs and help those in need. However, those days were a long way off. There would be much studying and many trials before that could become a reality.

That was definitely putting the cart before the horse, she scolded herself. She hadn't even been accepted into the Academy yet, and here she was, making grand plans for what her life would be like, as if her success were merely a formality. She battled against that self-doubt, gnawing at her lower lip as she took in the grandeur of the room.

Though she'd been forbidden from practicing her spellcraft in public, she'd stolen as many moments as she could to flee into the depths of the forest to be with her true love. There, at least, she couldn't be seen and punished for such an errant affair. Still, there were many things she didn't know, and within the walls of the Great Tower she would be expected to learn and control real magic. Powerful magic. Forces that could kill.

Volinette shuddered. Her father, when still pretending that he was afraid for her wellbeing, relished in telling the story of a young man from their village who had dabbled in magic he hadn't understood. The spell the boy had been working on backfired horribly, searing the flesh from his skull and killing him instantly. That could happen to you, he'd said to her. Wouldn't it just be safer to ignore this foolishness and do what you were born to do? She'd balked at the very idea.

Once he'd realized that Volinette wouldn't be dissuaded from her passion, he'd given up on her. Even when they crossed paths at home, he barely spoke to her. It was almost as if she'd been erased from his memory. He wanted to be rid of her as much as she wanted to become a Quintessentialist. Though her parents had been very careful to only whisper their fears in the deepest, darkest hours of the night, Volinette had still heard their heated arguments over her. No one in the family would be happy until she was gone. It had made the decision to commit to the Trial of Admission that much easier.

A handsome young man with an unruly shock of brown hair slipped his way through the crowd and came to stand near Volinette. He was tall and lean, with dirt under his fingernails and thick callouses that came from handling a plow. Volinette recognized him from his eyes. They were middling brown, the same color of the mud that caked the lower legs of his breeches. He lived in one of the farming communities that Volinette's family had passed through on their festival circuit. His face was broad and tan, with a crooked smile that made him seem younger than his years. He raised a hand in greeting.

"Hey Volinette! Surprised to see you here. Thought for sure you'd be soloing for the family by now."

Reanna made a strangled noise, but Volinette ignored her. Instead, she raised her own hand, returning the boy's salute.

"Sometimes even the purest note goes astray," she said with a grin. "I'm so sorry, I can't remember…"

"Baris Jendrek, of Wheatborne," he provided with an answering grin. "Don't worry. All us farm boys look the same after a while."

He laid a finger beside his nose and winked at her. A warm flush crept across her chest and up her neck, making Volinette's cheeks burn in a completely different way than they had just a short while earlier.

"Uh oh," Baris said, sobering suddenly. "Show's on."

A reverent hush raced through the room as a diminutive figure in a night-black cloak entered. The sigils on the cloak were silver, but seemed to pulse with a radiance that could only be attributed to magic. The Head Master's silver hair was pulled in a long braid that snaked down her back, standing out against black skin almost as dark as her cloak. It was a stark contrast to the royal purple robes she wore. Volinette knew, again from her beloved books, that there was no other Quintessentialist in all of Solendrea who wore robes of such a noble color. The purple robes were reserved for the Head Master of the Orders, and only the elected leader of the Quintessentialists could hold a claim to them. Maera climbed to the top of the platform and seated herself on the throne.

"Be seated, please." Maera's magically amplified voice bounced off the glass walls, penetrating the mind as well as the ear. She paused a moment, allowing enough time for the potential candidates and their families to settle. Then she continued.

"Welcome to the Great Tower of High Magic. You've traveled from the very edges of the Imperium to see your sons and daughters, your charges and students, participate in the trials that will determine this year's apprentices to the School of Sorcery. Many of these young people come well prepared for the challenges they will face. However, some of them may yet be too inexperienced to prevail. It is to them that I put forth the following warning:

"The tests are not intentionally designed to cause harm. They have been refined over hundreds of years to judge and weigh the aptitude and knowledge of the candidate. They are, by necessity, more challenging than anything you are likely to have faced before. Each of you has the potential to be a future Master within the Grand Orders of Quintessentialists.

"I will not lie to you and tell you that no one has ever died during the trials. Unfortunately, there have been incidents beyond our best laid plans that have caused some hopeful candidates to pay for their dreams with their lives. However, we will do everything within our power to ensure your safe completion of the trials.

"Now is the time for you to decide. There is no shame in stepping aside today and returning later with more knowledge and experience. Decide to stay, or decide to go, but either way, you must make a decision that could change your life forever. Mothers, fathers, siblings, and sponsors, it is time to say goodbye."

Maera stood up and cast an appraising eye over the crowd before sweeping down the small staircase and out of the room. Her exit seemed to spark a low murmur of excited conversation. Volinette dared to look at her mother for the first time since the Head Master had entered the room. Reanna's lips were still set in the thin white line that they'd been in since they had been outside in the courtyard. There was a fluttering lurch in Volinette's stomach, but she forced it away. She'd already made up her mind.

"Come, Mother, it's time to finish what I've started."

Volinette wove her way through the milling crowd toward an elderly Master standing near the doorway that led out of the High Council's Concordance. In one arm, he hefted a stack of parchment. In the other, he held an ornate quill. He smiled at her as she approached, and Volinette felt another flutter of uncertainty.

"I'd like to register for the Trial of Admission," she said with more confidence than she felt. "What do I need to do?"

Chapter Two

As a young girl, when Volinette would listen to the tales told of the Great Tower of High Magic and the powerful Quintessentialists that helped to protect the Human Imperium from all foes great and small, she would imagine that the registration all mages were required to go through when they came of age was a romantic rite of passage.

She was sorely disappointed when she discovered that the registration process was far more mundane than she'd ever imagined. After declaring her intention to participate in the Trial of Admission, the elder Quintessentialist directed her to leave the High Council's Concordance and proceed down the hall to where a Master would be waiting to assist her with her registration.

The Master turned out to be a man with glittering black eyes set too close together over a pointed nose. Volinette thought he looked a bit like a mouse and had to bite back a giggle when the irreverent thought popped into her head. The Master glowered at her, and she forced herself to put forward an appropriately sober appearance.

"As guardian or sponsor of the young person in question, do you release her into the care of the Academy of Arcane Arts and Sciences until such time as she is accepted into one of the schools *or* is returned to her home as an unsatisfactory candidate?"

Though the Master's voice matched his mousy appearance with uncanny precision, Volinette wasn't tempted to laugh this time. Instead, she looked to her mother. If she intended to interfere with Volinette's wishes, this would be her last opportunity to do so. Once she was released into the care of the Academy, there was no legal way for her family to interfere with her any longer. Even if she washed out of the Academy without being chosen for admission to any of the schools, she'd still technically be an Apprentice of the Orders. That meant, in the eyes of the One True King, that she was an adult and capable of making her own decisions. Never again would her parents have any say over what she did, where she did it, or whom she chose to associate with.

Reanna's lips returned to the same thin, white line that they had been in for almost the entire visit at the Great Tower. For a moment, Volinette was sure that her mother would force her to return home, to re-enter the life of virtual servitude as one of the players in the family business. She was surprised when her mother gave a curt nod to the Master.

"I do so release her into the care of the Academy," Renanna said to the Master. Then she turned to Volinette. "I hope you know what you're doing, Volinette. You know that your father will never welcome you back into his house after this. Are you sure this is what you want?"

There was a tiny part of Volinette that wanted to go back with her mother. To turn her back on the power she could feel thrumming at the base of her spine and go back to a 'normal' life. Or, at least, as normal as her family's nomadic existence could afford her. That, at least, she knew. It was familiar. If she continued with the Trial, nothing would be familiar again. There was so much that she didn't know that she would have to learn.

In the end, the tingle at the base of her spine, the subtle caress of the Quintessential Sphere, convinced her to face the unknown. She wanted to see what could happen. If she stayed with the family, her only prospects were working as a second-rate performer or working with the crowds. Volinette knew she would spend her life supporting better performers, like her brother or her sister Taryn. Father had said over and over that Taryn was going to be the best voice to come out of the family in generations. Why bother to compete with that when she could explore something that no one else in her family would ever do?

"I'm sure, Mother." Turning to the Master, she said, "I'm ready to participate in the Trial of Admission."

A small smile twisted the corner of the Master's mouth as he shook his head.

"Not just yet, youngster. There's much to do beforehand." He nodded to Reanna, his smile gone. "You've released your daughter into the care of the Academy of Arcane Arts and Sciences. You are dismissed."

The Master turned on his heel and began walking down the corridor. It took Volinette a moment to realize that she was supposed to be following him. She took a few steps and stopped, glancing over her shoulder at where Reanna still stood, motionless. She almost felt bad for her mother. She doubted that Reanna Terris had often been dismissed from anything, for any reason.

The Master cleared his throat, and Volinette hurried to catch up, stealing one last glance over her shoulder. This might be the last time she ever saw her mother. When she looked back, Reanna was striding up the hall in the opposite direction. It seemed they'd both made their choices.

"This way please," the Master said, directing her into a small office off the corridor.

Once she was inside, he closed the door and went to sit behind a cluttered desk. Stacks of parchment and paper littered the work surface, and towering bookcases lined every inch of wall space in the cramped office. Without seeming to look, he reached up, plucked a sheaf of papers from one of the bookcases, and sat them on his desk. He popped the cork from an inkwell and rummaged about in the drawer for a quill pen that Volinette was certain he'd been using since his days as an apprentice. It was far more drab and utilitarian than the quill the Master in the hall had been using.

The Master dipped the quill in the ink and hovered his hand over the first page of his stack. At last, he looked up at her, seeming surprised to see her still standing near the door where she'd stopped upon entering the room. He motioned to the chair across from his desk with the tip of the battered feather.

"Sit, sit. There's much to do before you can begin the Trial. Name?"

"Volinette Terris."

"Place of Birth?"

"Dragonfell."

"Date of Birth?"

"20th of Wyrna, 5764"

"Are you here of your own free will, without coercion or bribery?"

"I am."

How long the questioning went on, Volinette couldn't guess. She continued the rote recitation of facts about her family, life, and childhood until the Master seemed satisfied that he'd checked every box in his stack of forms. Finally, he took a shaker of white powder from his desk and sprinkled it over the ink on the papers. He stacked them and set them aside, then folded his hands atop his desk.

"Very well, Volinette Terris of Dragonfell. You've been registered in the records of the Six Orders."

"Okay." Volinette chewed her lower lip, debating whether or not to unleash the torrent of questions that was raging in her head. "What does that mean?"

"All potential Quintessentialists are registered with the Six Orders by decree of the One True King. It's Imperium law that anyone capable of tapping into the Quintessential Sphere be instructed by the Academy of Arcane Arts and Sciences to control their power. Those that refuse to register are considered rogue mages and face censure by order of the King."

"Censure?"

The Master snorted.

"Didn't have too many Quints where you come from, did they girl? Censure is the horror that all mages fear in the night. Censure cuts your ties to the Quintessential Sphere. That feeling in the pit of your stomach, that almost impossible to hear buzz in your head that connects you to all things, imagine having that severed."

The Master made a motion with his hand, like a pair of scissors cutting off a thread, and Volinette shuddered. She hadn't realized that her connection to the Sphere was something that could be reversed. Though she'd thought she was going mad when she first realized she could feel the pull of all things, the intertwining of the infinite number of threads that intersected in the Quintessential Sphere, she couldn't imagine being without it. No wonder the Master described it as a nightmare.

"I never introduced myself, girl. My name is Fulgent Casto. You'll be my responsibility until the Trial begins. So if you've any more questions, now's the time."

"When does the Trial start?"

"Not for a few hours yet. All the candidates are busy being interviewed and registered, just as I did with you. That takes some time."

"What happens when it starts?"

Fulgent waved a finger at her with a tolerant smile.

"I can't tell you that. There are things you're just going to have to figure out for yourself. You'll be placed into a holding area with the other candidates before the Trial begins. From there out, you're on your own."

Volinette swallowed audibly, and the Master settled back in his chair, a grin showing his yellowed teeth.

"I will give you a bit of free advice, Volinette. Play to your strengths and keep your head. A lot of the candidates, especially the youngsters, tend to freeze up when they get out on the Trial Field. Remember to breathe and remember to move, and you'll be fine."

There was a loud pop, and Volinette shrank back from the sudden noise. A shower of sparks, every color of the rainbow, cascaded down over the desk, flickering out just as they reached the cluttered surface. Volinette blinked a few times, as if by that motion she might rid herself of the hallucination she was obviously having.

A tiny creature, about a foot tall with rapidly beating pearlescent wings, was hovering over the desk. It appeared to be a miniature woman, with skin so pale that a fine pattern of faint blue veins could be seen tracing up and down her bare arms and legs. Her hair was a shade of red that would have been more appropriate on a ripe strawberry than on a living, breathing thing. She wore short breeches and a tiny tunic that would have been too small for the dolls Volinette played with as a child, yet they were finely woven with intricate details almost too small to see.

She spun in a lazy circle, the gentle breeze from her wings buffeting the papers scattered about the desk. Volinette was surprised at the size of the thing's eyes. The violet orbs seemed to be much larger than they really were, drinking in every detail in the room. She almost felt as if those eyes could see right into her soul, and the thought sent a shiver up Volinette's spine.

At Volinette's involuntary chill, the creature smiled at her, revealing two rows of sharp teeth. Volinette wanted to bolt from the office, but Fulgent was still slumped back in his chair as if this were an ordinary occurrence.

"What?" Volinette asked, but couldn't manage to get more than that single word from her suddenly dry mouth.

"Not what," Fulgent corrected. "Who. Good day, Lacrymosa. Are they ready for the candidates?"

"Yes, Master Casto," the creature replied in a voice like a songbird. "Head Master Maera asks that you have Volinette join them in the antechamber."

"Very well. That's sooner than I expected. Volinette, this is Lacrymosa. She is of the Pheen."

"Pheen aren't real," Volinette blurted.

"I'm very real, thank you very much," Lacrymosa said, landing on the surface of the desk and stamping one foot. The tiny creature's eyebrows drew together in a scowl. "Maybe you're not real!"

Fulgent chuckled.

"You're scaring her, Lacrymosa."

"Am I scaring you?" Lacrymosa asked, cocking her head to the side as she looked at Volinette.

Words seemed too difficult to procure and she didn't want to offend the Pheen, so Volinette just nodded. Lacrymosa flicked her wings to her back, walked to the edge of the desk, and plopped down, sitting across from Volinette with her tiny legs crossed one over the other.

"I'm sorry, child. There's no reason to be afraid. I have no desire to harm you."

"But…a Pheen? Why? How?"

"I find humanity fascinating, don't you? I came to study humanity and I've just never found a good reason to leave. I like it here."

Volinette glanced toward Fulgent, who shrugged.

"She's been here as long as our written history has been recorded," he said with another shrug. "Who's going to argue with a god?"

Lacrymosa snorted.

"The Pheen aren't gods. We serve the will of the Eternals."

"The will of the Eternals?" Volinette asked. It seemed that every moment she remained inside the Tower, there were two more questions she wanted answers to. Was this how the rest of her life was going to be? A constant stream of unanswered questions?

"No time for an answer, even if she'd give you one," Fulgent declared, pushing himself to his feet. "We need to get you to the Trial Field. Lacrymosa, will you please tell the Head Master we're on our way?"

"Of course, Master Casto."

With a loud crack and a shower of sparks, Lacrymosa disappeared from view.

"She certainly knows how to make an exit," Fulgent remarked as he opened the door to the office, motioning for Volinette to proceed him into the corridor beyond.

"Does that always happen?"

"What's that?"

"The light and sparkles and bang?"

Fulgent chuckled.

"Oh yes, she's quite theatrical about the whole thing. She swears that it's a function of the way the Pheen manipulate the Quintessential Sphere, but I think she's probably just pulling one over on us. Not like we'll be able to call her out on it. Unless another Pheen comes visiting sometime soon."

"Which isn't likely to happen?"

Fulgent stopped in the threshold of the doorway and gave Volinette a quizzical look.

"No, not likely. Lacrymosa's the only Pheen to ever reveal herself to us, the lowly humans. There are those in higher circles who question whether she's actually Pheen at all, but I prefer to believe she's being honest with us. I'm not sure she has anything to gain by lying."

Further discussion of one of the most powerful species in Solendrea was interrupted by their insertion into the teeming chaos in the corridor beyond. It was clear that Volinette's summons hadn't been the only one. Scores of hopeful candidates were moving up the hall alongside their proctors. Fulgent took her gently by the elbow and led her into the mass of bodies making their way to the Trial Field. A strange sensation flashed up her arm, and she glanced at Master Casto.

"Remember, just play to your strengths and do the best you can," he was saying, but Volinette could barely hear him over the incessant fluttering of the butterflies in her stomach. She was sure his advice would come in handy, but she just couldn't force herself to focus on what he was saying when they were so near the beginning of the next chapter in her life.

Light blossomed up ahead, dazzling her eyes and making purple spots dance in her vision. Then they were outside, milling about in a sandstone courtyard on the far side of the Great Tower. A low stone wall ran around the perimeter of the courtyard, a space wide enough that even the largest crowds that had come to see her family perform could have fit into it with room to spare.

Volinette turned to thank Fulgent for his encouragement, but he was gone. In a minor panic, she scanned the faces around her and found that all the proctors had left their charges. They were on their own now, Volinette knew. They would prevail and be accepted into an ancient and prestigious order of mages. Or, they'd fail and be returned to their hometowns to live out their lives as people apart. Marked by something greater, but not allowed to call on the talent that would beckon to them like a forbidden mistress for the rest of their lives.

A hard knot of resolve began to form in her stomach, displacing the fluttering butterflies for the most part. She needed this. There was no way she could return to her family now, not after seeing the magic and wonders the Great Tower held for those that lived and worked there. A tune came to her, a heroic march well-suited to the challenge she would soon face.

"Would you *please* stop making that racket?" a shrill voice asked from behind her. "Some of us are trying to concentrate!"

Volinette hadn't even realized she'd been humming to herself. She turned to see who had taken such offense at the simple tune and found she was being stared at. A girl with a blonde topknot stood behind Volinette, her arms folded across her ample chest and eyes the color of cut sapphires blazing with indignation. Beside her was a smaller, younger, copy of the girl. She had the same topknot, the same blonde hair. Only the eyes and the softer expression convinced Volinette that the smaller girl wasn't an exact replica of the taller, surly creature that was still staring at her.

"I'm sorry, I didn't realize—"

"No, I'm sure *you* didn't. The rest of us did, though. Right, Tenika?"

The blonde girl turned to her copy, who nodded dutifully. "Right, Janessa."

"Well, I said I was sorry." Volinette made to turn away, and Janessa caught her by the arm. That same strange feeling flashed through her arm. A tingle, almost a shock. It was the same as she'd felt when Master Casto had taken hold of her elbow.

"You might not be serious about making it through the Trial, but we are. My sister and I are going to be the youngest Masters to graduate from the School of Sorcery, aren't we, Tenika?"

This time the younger girl's nod was accompanied by a grin and a show of her skill. Tenika held out her hand, summoning a ball of flame that hissed and spat. The fireball rocked in the palm of her upturned hand before she tossed it toward Janessa, who caught it with both hands. She turned to Volinette, opening her hands and displaying a perfect sphere of ice.

"We've been doing this since we were born. How about you?"

Volinette suddenly felt as if she wasn't ready to be here. She'd only been practicing her command of the Quintessential Sphere for a few years, and even then, only when she could steal away from her other duties to hide some place she wouldn't be discovered. These girls not only had skill, but they obviously had come from a family that knew about and embraced their magic. That was an advantage that Volinette couldn't hope to compete with.

She muttered something under her breath, hoping that the less than forthcoming answer would convince Janessa and her sister to go elsewhere. She was to have no such luck.

"What? Speak up! You'd think someone who can hum so loud would be able to speak properly."

Janessa turned to Tenika and they laughed. They laughed far too long and too loud for a joke that wasn't even funny, and Volinette was very aware of others turning to look in their direction. Her cheeks burned with the flush of blood that had crept up her neck and prickled at the back of her eyes.

Volinette clamped down on that urge right away. They might embarrass her as much as they could, but she was not going to allow them to see her cry. Fleeing, however, wasn't out of the question. She turned on her heel, preparing to put as much distance between herself and her tormentors as possible, and nearly ran over Baris.

"Hey! Careful now!"

Baris's startled exclamation brought a renewed round of howls from Janessa and her sister, who were now slapping their thighs and pointing at Volinette as if she were the funniest thing they'd ever seen.

Recovering quickly from the surprise, Baris cocked his head at Volinette and cast a critical eye upon her.

"Everything alright, Volinette?"

"Fine," she managed through gritted teeth. "I was just going to find somewhere else to ready for the Trial."

"Because of them?" Baris peered over her shoulder at the sisters, who were now huddled together, conversing in conspiratorial whispers.

"Yes, please, just let me go."

"No place to run in the Trial," Baris said in a firm, but not unkind voice. "Can't let others push you to the outside. What got them started?"

"I was humming to myself. They said I was disturbing them."

"A little humming got them riled up, did it?" Baris asked, his eyes sparkling. "Wonder how a proper duet would do them."

"Baris!"

"Volinette! You remember *The Power and the Blood*, don't you?"

"Of course."

Leave it to Baris to choose the ballad that her father had forced her to sing at festival every year. The story of a young girl torn between duty and love had always been a favorite of Volinette's. It was one of the only things that made performing at her father's demand even marginally tolerable.

Without missing a beat, Baris launched into the male part of the duet. His voice was throaty and rough, better suited to singing work songs in the field or tavern tunes than a delicate duet usually reserved for the finest minstrels and bards.

Still, when the moment came, Volinette found herself responding to the prompt of the song, picking up the fragile descant, raising her voice and singing from deep in her belly, as she was taught to do so long ago. She lost herself in the story of the song, feeling it burst from within her soul as if it had been imprisoned there. The hairs on the back of her neck stood on end as they sang together, their verses chasing each other until they finally reached the final note, which echoed away across the courtyard.

An explosion of cheers and applause erupted around them, making Volinette jump and clutch at Baris until she realized that it was the other candidates and the crowd beyond showing their appreciation for the impromptu song. A flush crept across Volinette's face and she grinned, offering a self-conscious wave for those who were still clapping or pointing at the pair.

Volinette glanced behind her and saw Janessa and her sister, their faces twisted in matching grimaces. She and Baris might have entertained the rest of their contemporaries, but Volinette realized now that there would be no appeasing those two. It would be in her best interests just to avoid them altogether.

"Just ignore them," Baris said when he saw the direction of her gaze. "There's no pleasing folk like that."

"I was just thinking the same thing." Volinette smiled. "Thank you for that, Baris. I'm feeling much better now."

"My pleasure, Volinette. Any time." He winked at her, then scowled. "Just remember to keep an eye on them. The Tower is a big place, but not so big you'll be able to get around them forever."

"Mother always says you catch more flies with honey than with vinegar."

Baris shrugged.

"Maybe, but some flies bite. Best not to catch those at all."

Chapter Three

The crowd that assembled at the edges of the stone wall to witness the Trial were no less boisterous and excited than those who had come to the music festivals Volinette had attended all her life. They shouted good-natured advice and encouragement from the sidelines, though most of what they said was torn away by the distance and the low drone of the candidates murmuring to each other.

A sudden hush fell over both crowds as a figure emerged from the depths of the Great Tower. The Head Master had returned to oversee the administration of the Trial. Her black cloak, emblazoned with arcane symbols and runes in silver, seemed to drink in the light of the sun, making her appear larger than she really was. Maera was a titan who was only a bit shorter than Volinette herself. Her dark skin was a stark contrast to the whiteness of her teeth, which shone in a wide smile as she waved and acknowledged both the apprentices-to-be and the spectators who were in attendance.

Maera's amber eyes, unlike any Volinette had ever seen, danced with uncontained excitement as she swept into the center of the courtyard. She raised her hands for silence, an unnecessary gesture, as the hush that had begun at her entrance continued unbroken. She dropped her hands, spreading her arms out in front of her, encompassing everyone standing in the courtyard. A shiver went up Volinette's spine as she realized the gesture included her. This was it. This was the moment that could change the rest of her life forever. Either she'd succeed and leave the field today as an apprentice to one of the Great Orders of Quintessentialists, or…she wouldn't.

Volinette cut off that line of thought. This wasn't any time to doubt why she'd come so far, or what she was fighting for. Still, there was a voice in the back of her head that wouldn't shut up. *Only a musician,* it said, *and a half rate one at that. Never as good as your brother. Never better than your sister. Never quite good enough.*

She gave her head a violent shake, trying to rid herself of the voice that was both nagging her and preventing her from giving her full measure of attention to the speech Maera had begun. Janessa must have noticed the motion, because out of the corner of her eye, Volinette could see her smirking. If nothing else, Volinette didn't want to give the girl the satisfaction of her discomfort. She schooled her features, forced her mind to order, and focused on the magically amplified words of the Head Master booming out across the Trial Field.

"Candidates, the time has come to put all your practice into action. Those who have opted to sit out this year and return later have been removed from your ranks. Those you see around you are those who you fight against for your entry into the School of Sorcery."

The Head Master raised a warning hand and swept her disconcerting gaze around the field. Volinette felt it slide over her, as if she'd been doused in cold water, and wondered what magic could imbue a simple look to make it feel so foreboding.

"That said, I offer you the following warning: though the Trial of Admission is intense, you are not to turn on each other. Any candidate found using their magic against their fellow mages will be immediately expelled from any consideration within the Academy and will face censure as punishment for their dishonor. Though you compete against each other, you must always remember that you fight for the greater good of the Order to which you eventually swear your loyalty and to the entirety of the Imperium."

Maera glanced around the crowd a second time, her gaze seeming to linger longest on the few people who seemed to be bored or disinterested in the entire process. There was a boy and his friend who had been talking in hushed tones throughout the entire delivery, and Volinette wondered how arrogant one had to be to speak at the same time as one of the most powerful mages in the Imperium was speaking.

Sudden doubt flooded through her, a torrential downpour of uncertainty. What had she been thinking? At least up on the stage, her brother and sister were there to take the worst of the criticism. Now she was on her own, standing in a field full of strangers who wanted the same thing she did. What if they wanted it more? What if they were better? What if they were stronger, or faster, or, or, or! When the Head Master spoke again, it was with a grave finality that made a shiver run up Volinette's spine.

"Once the test begins, the arena will be sealed. You have only your magic to protect you, so use it wisely. There is room for eight of you to enter the School of Sorcery. The last eight of you to remain standing on the field of battle will enter the Academy this year with the remaining candidates from other Trials. Do you understand?"

Volinette and the other candidates nodded, indicating their acceptance of the test that was about to begin. The courtyard was quiet as a grave as the last echoes of Maera's instructions died away.

"Good. Let the Trial of Admittance begin."

The silence was shattered by a crack and rumble, like nearby thunder. Maera had disappeared from the courtyard and only the candidates remained.

The hairs on the back of her neck stood up and Volinette looked skyward, sensing the presence of the magical dome that had been erected to contain the Trial of Admittance. It was like a smudge in the sky, a blurring of the air that made the spectators at the edge of the field appear as if through eyes just emerging from a deep sleep and not yet wiped of the night sand that sometimes accumulated there.

A terrified scream snapped Volinette's attention back to the task at hand. Tenika stood a short distance away, one hand covering her mouth as if she could reverse her scream. The other arm was locked in a rigid line. Volinette followed the direction the girl was pointing and saw a skeleton clawing its way out of the earth, its empty eye sockets alight with a sinister orange glow. A quick glance around her, and she saw other skeletons popping up like spring blooms of terror, shuffling toward the candidates who seemed frozen, lost, uncertain of what to do.

Volinette forced her feet to move, separating herself from the hesitant mass of her colleagues. Across the dome, she could see Baris hurling miniature bolts of light at the desiccated corpses, detonating them in bursts of bone fragments and dust.

One by one, the others were catching on, each fighting according to their own talents. Janessa arched her fingers above her head, drawing a ball of magical flame from the air and sending it slamming into her foe. She crowed in triumph. *Her practice must be paying off now,* Volinette thought with no small amount of bitterness.

She felt icy fingers clutching at her flesh and whirled to find herself staring into the face of death. Dropping to her knees, she rolled away from the creature's grasp. She vaulted backward, a dance movement that often thrilled the crowds, and ended up standing behind her attacker. Volinette wove an intricate pattern in the air with her fingers while speaking words of power. She called on a very powerful memory of a beautiful spider she'd once seen spinning a web in the crevice of a barn door. She felt the power of the Quintessential Sphere flow through her, an icy river burning within her veins. Strands of tacky webbing flew from her fingers, cocooning the skeleton. Enshrouded in strong silk, it teetered and fell to the ground, unable to move.

Volinette stared at the spot where the shrouded form lay. It seemed almost impossible that she'd done that. Still, it had happened and she'd managed to save herself from the attack. A scream nearby told her that there was no time to rest.

Looking over her shoulder, she saw a pair of menacing undead fall on a boy younger than Volinette. The boy panicked, shrieking and trying to run from the creatures clawing at him. There was a burst of light and

Volinette had to look away. When she glanced back, both the boy and the skeletons were gone.

As the candidates managed to destroy the skeletons, more horrific creatures appeared. Noxious trolls materialized from out of thin air and entered the fray, their battle-axes swinging in wide arcs of death. Volinette watched in horror as a boy no older than twelve was cleaved in half at the waist, the wicked blade spilling his entrails onto the cobblestones. Volinette felt sick. Not even the finest cleric could heal a wound of that magnitude. The boy and his attacker vanished in another burst of light.

The candidates split into pairs, trying to deal with the new threat in teams. Volinette cast a web around one of the trolls, but it broke free without any effort. The trolls were much stronger than the skeletons had been. Volinette concentrated on the cold snows of winter, calling a cone of razor-sharp ice from the Quintessential Sphere and directing it at her target. The troll roared as shards of frozen water tore into its flesh. Gouts of thick gray blood spurted from the wounds, making the sandstone courtyard dangerously slick.

Volinette felt something hit her foot and looked down to see the head of a troll that had rolled across the courtyard. She jumped back involuntarily, not knowing she was stepping into the path of a swinging ax blade. Baris tackled her, dropping them to the ground just as the blade swung overhead. Janessa stepped over them, flames from her hands reducing their attacker to a pile of cinders.

"Awful time to fall for me," Baris quipped.

Volinette flashed him an apologetic glance and then rolled from under him. He sprinted away as she got to her feet, ready to fight. Almost all of the trolls had been destroyed, and she waited to see what new horror the test had in store for them. The butterflies in her stomach were almost too much to bear.

Nothing happened. Volinette and the others looked around, surprised not to be the target of a new onslaught. It seemed, at least for the moment, that they were out of immediate danger. That was almost worse on her frayed nerves than the steady pulse of the expected attack had been.

Baris was crouched nearby, waiting. Janessa, her sister, and some other girls were crouched by the edge of the dome, waiting like animals penned for slaughter. Deciding there might be safety in numbers, and not liking her chances with the girls, Volinette turned toward Baris.

As she approached him, her feet sank into the stone, throwing her off balance. That wasn't right. She struggled with the thought. How could she sink into stone?

A magical spring had welled up in the center of the courtyard, seeping through the pavers. The apprentices watched, waiting for a water demon or sea monster to leap out at them. Nothing emerged from the water, but the spring did not stop flowing. In fact, the flow increased, reaching the edge of the magical barrier and lapping against it. A sudden geyser of water erupted, spreading outward like a raging river. Panicked though she was, Volinette made herself focus on creating a bubble of breathable air in the midst of the swirling tempest.

Tenika was nearby, tears streaming down her face as she tried again and again to pronounce the words of power that would save her from the new threat. Her eyes were wide with panic and her voice had taken on a jabbering quality, as if she were trying to cast any spell that came to mind. Volinette wanted to help her, but the flow of water had increased yet again, waves crashing against the edges of the dome and racing back toward them. There wasn't enough time to save everyone. Volinette finished her spell just as the water reached the top of the barrier.

Candidates that hadn't protected themselves quickly enough thrashed about in the water, their eyes wide with terror. Then they were still. Their bodies bobbed in the water around her, and she couldn't understand why they hadn't vanished like the others who had been struck down during the trial. Volinette's stomach turned as Tenika's body floated past her bubble, drifting in an unseen current, her eyes wide and staring. The girl's fingers were curled into claws, as if she'd been in the midst of a spell when the water had overtaken her.

As quickly as it had appeared, the water began to evaporate, like a puddle in summer sunshine. Volinette allowed herself to be carried to the ground, releasing her control over the bubble and allowing it to dissipate. She was cold, wet, and tired, but she knew she couldn't give up. There weren't many of them left, which meant that the test was almost complete.

Many of the remaining candidates scurried to and fro aimlessly, trying to cope with the horror that had been inflicted on them. The ground began to tremble with the force of an earthquake. Huge rocks thrust up from the earth, moving under the accord of some supernatural power. Volinette stood rooted in place by fear as a huge stone elemental pulled itself out of the earth.

The creature was monumental, easily twenty-five feet high, its limbs the size of massive tree trunks. The monster swayed uneasily for a moment before stumbling toward a couple of candidates cowering at one edge of the dome.

They scattered. Two younger men paired up to throw lightning at the huge elemental, but succeeded only in chipping its stone skin. With a shriek that threatened to split her head, the elemental slammed a fist into the boys, killing them instantly, and leaving a red smear on the stone where they'd been standing. The force of the impact was enough to throw the others to the ground.

There were eight of them now, Volinette thought, scrambling to her feet and doing a quick count of the candidates left in the courtyard. The test should be ending! She ran to the edge of the dome and peered out. Through the haze she could see the Masters running along the circumference of the barrier, tracing intricate symbols in the air. She could hear their shouts, but she couldn't make out what they were saying.

It wasn't supposed to happen this way! The test was supposed to be over when there were eight candidates left. Volinette once again felt icy claws of panic tighten around her stomach. Could the Head Master have lied about the test?

Most of the others had lost all composure. Baris stood behind the elemental, his eyes filled with blank confusion. Janessa was crouched by Tenika's body, weeping. Across the field, Volinette could see a group of candidates pounding on the barrier with their fists, shouting, unaware that the elemental was approaching.

Volinette gathered breath to shout a warning, but a single clear note came instead. Sudden inspiration struck her. An otherworldly voice whispered in her ear, like chimes in the wind. Maybe all her years training in music could be useful after all! She took a deep breath from the belly and let the song burst forth. The high sweet notes of an old folk melody cut through the terrified screams of the candidates. Volinette raised her arms, calling forth the power of the Quintessential Sphere, braiding streams of energy together and binding them to the rhythm of her song.

The elemental stopped and turned toward the sound. As Volinette continued to sing, she could feel her power growing. It filled her, tendrils of ice in her mind and soul, and spilled out of her, sparking and shimmering in the air around her. It felt as if her blood was boiling, the pleasure-and-pain combination that washed over her whenever she cast a particularly difficult spell.

Stretching her hands out before her, she released her control, letting the magic merge with her melody. A few premature sparks showered from her fingertips but she paid them no heed, concentrating instead on the song bursting from her lungs. The magic would come. It would heed the call of her song. She was sure of it, though she didn't know why it seemed like such a certainty.

As she reached an ear-shattering crescendo, there seemed to be a solid, pulsing shaft of energy linking her to the elemental. The last note of the song echoed across the courtyard. There was a flare as bright as the sun. The elemental exploded, showering Volinette and the rest of the candidates with pebbles and stone dust. Unable to remain on her feet, she collapsed, spent. Baris was with her in a moment, on his knees next to her.

The barrier collapsed and the Masters rushed into the courtyard, calling for clerics and healers as they reached the few apprentices who remained.

Volinette curled herself into a ball, unable to move. She felt as if all the bones had been torn from her body, and her head throbbed to the beat of an unseen drum. Baris was saying something to her, but she couldn't quite make out the words. It wasn't until the Head Master appeared that she managed to almost be able think again.

Maera dropped to her knees beside her.

"Are you alright?" Maera asked urgently, her eyes blazing.

"I don't know." Her answer seemed tactless, but honest. Volinette didn't have the strength for tact. Then, remembering that she was participating in the Trial, she added, "Did I pass?"

One of the Masters standing beside them chuckled in spite of the circumstances.

"She's going to be a handful, Maera."

The Head Master looked at her and smiled.

"My girl, you did much more than merely pass. The elemental wasn't part of the test. Nor was the flood."

"It wasn't?" Volinette shuddered, unable to control the new fear that overwhelmed her.

"It wasn't. Someone in the group, we don't know who yet, manipulated the Trial with magic they couldn't control. They obviously wanted a place in the Academy very badly. The elemental you defeated was not a test, but a very real, very powerful magical monster."

A chill ran up Volinette's spine but she managed to squelch her fear. After all, she had been triumphant.

"Not only did you defeat the elemental," Maera continued, "but you saved the other apprentices from a gruesome fate. The Masters have agreed that you need more instruction, but that your place is here, with other mages. In keeping with such bravery in the face of danger, the High Council has decided that you should advance immediately to become an Acolyte in the Order of the Ivory Flame."

"An Acolyte?" Volinette squeaked, unable to believe her ringing ears.

"Yes, you'll need to train with the rest of the apprentices for a time, but you'll progress much faster than they will. You're a natural. Now is the time for rest, girl. There will be plenty of time for you to start your lessons tomorrow."

Maera stood and left Volinette to the ministrations of the healer who approached them.

Volinette lay in the courtyard, thinking. She knew the history records well enough to know that she was the youngest Acolyte in the Order's history. Perhaps now her mother could be proud. Not only had she gained entrance into the School of Sorcery, but also she had found a way to keep her passion for music alive. Her father could say many things about her, but not that she was a failure.

As they lifted her in a litter, Volinette drifted off to sleep, secure in the knowledge that she would always have both music and magic.

Chapter Four

Any dreams of a grand entrance into the Great Tower of High Magic after her Trial were dashed by the fact that she was carried, on a litter, to the infirmary by two orderlies who seemed totally uninterested in telling her anything about where they were going or what was going to happen to her when she got there. They repeatedly told her to relax and lie still, and that was all. Fortunately, the trip across the Academy grounds to the squat brick building didn't take all that long.

The interior of the building wasn't much more exciting than her attendants had been. Pale green walls were illuminated by bright oil lamps. Healers and clerics bustled to and fro, calling to each other in a language that was most certainly common, but favored terms Volinette had never heard before. However, they seemed both confident and proficient, so she resigned herself to their care, even if she felt as if all she needed was a really good nap.

The orderlies moved her from the litter onto a bed in a small cubicle. They pulled a curtain across the entrance of the small room and then disappeared beyond it, leaving her alone without any further explanation of what to do or what to expect. Volinette's stomach sank. All in all, a rather banal entrance into the place that should have been an exciting start to the rest of her life.

She glanced around the small room. There was the bed on which she'd been placed, a simple wooden chair, a small table, a basin and pitcher of water, a lamp on the wall, and not much else. Beyond the curtain, she could hear other people speaking in hushed tones. They were quiet enough that Volinette couldn't make out what they were saying, so eavesdropping, rude as it might be, was out as a means of entertaining herself while she was detained. Even though the cubicle was graced with a window that let light into the cramped space, it was too high up and beside the bed, which made it impossible for her to see what was beyond. Maybe if she stood on the chair…

With a bit of a struggle, Volinette managed to sit up, then realized there was a reason they'd carried her from the trial field. Her head swam and her vision went gray around the edges. Her gorge rose and she flopped back against the pillow before the nausea could get the better of her. She scrunched her eyes closed, fighting with all her will not to be sick. After a few moments, the queasiness passed and she was able to take a deep breath, which further calmed the raging storm in her stomach. She opened her eyes and yelped in surprise. There was a young woman standing in her cubicle.

She was dressed in a simple white linen tunic, with a sea foam green sash tied around her narrow waist. Her oval blue eyes flicked over Volinette from head to foot, and she felt as if she were being weighed and measured. When the woman in white brushed her straw yellow hair back from her forehead, she tucked it behind ears that rose to a gentle point.

"You're…" Volinette managed, but then the capacity for speech departed and seemed unwilling to return upon command. Instead, she sat there with her mouth working soundlessly.

"An elf, yes," the woman replied, the corner of her mouth turned up in a little smile. "You may call me Qadira. I'll be attending to you while you're here in the infirmary. How are you feeling? Any pain? Any sickness?"

"I'm sorry," Volinette stammered, her cheeks going red and the tips of her ears burning as if they were on fire. "That was tactless. I mean, I'm pleased to meet you."

"It happens often, but my questions are more important. Any pain? Sickness?"

"I felt ill when I tried to sit up," Volinette admitted with no small amount of hesitation. "I had to lay back down."

Qadira nodded.

"I should think so, young Acolyte. You've been through quite an ordeal today, but we'll see you through the worst of it."

A commotion from outside the cubicle's curtain drew Qadira's attention and she raised a finger, indicating that Volinette should wait. As if she had anything better to do. Even straining, Volinette couldn't make out the hushed argument that was being conducted just beyond her door. She clenched her fists and savaged the bed sheet between her fingers. She was close to everything but couldn't understand anything. It was infuriating.

Qadira reappeared, smoothing the lay of her tunic with long fingers. She took a deep breath and let it out in a long sigh, as if she were trying to regain her composure. Volinette raised an eyebrow, but the elf shook her head. The elven woman's eyes, a bright shade of amethyst, sparkled with anger, but not directed at Volinette.

"Nothing for you to worry about, Acolyte. What happens beyond that curtain is my problem, not yours."

When Qadira approached the bed, she seemed to glide instead of walk. It was almost as if she'd floated from the doorway to where Volinette lay. She laid a cool hand on Volinette's forehead.

"Ow!" Volinette exclaimed. She jerked away from the touch as pain lanced through her temples.

"I'm sorry," Qadira said, inclining her head in apology. "Link shock is always worse when you've recently overextended your abilities. Even so, it needed to be done, but it's over now. You can relax."

"Link shock?"

"Haven't you ever touched another mage and felt a tingle or burning in your fingertips?"

Volinette thought back to the first time she'd met Baris. Clasping his hand in greeting had sent a tingle running up her arm, but she'd paid no attention to it at the time. Then there was the touch of Master Casto and later, Janessa. Even so, it was certainly nothing like what she'd felt when Qadira had touched her forehead.

"Yes," the girl admitted slowly. "But I didn't know what it was."

"That's link shock. It's the power of the Quintessential Sphere jumping between two vessels."

Volinette blushed again. There was a great deal she needed to learn before she could fulfill her dream of becoming a Master. Still, Maera had made her an Acolyte just based on the outcome of the Trial of

Admission. Surely that meant something, that she had something unique about her.

Qadira reached up and turned down the wick on the lamp, lowering the light in the small room to just that which came in through the high window.

"You need to rest. I'll be back soon with something to eat."

She'd pushed out through the curtain before Volinette could protest. The thought of eating anything made her stomach roil in a way that reminded her of the near sickness she'd just recently overcome. Determined not to let it get the best of her, Volinette settled back against the pillow and closed her eyes. Perhaps if she were able to get a little nap in, she'd feel better by the time the cleric returned.

Volinette was just about to drift off to sleep when the rustle of the curtain announced a visitor.

"Forget something?" she asked, without opening her eyes. Qadira seemed as if she'd be able to take a joke, with her quick smile and lively eyes. Anything to help pass the time would make Volinette happy.

"I'll never forget you, or what you've done. She's dead and it's all your fault. Maera may think you're something special, but I think you're just a murdering piece of filth, and I'll make sure you pay."

Volinette's eyes snapped open and she saw Janessa standing at the foot of the bed. Her face was flushed, her eyes squeezed into narrow slits that never wavered from Volinette's gaze. Janessa's arms were straight down to her sides, her hands balled in fists so tight that it was easy to see the whiteness of the knuckles where the skin was drawn taut across them. Her hair was free of its topknot, dirty and tangled. The cut sapphires of her eyes were dark now, deep blue shards of ice that bore into Volinette.

"I...I mean," Volinette stammered. "I'm sorry. I couldn't—"

"You could have saved her," Janessa spat, her lips curled in a snarl. "You could have, but you didn't. You saved yourself, and now Tenika is dead!"

Janessa's voice had risen from a threatening whisper to a harsh cry that seemed to explode from her chest like a startled crow. Volinette pressed herself backward into the pillows. Janessa stepped around the foot of the bed, approaching Volinette with malice glittering in her icy blue eyes. Volinette tried to scream but all that came out was a raspy squawk. Janessa was almost on top of her when the curtain was yanked back and a figure appeared in the opening.

Fulgent Casto stood in the doorway, his black eyes burning with an intensity Volinette could feel from several feet away. His mousy appearance had been transformed by the palpable power that was oozing off him in waves. The Quintessentialist now looked less like a mouse and more like a mean street rat out for blood. His bushy eyebrows were drawn together over his eyes, which darted back and forth between Janessa and Volinette. In that moment, Volinette was sure that the mage hadn't missed a single detail in the scene that was unraveling before him.

"Apprentice Janessa," he said, his voice sharp. "You were told not to leave your cubicle. You'll return there at once."

The girl whirled on him, her hair standing out from her head like an aura. Her eyes had taken on an intensity that matched his. When she spoke, her voice was little more than a malevolent hiss. Power sprang up around her, pushing back at the force that had entered the room with Fulgent.

"Who are you to tell me what to do, Fulgent? Do you know who I am? Who my parents are?"

Janessa raised her hand as if to strike the mage, and there was a flash of crimson light so bright that Volinette had to shield her eyes with her hands. She heard Janessa's cry of pain and a loud clatter as the girl was thrown into the stand that held the pitcher and basin. The pitcher rocked free and crashed to the floor, shattering in a hundred pieces and spraying water everywhere.

When Volinette dared look again, Fulgent was standing over the fallen apprentice, his long forefinger outstretched and pointed in her face.

"I do, indeed, know who you are, Apprentice. Your parents would have done well to raise you knowing better than to raise your hand to an elder. I believe I've filled the gap in their education. However, if you're particularly stubborn, or stupid, I will be happy to provide another demonstration if necessary."

"No, thank you," Janessa grunted, scrambling to her feet. She shot a last dagger-laden look at Volinette before turning toward the open curtain. "If you'll excuse me, *Master* Casto."

The simpering familiarity in Janessa's tone turned what should have been an honorable title into something just shy of an insult. She slid sideways past the Quintessentialist and disappeared down the corridor beyond. Before Volinette could say anything, Qadira appeared with a laden dinner tray.

"And what happened here?" Qadira asked. With one hand, she slid the tray across Volinette's legs. With the other, she tucked another pillow down behind her, propping her up sufficiently to eat.

"Nothing I couldn't handle, Qadira." Fulgent waved a hand and the pieces of the pitcher leapt off the floor and reassembled themselves. With a flick of his wrist, he settled the restored vessel in the basin and brushed his palms against his robes. He flicked a hand at the scowl Qadira was giving him. "Don't start with me, Elf. You do magic your way, I'll do it mine."

"A mage's power isn't to be used in place of honest labor," Qadira retorted.

"Yes," Fulgent agreed. "And I remember teaching you that when you were yet a whelp, so in this case, listen to your old teacher when I say that I was just sparing someone a nasty cut on one of those shards."

Fulgent winked at Volinette and indicated the floor with an outstretched finger.

"That water will need to be cleaned up before someone slips. I'm sure you don't need a mage's power to pick up a mop."

"Get out," Qadira snapped. "Out. Out. Out! I have a patient to attend to."

"Then perhaps you should see to it."

With another wink at Volinette, Fulgent slipped from the cubicle and slid the curtain across the door. Qadira disappeared and returned a moment later with a mop, which she used to clean up the spill while muttering under her breath in a light, lilting language that Volinette couldn't understand.

Instead, she focused on the meal the cleric had brought her. There was a bowl of rich brown broth, a hunk of crusty bread, and a cup of water. Even that meager repast seemed to be too much. Volinette lifted the bread from the tray, turning it over in her hands as if she were seeing bread for the first time.

"Tsk," Qadira said with a sigh. "You're supposed to eat it, not play with it."

Volinette glanced over at the elf who was leaning on the mop. Qadira's eyes were bright, but Volinette couldn't figure out if it was in amusement or annoyance. Perhaps both. Determined not to make another enemy in the Academy, Volinette dipped the bread into the rich broth and took a bite.

Much to her amazement, her stomach not only accepted the offering, but demanded more. For having felt so sick so recently, Volinette was surprised that her hunger had returned with such force. It wasn't long before she'd finished the meal that Qadira had brought her, right down to draining the last few drops from the mug of water.

The cleric, who had gone to attend to other charges while Volinette ate, returned with a promptness that made her wonder if Qadira wasn't using magic to attend to her.

"No magic here," she said with a smile, as if she was reading Volinette's thoughts. "Just many years in service of my trade and craft. One develops a second set of senses when they're practiced long enough. Just like a singer's voice, no?"

Volinette's back went rigid at the question, and Qadira raised an eyebrow at her.

"How did you know?" Volinette stammered, the tips of her ears going red with embarrassment. She'd thought she'd have some sort of anonymity in the Great

Tower, but now that she thought about it, she didn't know why she'd had such a notion.

"I've seen your family perform at the spring festivals, Volinette. You're hardly the first young person to enter the Great Tower with hopes and dreams of leaving their past behind."

The cleric lifted the thin blanket from the foot of the bed and spread it across Volinette, tucking the ends under her with deft fingers.

"Don't worry," Qadira said, smoothing down the worst of the wrinkles in the blanket. "Your secret, such as it is, is safe with me. Everyone deserves a second chance. Now get some rest."

Volinette felt as if there should be something else to say, but in the few moments that it took her to wrap her mind around Qadira's words, the cleric had turned down the wick on the lamp for the second time and retreated from the cubicle, drawing the curtain closed behind her.

A glance at the high slit window showed Volinette that evening had descended over the Imperium. The sounds of the infirmary had quieted to a distant murmur, and Volinette suspected that the other patients were being put to bed in much the same way that Qadira had treated her.

Without much else to do, Volinette nestled down into the bed and closed her eyes. It wasn't long before the quiet shuffling of the healers and the muted sounds of the hospital lulled her into a fitful sleep.

When her dreams came, they were disjointed fragments of the Trial and its aftermath. The boy who'd had his intestines spilled. Crimson streaks on the stone from where the boys had been smashed by the elemental. Pressure, the water that had flowed over them, ripping many of the candidates from the lives they were fighting for. Tenika's body flowed past her again and again, the glazed eyes staring at her in mute accusation.

"You killed her!" Janessa's unseen voice shouted. "You did it! Murderer! Filth!"

Volinette sat bolt upright. Silence blanketed the ward. Not even a quiet conversation shattered the stillness. Night outside the slit window was pitch black. Morning wouldn't come for several hours yet. She rolled over, willing with all her might to fall asleep. Eventually, she did.

Chapter Five

After a couple days in the infirmary, Volinette was convinced that she was falling behind the other students who had been in her Trial of Admission, and that she had become, she had to admit to herself, a whiny mess of a child. Qadira had taken this shift in attitude with the same grace and aplomb that she had shown since Volinette had first met her.

"None of the others of your class have moved on from their time in the infirmary yet, either, Volinette." Qadira's tone was calm, meant to be soothing, but Volinette found that almost even more infuriating. "You will all be released when the last of you is ready for instruction. Until then, you are my guest here."

Though Volinette ground her teeth at the restriction, she had to admit that there were worse ways in which to be kept captive. After the first day, she'd be allowed to roam the gardens that surrounded the ward where she was kept. Afraid of going out of her mind with boredom, she had asked for something to do, and Qadira had allowed her to help with some minor tasks like cleaning vials and folding linens. It was during these tasks that Volinette learned that very few of her classmates had escaped the Trial unscathed. Some were wounded more seriously than others, but all were recovering well under the skilled hands of the clerics who had been assigned to their care.

Volinette wasn't upset, however, the morning that Qadira entered her cubicle and informed her that her stay within the infirmary had come to an end.

"Get out," the elf said, though not unkindly. "This bed needs to be put to better use, and the rest of your class is ready to move on. You're to assemble in the Apprentice's Instruction Room."

Now that she was faced with leaving the safety of the infirmary, Volinette found herself balking at being moved on in such a perfunctory manner.

"Are you sure I'm ready?" Volinette's voice cracked, and Qadira smiled.

"You've been ready longer than most, Volinette. Besides, it isn't as if you'll be bereft of a friendly face. Master Casto is your class advisor.

"Fulgent? That doesn't sound so bad."

"No, Master Casto." Qadira waved a finger at her. "Remember that you're a Quintessentialist now, Volinette. You'll be expected to adhere to the ancient laws and customs. Including the respect due your elders."

Volinette blushed and Qadira grinned.

"Don't worry so much, Volinette. You won't be the first apprentice to forget a title or an honorific. You'll be fine."

"But I'm not an apprentice," Volinette protested. "I'm an Acolyte, in an Order. What if they expect me to know more than the apprentices?"

Qadira clucked her tongue.

"I'm sure the Head Master has her reasons for placing you as she did." The cleric trailed off, leaving Volinette sure that there were other thoughts left unvoiced. "Master Casto and the others will ensure that you know everything you need to know."

No amount of additional hedging would prevent Qadira from pushing her out of the small cubicle in the infirmary. The cleric gave Volinette a rudimentary set of directions that would lead her back to the instruction room and then all but shoved her out of the door. Volinette wondered if the sense of foreboding that settled into the pit of her stomach was what baby birds felt when they were shoved unceremoniously from the nest into the cruel world.

As Volinette made her way through the gardens and courtyards of the Academy of Arcane Arts and Sciences, she looked at the Great Tower and began to fully appreciate the beauty of the obsidian monolith that would dominate her days until she finished her instruction.

The Great Tower of High Magic was the pinnacle of Quintessentialist achievement. A towering construction of glass crafted from the nearby beaches of fine black sand that gave the city its name. It had taken the life's work of hundreds of mages to create the maze of walls, rooms, and caverns that had become the central pillar of all magical knowledge within the Human Imperium.

"Hey! Watch where you're walkin'!"

Volinette, consumed as she was by the awe and beauty of the tower, had walked right into a young man stocking a cart that sat on the path toward the building that housed the School of Sorcery. She stumbled backward, tripping over her feet, and landing hard on her rump. The stall-keeper was crouched by the cart, picking up the fruit she'd carelessly scattered and brushing off the worst of the dust on the plain tunic he wore belted around the middle.

"I'm so sorry," she stammered, scrambling to help pick up the round red fruit she'd knocked from the cart.

The young man took the fruit from her trembling hands and dropped it, without ceremony, back on the pile. He offered her a hand, helping her to her feet.

"Fresh meat, huh?" he asked, casting an appraising eye over her with a twisted grin. "No lasting harm done. Pretty impressive, huh?"

He hooked a thumb over his shoulder, indicating the building that had consumed so much of her attention that she'd forgotten to watch where she was walking.

Volinette blushed, her cheeks going as red as the fruit she'd just helped return to the cart. She tried to reply, but found that the words just wouldn't come. Instead, she stood there under the gaze of the stall-keeper, wishing she could just melt between the stones under her feet.

The young man looked at her a moment longer, then laughed. His guffaw seemed to snap Volinette out of her paralysis, and she gave him a sharp look before she also started laughing.

"I'm sorry," she said, wiping a tear from her eye. "I must seem the total moon-brained fool. I'm Volinette."

"A pleasure, Volinette." The young man thrust his hand out at her, staring at her until she seized it and gave it a good pump.

The merchant plucked a piece of fruit from the basket and shoved it into her hands, folding them over the sphere. He winked at her and nodded toward the footpath.

"I suspect you don't want to be late, so you better hop. Take this. Consider it a gift from the Merchant's Guild."

"Oh, I couldn't."

"You can and you have. Otherwise, you'll have offended me, miss."

Volinette peered at him. He appeared to be completely serious. Not wanting to offend him, she tucked the offering in the pocket of her tunic.

"You're very kind. Thank you."

"Don't mention it. Better move."

The rest of her journey to the classroom where she'd be taking her instruction was uneventful. A squat stone building, built with massive blocks of gray stone, dominated one corner of the Academy grounds. A sign over the doorway declared it to be the School of Sorcery, founded in 3623. For over two thousand years, Quintessentialists had been attending the Academy of Arcane Arts and Sciences. That wasn't daunting. Not at all.

Volinette poked her head into the room and looked around before she dared enter. There were already a few apprentices scattered around the room. Most were alone, but a couple had formed loose knots, banding together against the unknown that faced them. There were a few faces she recognized, but more that she didn't. Stepping into that room seemed as dangerous as walking into the open jaws of a slavering bear.

"Hey! Volinette! You made it!"

The voice that called out to her seemed far too loud for the small room, and a number of apprentices turned to stare at her. She slipped into the room, wishing that her entrance hadn't been noticed by quite so many people. She'd have preferred to enter unnoticed. Unfortunately, Baris had other plans.

"Hello, Baris," Volinette replied quietly. She hoped that the young man would take her lead and lower his voice. "It's good to see you."

"Too right!" Baris slapped his knee. The young man seemed oblivious to the fact that the others in the room were watching his antics and talking amongst themselves. Volinette could only wonder what they were saying, but she doubted it was very complementary. "I'm glad you made it through, always nice to have a friendly face."

"Perhaps we should be a bit quieter?"

"Pshaw," Baris snorted, jerking his head at the other apprentices. "Don't worry about disturbing that lot. They're all just a bunch of temple mice. Live a little, that's what I say."

"Some people don't deserve to live. Even a little."

Volinette and Baris turned at the same time to see Janessa standing on the threshold. The cold malice that Volinette had seen in the infirmary still lurked behind the girl's blue eyes. Volinette took an involuntary step back, but Baris drew himself up to his considerable height. He towered over Janessa, looking down into her reddened face.

"Shove off, Janessa. Tenika knew the risks just like the rest of us. Just because you couldn't save her doesn't mean that it was anyone else's responsibility to do it for you. Maybe you should stop taking out your failures on others."

Janessa's mouth worked slowly, but no words came out. After a long moment, she shoved past Baris and stalked across the room. A group of girls there folded her into their midst and looked back at Baris and Volinette with darkened eyes.

"Don't let her get to you, Volinette." Baris was still looking at Janessa and the girls who had surrounded her. "She's rotten on the inside."

"You know her?" Volinette was surprised. She didn't know Baris all that well, but she doubted that a boy from a farming village would be likely to travel in the same circles as Janessa.

"I know the Navita family by reputation," Baris said with a shake of his head. "Her parents are Masters on the High Council. Purebred Quintessentialists for the last thousand years. Guess all that refined blood didn't save her sister, did it?"

"Baris!" Volinette was aghast at his tactlessness. She was beginning to wonder if having Baris as an ally wasn't just as bad as having Janessa as an enemy.

"What?" He shrugged. "It's true, isn't it?"

He seemed to see Volinette's expression for the first time and ducked his head.

"Alright!" he exclaimed. "I'm just saying she knew the risks like the rest of us. If Tenika couldn't handle the trial on her own, she shouldn't have been there in the first place. If Janessa was supposed to be there to help her, she should have been. It isn't anyone's fault but her own."

"A little compassion goes a long way, Apprentice Jendrek."

Volinette recognized the new voice from the doorway and she hung her head. How much worse could today get? Master Fulgent Casto stood in the doorway behind them. The look he turned on Baris was enough to make even the impertinent former farmer hang his head.

"I don't appreciate her attitude either," Fulgent said candidly. "However, that does not negate the fact that she lost a sister to the Trial, and it would do you well to remember that any one of you could have lost your life in the same manner."

With a final long look at Baris, Master Casto stepped into the room and raised his arms for attention. It took a few moments for the apprentices scattered around the room to recognize the gesture and fall silent.

"Welcome, Apprentices. As many of you know, I am Master Fulgent Casto, and I will be your class advisor until you've ascended into the ranks of the journeymen. This means that we could potentially be together for many years, so I recommend that we try to make the best of our association."

It wasn't lost on Volinette that when Master Casto's gaze swept the room, it lingered longest on Janessa, Baris, and herself. Though she'd made a friend in Fulgent from the time she'd entered the trial, Volinette knew that the kinship they'd shared would not extend to her instruction. He struck her as nothing if not eminently fair. That suited Volinette just fine. The less reason Janessa had to continue her crusade against her, the better.

"Tomorrow, we will begin our instruction in earnest. Today, you will receive the materials you need to begin your instruction in the arts and sciences of the Quintessential Sphere. I will also be dividing you into pairs for certain parts of your instruction. These pairings are permanent for the duration of your time spent here as apprentices."

Please, Volinette begged inwardly. *Please pair me with Baris. Please. Please. Please.*

It took what seemed like hours for Master Casto to make his way around the instruction room, pairing the apprentices off. Volinette's heart sank early on when Baris was paired with a girl named Syble. She'd been one of the three girls who'd been clustered with Janessa after her entrance into the classroom. Volinette caught his eye from across the room, and he pantomimed choking to death behind Syble's back. She couldn't really blame him, but Volinette had greater concerns. The pool of apprentices was dwindling and Janessa hadn't been partnered with anyone yet.

"Volinette Terris," Master Casto said, startling her out of her ruminations. "You'll be partnered with Janessa Navita."

Volinette felt as if she'd been thrown into a fire. Her skin burned from the base of her neck to the tips of her ears. It took every bit of willpower she possessed to keep the tears that prickled the back of her eyes from slipping down onto her cheeks. Why had Fulgent done that to her? He was well aware of the animosity Janessa held for her. How could he do such a thing?

Neither Janessa nor Volinette said a word as Master Casto finished pairing off the apprentices and announcing the partnerships. Nearby, Halsie and Nixi, the other girls who had been clustered around Janessa, were huddled together, talking in whispers. Their continued glances at Volinette made it easy for her to guess what and whom they were talking about.

When Master Casto retired from the training room to retrieve some materials, the girls sidled over to Janessa, clucking conspiratorially.

"What are you going to do?" they asked Janessa, as if Volinette weren't standing a few feet from where they gathered around their friend. "How can they expect you to work with that?"

Janessa smiled and Volinette was reminded of the predatory fish that patrolled the shallows along many of the beaches in the Imperium.

"Oh, I'm sure we can convince her that her talents are better suited elsewhere. After all, she's just a show off. We know who has the real power here, don't we?"

Syble had joined the other girls, forming a loose circle around Volinette. Halsie, Nixi, and Syble snickered at Volinette, and it wasn't until a moment later that Volinette realized that Janessa was muttering the words of a spell. Somewhere behind her, Baris called a warning, but it was too late. A fine green mist crept from Janessa's palms, wafting over Volinette's face.

The mist seemed to claw at her nose and mouth, slipping into her no matter how much she fought against it. The thin green tendrils seemed to wrap around her stomach from the inside, clenching it in a grip like a vice.

Helpless against the power of the spell, Volinette gasped for breath that seemed to burn in her lungs. She opened her mouth to cry out, but the only thing that came was a thick green bile that spilled down the front of her tunic and onto the floor by her slippers.

Janessa and the others crowed with laughter, jumping back away from the mess Volinette was making, unable to stop herself from retching. She collapsed to the floor, doubled over against the pain that wracked her. Volinette was only vaguely aware of

Master Casto's return. He rushed to her side, invoking a counter-spell that eased her misery. However, no spell could undo the humiliation she felt at being cowered on the floor in a pool of her own vomit.

"What is the meaning of this?" Master Casto demanded, still standing over Volinette's pain-wracked body.

"She tried to attack me, Master," Janessa simpered. "I was merely defending myself."

Though Halsie, Nixi, and Syble were quick to back Janessa and her story, Volinette took some reassurance in both the loudness and vehemence of Baris's defense of her. Much to her disappointment, the rest of the apprentices seemed content not to take sides, perhaps afraid of what might become of them if they did.

"You'll need to see the Quartermaster and get new clothes, Volinette," Master Casto said, helping her to her feet. She wasn't so sick that she couldn't see him wince when he helped her up. A fact that only deepened the sense of shame and humiliation she already felt. "Baris will go with you. Return here once you've had time to clean up."

Volinette wanted to argue, to tell him that it was unfair that she should miss out on any instruction because of the unwarranted attack Janessa had made on her. By the time she felt strong enough to say anything though, Baris had a hand under her arm and was guiding her from the training room toward the commissary.

They didn't say much on their way to the Quartermaster's office. Volinette was too angry to form much of a coherent argument, and Baris was smart enough to keep his mouth shut until she'd regained her equilibrium.

The Quartermaster was a stout old man with a huge, bushy white beard and a tunic that bore the faded crest of the Merchant's Guild. After getting a whiff of Volinette, he demanded that they conduct business at arm's length. She was asked for her measurements and gave them, miserably. The Quartermaster disappeared into the back room of the dispensary and reappeared with an armful of garments, which he pointedly handed to Baris.

As they walked back toward the girls' dormitory, Baris flipped through the clothing. There was a simple linen tunic and breeches, both in a natural brown, and a tightly braided rope belt to cinch the tunic closed.

"Not much to look at, are they?" he groused. "No flair, whatsoever."

"I'll just be happy that they're clean and dry."

Of all the ways Volinette had imagined her first day of classes at the Academy, the reality of it hadn't even made the list.

Chapter Six

"I don't know how much more I can take, Baris. She's awful. Every time Master Casto looks away, she's doing something horrid. I just can't take it anymore."

Baris swung his legs and stared out at the waves breaking against the beach. They'd been sitting on the breakwater since mid-morning, and now the sun was nearly halfway to the western horizon. After a long minute, he glanced at Volinette and shrugged.

"Syble isn't exactly an ideal partner either, you know. I have no idea how she got through the trial. It seems like everything she touches turns to dung. She struggles with even the most basic spells. You'll never convince me that she didn't have help getting to the Academy."

"Probably Janessa and her other cronies," Volinette said, wrinkling her nose. "Those four are thick as thieves."

"And just about as honorable," Baris agreed. He picked up a rock from the edge of the breakwater and tossed it out into the waves. They watched it skip once or twice before it sank into the murky water. Neither of them said anything for a long time.

"Still, at least Syble isn't trying to kill you."

Baris chuckled without much humor. He looked at Volinette, his eyes scanning hers.

"Maybe not on purpose," he sighed. "It certainly seems like I get the brunt of her accidents though."

He rubbed his arm just under the sleeve of his tunic where a fresh scar was just beginning to turn pink with new flesh. It'd been a nasty burn, requiring the attention of a cleric and a healer and keeping Baris out of class for two days while the wound was tended to. They had been two of the longest days that Volinette had spent in the Academy. Her interactions with Baris were the only things that kept her sane when she had to deal with Janessa day in and day out.

Volinette took a deep breath and blew it out in a gusty sigh. They'd spent most of the rest day hanging around the docks, and she wasn't very keen to return to the dormitory she shared with the other girls. It seemed so old fashioned and arbitrary that the boys and girls had to be segregated from each other. Still, that was the way things were done in the Academy, and she'd learned that some things just weren't worth questioning.

"I guess we better get back," she said at last, drawing out the words as if by sheer force of will she could slow time and keep from having to go back.

Baris shrugged. "I guess."

They slipped off the breakwater and began the walk back toward the Academy grounds. Baris didn't say much as they wound their way through the streets back toward the school. That was fine with Volinette. She really wasn't in much of a mood to talk anyway. She knew that the night in the dormitory would be just as miserable as every other night had been so far. No sense in hoping that things might be different tonight. She'd just have to deal with it. Shorted sheets, snakes in her bed, her clothing dumped in the privy or hoisted into the trees outside her room. Volinette had to give it to the harpies, at least there was creativity in their evil.

Passing through the Academy gates was their cue to say their goodbyes. Neither of them had much to say, so they just drifted apart as the sun slipped below the horizon, plunging the ornate gardens into semi-darkness.

Unwilling to go back to the dormitory just yet, Volinette made her way into the largest of the gardens. There was an ornate fountain in the center, carved with the likenesses of Quintessentialists long dead. A small bronze placard on the edge of the fountain named the mages who had been immortalized and their contributions to the Academy of Arcane Arts and Sciences. One had been a Master Cartographer, whose maps still hung in the large library. Another had advanced the School of Sorcery to new and exciting heights. A third had been one of the first and most beloved Head Masters of the Academy and a vaunted member of the Order of Ivory Flame.

Volinette plopped down on the edge of the fountain, trailing her fingers through the cool water. How was she supposed to meet her full potential when Janessa was opposing her at every turn? It wasn't that she blamed Janessa for being angry about Tenika's death. She had every right to be upset about that, but there was no reason Janessa should be taking it out on her. Complaints to Master Casto had fallen on deaf ears. It was unfortunate that Janessa blamed Volinette for Tenika's death, he'd said, but it was something she'd need to work out on her own. One couldn't be made to see facts they didn't want to see.

No matter how Volinette tried to explain that Janessa's intentions were more than a grudge, Master Casto's advice was to keep working at a reconciliation. Mages needed to work together, he'd said, pointing to the Great Tower in the distance. How else did we learn and grow? Secretly, Volinette wondered if there wasn't a way for her to grow without Janessa's constant interference.

There was a noise deeper in the garden, and Volinette huddled up against the side of the fountain. Whoever was lurking about out there, she didn't really feel like talking. She breathed a sigh of relief when a page strolled down the manicured path, lighting the lanterns that lined the walkway. At least she wouldn't be required to have a conversation with the page. He had his duties to perform and wouldn't be concerned with her. In fact, as he passed through the courtyard on his way across the garden, he only acknowledged Volinette with the briefest of nods.

The night deepened as she sat there, listening to the gentle babble of the water falling into the pool. Of everywhere on the school grounds, this was one of her favorite places to sit and think. It was quiet and serene and helped soothe the nerves that were almost always frayed to the point of breaking by the end of the day.

"Oh, look, it's the murderer."

Volinette jumped at the cold voice behind her. She whirled to find Janessa standing there with her arms folded across her chest. The three other girls, shadowing their leader, stood a few steps behind, their arms similarly arrayed.

"Oh give it a rest, Janessa," Volinette snapped. She was too tired to be tactful and really didn't care to try anymore. Every day was more of the same, and for Janessa to start up with her on a rest day was just the final straw.

"I'll give it a rest when you pay for what you've done."

Before Volinette could really credit what she was doing, she'd leapt to her feet, inches from Janessa's face. The taller girl took a step back, only registering a moment of surprise before she schooled her features into the sneering mask she normally wore around Volinette.

"I haven't *done* anything," Volinette exploded. "It wasn't my fault that Tenika couldn't handle the Trial. If you were so worried about her, why weren't *you* there to protect her? She was your sister, after all, wasn't she? What kind of sister are you to just let your sibling *die?*"

Volinette was trembling from head to foot. She wasn't sure what had gotten into her, other than she was just so tired of Janessa's attitude and constant accusations. Something had to give. Volinette felt as if something deep inside her had snapped, unraveling in a flood of words that she had no control over. She stood there, shaking, watching the furtive look that Janessa shot to her companions. For the first time, it seemed as if Janessa didn't know what to do about the monster she'd created.

All at once, Janessa seemed to regain her composure. She flicked her fingers forward, intoning the words of a spell that she'd used on Volinette before. This time, though, Volinette was ready for her. The words that came from Volinette's mouth were carried on a melody, a song that she'd known since her childhood, which she'd sung with her family on warm spring nights in front of crowds who bobbed and swayed along with the music. The lyrics, however, were different. Instead of the words she'd learned as a child, Volinette heard a whispered voice in her head, like chimes. She repeated the words as they came to her, weaving them into the familiar notes of the song.

A flash of brilliant white lit the courtyard. Janessa and the others were blown backward, sailing through the air as if they'd been picked up by a giant invisible hand and thrown away from where Volinette was standing. The sudden burst of power left Volinette unsteady on her feet, and she wobbled where she stood, trying to remain upright. Across the courtyard, she could hear the girls whispering to each other in hushed tones. There was some sort of argument, and the others fled from Janessa as the girl got slowly onto unsteady feet.

"You don't know who you're going up against, I promise you."

Janessa stepped back into the light around the fountain, and Volinette saw that her face was stained with fresh blood from her nose and upper lip. Volinette hadn't meant to hurt her or any of the others. She just wanted them to leave her alone.

"I think, perhaps, that you underestimate who you're up against, Apprentice Navita."

Both Janessa and Volinette whirled to face the new voice. Maera was standing at the edge of the courtyard, her rich purple robes seeming to drink in the little light that the lanterns provided. Even from where she was standing, Volinette could feel the muted power that seemed to waft off the Head Master in pulsating waves.

Her amber eyes glittered, unsettlingly bright in the meager light, and they never left Janessa's face.

"Please excuse me, Head Master," Janessa managed to mumble through her split lip. She turned and trotted from the courtyard before Maera could dismiss her. Volinette wondered how the girl could get away with such blatant disrespect.

Volinette didn't trust herself to stand any longer, so she sank to the edge of the fountain, risking disrespecting the Head Master in her own way. She fought back the urge to break into tears.

The Head Master sat beside her, smoothing her voluminous robes around her legs as she perched on the edge of the fountain. It was a long time before she said anything. With each passing moment, Volinette was sure she was going to be kicked out of the Academy. Her journey to become a Master in the Order would be over before it ever really began.

"I know it isn't fair, the way she treats you," Maera said, her voice so soft that Volinette had to strain to hear it over the rushing of the fountain. "However, you must learn to keep your temper. A Quintessentialist as powerful as you must learn to use her gifts only when absolutely necessary."

"I didn't do anything wrong," Volinette replied, with much less tact than she would normally have hoped for. "She blames me for something I had no control over. I can't fix it. I would if I could."

Maera nodded, her curious amber eyes scanning Volinette's face in the faded light.

"Janessa Navita comes from a long line of powerful Quintessentialists. What most people don't know is that, as bloodlines go, Apprentice Navita wasn't blessed with the skill of her parents. She is, at best, a mediocre mage."

Volinette gasped. She couldn't believe that the Head Master, one of the most powerful Quintessentialists in the Imperium, had just laid one of her students and charges out so low. Maera raised an eyebrow.

"I trust in your discretion in this matter, Volinette. It wouldn't do for me to appear to be playing favorites. Even if there is some truth to the accusation." Maera smiled at her. "You remind me of me, when I was your age, young Acolyte. However, that doesn't mean that I can interfere in your training. That is the bailiwick of Master Casto, and if he believes that you should have to stand on your own against Janessa and her ilk, then I must respect his decision."

"It's just so hard," Volinette blurted, the tears coming dangerously close to slipping free of the dam she'd put them behind. "Every day she's just so horrible!"

"Have you ever considered, Acolyte, that she's so horrible because she's jealous of your abilities?"

Volinette's bark of laughter surprised both of them.

"Jealous? Of me? Why? Her entire family has been through the Academy. She was never punished for her magic. She was trained and groomed and knew that she was destined to be a Master from the day she was born. What do I have that she could possibly be jealous of?"

Maera shook her head, a slow smile creeping across her exquisite features.

"There are many things you have yet to learn, Volinette. The likelihood of Janessa Navita ever ascending to the Mastery, in any Order, is exceedingly slim. Advancement in the Academy of Arcane Arts and Sciences isn't all about power. She has power, though it is woefully underdeveloped compared to yours. Power isn't everything, though. She lacks a humility that the best Masters of all the Orders have. Something you have naturally, I might add."

"It doesn't seem to be doing me much good," Volinette groused. She knew she was being peevish, but couldn't help it.

"Neither will feeling sorry for yourself," Maera said, somewhat sharply. "You and Janessa have undoubtedly gotten off on the wrong foot. She accuses you for something that you had no control over. It's up to you to either educate her in the futility of her actions, or learn to live with her in such a way that you can peacefully coexist."

"How am I supposed to do that?"

The Head Master stood, smoothing out the robes that billowed out around her. She glanced at Volinette and gave her a fleeting smile.

"You'll figure it out. I have faith in you. You're a clever girl."

Maera gave her a nod, then stepped into the darkness. Volinette listened until the night and the fountain drowned out the Head Master's retreating footsteps. The sun had slipped beyond the horizon, and now the only light that illuminated the gardens came from the lanterns the page had brought to life earlier.

Getting to her feet, Volinette started down the path that would lead to the girls' dormitory. She encountered no one on her way to her chambers. The common room was empty of Janessa and her entourage. Though she might pay for the night's adventure tomorrow, she doubted that even Janessa was foolish enough to press the matter tonight.

As Volinette got into her nightshirt and slipped into bed, she replayed her encounter with the Head Master time and again. She was stronger than Janessa. Maera had all but said that. However, she'd also said that she needed to control her temper. Volinette was sure that another outburst like the one she'd had tonight wouldn't go unnoticed by the Head Master, and Maera wasn't someone to be on the outs with. In fact, Maera had provided her with a wealth of information in their short meeting. It was information that Volinette was determined to use, but use judiciously. There was no sense in antagonizing Janessa any more than necessary.

Volinette reached over and turned down the wick on her table lamp, plunging the room into darkness. As she nestled down under the warm comforter, she couldn't help but smile. Even if she could never reveal what she knew of Janessa, she had a secret, and that was a power all its own.

For the first time in many nights, sleep came easily and without worry about the day to come.

Chapter Seven

Volinette stood and stretched, her back popping as she extended her arms over her head. She scanned the classroom, hoping to catch Baris's eye before he left. It seemed that he had already escaped. She stifled a sigh. It was harder for her to leave the room, since she and Janessa shared a worktable near the wide desk that Master Casto used as both a demonstration space and a podium for his lectures.

"Can I talk to you for a minute, Volinette?"

It took Volinette a few seconds to register the fact that it was Janessa who had spoken to her. Not just spoken to her, but in a quiet voice that was nothing like the one that she normally used when calling her names or accusing her of murder. Volinette wasn't quite sure what to say. Her mind whirled with possibilities and implications.

"Um. Sure. I guess. What do you need?"

"I just—" Janessa broke off, glancing around the room as if she were afraid someone else would be listening in. She needn't have worried. Everyone else had left the room. Even Master Casto had gathered his belongings from the desk and slipped out before Volinette could free herself of Janessa's attendance.

Volinette stood there, watching Janessa shift from foot to foot and wishing that she hadn't picked this moment to have a heart-to-heart talk. She almost wished that Janessa would go back to threatening her. At least that was expected. This was just, well, strange.

"I wanted to say that I was sorry," Janessa blurted out in a rush, as if she didn't dare pause between the words. "I know you're not responsible for what happened during the Trial, and I've been pretty hung up on it. So I wanted to say, you know, I'm sorry."

Of all the things that Volinette might have expected Janessa to say, offering up an apology for her behavior was probably the last thing she'd have written down on the list. It just seemed too unnatural, especially after so many weeks of Janessa and her friends making Volinette's life as miserable as they could manage without getting caught.

"I, um…I'm not sure what to say," Volinette answered, deciding the honesty was probably the best course to take. On the off chance that Janessa was genuinely sorry for her actions, there wasn't anything to gain by making the process harder for her than it needed to be. "Thanks, I guess."

"I don't blame you for being suspicious. I think I would be too. I don't expect us to be friends." Janessa ducked her head, as if embarrassed by the admission. Volinette just stared at her. "But I wanted to say I was sorry, that's all."

Janessa fled from the room before Volinette could form an answer. She stood there by the worktable for several long moments, staring at the door that Janessa had made her hasty exit through. Baris appeared in the doorway, his eyes wide.

"I wasn't trying to listen in," he blurted. "Did she just apologize to you?"

Volinette nodded. Baris shook his head.

"What did you *do* to her?"

"I didn't do anything to her," Volinette snapped, unsettled by the awe in Baris's question. "I kept her from casting a spell on me, that's all. I protected myself."

Baris shook his head again.

"I don't think that would do it, Volinette. I think you need to keep an eye on her. Apology or not, I don't think she's going to let you off the hook that easily."

"I'll be careful," Volinette said absently. She was still thinking about how uncomfortable Janessa had been during their brief exchange. She wasn't sure Janessa could fake it that well.

"You better be," Baris said, his voice dire. "I still think she's got it out for you."

"You might be right. Either way, I'll be careful."

"Good." Baris eyed Volinette as if he didn't believe her, but he let it go. Volinette was glad he did. She really didn't want to talk about it anymore.

"Why did you come back?"

Baris sighed.

"I was hoping you were hungry," he said, rather plaintively. "I don't feel like eating alone again."

"What? You don't want to sit with Syble?" Volinette knew full well that Baris hated Janessa's shadow nearly as much as Janessa had, until today, appeared to hate Volinette. Still, she couldn't resist needling him over the pairing.

"No! She's a—"

"Baris!"

"Well she is! You should hear the way she talks about Janessa. You'd think that she was the Head

Master or something. It's always 'oh, she's so smart' or 'oh, she's so clever.'"

Baris clutched his stomach and pantomimed retching on his feet. He was exaggerating so much that Volinette couldn't help but to burst into laughter. She wiped the tears from her eyes and clapped Baris on the shoulder.

"I'm so glad you're here with me. I'm not sure what I'd do without you."

"So, you'll come have lunch?"

"Yes," Volinette laughed. "I'll come have lunch. I promise I won't leave you to the ravages of Syble and Janessa's other cronies."

Baris shifted from one foot to the other while Volinette gathered her books and scrolls from the worktable. He was not at all pleased when she wanted to stop at the dormitory to drop off her things, but he kept his complaints to a minimum. It wasn't long before they entered the bustling cafeteria across the courtyard from the dormitory.

Janessa and her friends were gathered together at the farthest table from the door. When Volinette and Baris entered, they bent their heads together in a conspiratorial fashion. Volinette ignored them, instead following Baris to pick up a tray and get in line for refreshments.

They made their way through the line quickly, picking and choosing from the food that was available. The Academy cafeteria employed some of the greatest cooks in the Imperium, or, at least, that's what they were told. What Volinette knew for certain was that there was never a lack of people in the cafeteria, from lowly apprentices up to the Head Master herself.

Volinette and Baris took up seats opposite each other on one of the open tables near the door. While Volinette began to eat, Baris sat with a fork in his hand, staring over her shoulder. It wasn't hard for Volinette to decode his bizarre behavior.

"Let it go, Baris. They're not going to do anything here. There are too many people around. Janessa might not have respect for anyone, but the others are still afraid enough of the Master Quintessentialists to cause too much trouble."

"I guess." He glanced at her tray, seeming to see the food for the first time. "Hey, are you going to eat that?"

Volinette poked him in the hand with her fork.

"Eat your own, you have plenty."

Baris stuck his tongue out at her, but set into his own food as if it was the first meal he'd had in days. They spoke very little as they worked their way through the food and, once finished, deposited their trays in the slot at the end of the long room. A quick glance around the cafeteria showed Volinette that Janessa and the others had left sometime during their meal. That was just as well, she thought. She didn't really want to deal with Janessa again so soon.

"Want to go down to the breakwater?" Baris asked as they stood idle near the cafeteria doorway.

Volinette wrinkled her nose. "No, not today. I heard a fresh batch of ships came in, and I don't want to be upwind of their cargo. I was thinking about going to the library."

Baris wrinkled his nose in an almost perfect mimicry of the grimace she'd just made.

"No thank you. I'll find something better to do with a half-day free of work and studying. I guess I'll see you around then."

She gave him a smile and sent him off with a little shove. Baris was a good friend, but his lack of interest in any learning that wasn't mandatory both aggravated and amused her. He was often the last student into the classroom and the first one out. His objections to self-study were loud and drawn out, often earning the ire of Master Casto. Sometimes lowering the Master to the point where he'd rap the back of Baris's hands with the long willow pointer he carried around while teaching.

Volinette made her way from the cafeteria back to the squat stone building that held most of the teaching rooms for the younger students. Though Master Casto had given them the afternoon off from their studies, not everyone in the Academy was so lucky. There were still many classes in session. She lingered in the hall outside some of the open classrooms, hoping to catch an interesting fact or turn of phrase.

This wasn't the first time that she'd spent a free afternoon just wandering the halls of the Academy. None of the Masters seemed to mind, so long as she stayed out of view and didn't interrupt. She'd been caught on a number of occasions, lurking outside a room listening. Most of the Masters just gave her a smile and a tolerant shake of their head before moving on.

Her favorite classes to eavesdrop on were those that dealt with the history of the Great Orders, famous Quintessentialists, or the struggle the mages faced in the growth and expansion of the Human Imperium. It wasn't unusual for Volinette to hear something she found fascinating during one of her wanderings and then rush to the Great Library and dive deeply into whatever books she could find on the subject.

She stopped outside an open classroom and strained her ears. What she heard wasn't any of the Masters she was familiar with. It was a hushed conversation, not at all like a normal lesson.

"Do you think she's really gone soft?" a girl's voice asked. The voice was familiar, but Volinette couldn't quite place it. She flattened her back against the corridor wall, closing her eyes so she could focus on the softly spoken words.

"I don't know," another girl replied, her voice sharp. "I only heard a little before that simpering fool came back."

"She's very clever," still another girl said. "She has to have a reason. She has to."

Volinette flushed, going red from the base of her neck to the tips of her ears. That last voice was one that she'd be able to recognize anywhere. Syble had a very distinct timbre to her speech, and Volinette could see her in her mind just as clearly as if they were in the same room.

"I still don't like it." That was Nixi. Now that she knew whom she was listening in on, it was easier for Volinette to pick out the girls' voices.

They were obviously talking about Janessa, probably about her apology and attempt at reconciliation. If Janessa's harpies were confused by her actions, maybe they were genuine after all. The girls certainly wouldn't be likely to turn their back on Janessa unless she'd given them a very good reason.

"Let's get out of here. We can talk about it later."

Volinette's eyes snapped open and she scanned the hallway, searching for a way to escape. All of the other classrooms were occupied and closed. She couldn't just barge into one of them to get away from the girls. Their footsteps were getting closer to the door. Forcing herself to move, Volinette turned from the door and walked as fast as she could toward the opposite end of the hallway.

"Well, well, look who it is."

Her flight hadn't carried her far enough. Halsie's sing-song voice echoed down the hallway, making Volinette's spine go rigid. She didn't care for her odds against the three girls. Fighting the urge to turn and face them, she continued on as fast as her feet would carry her.

"Aw," Halsie said, in a voice far too loud for the quiet hall. "The murderer doesn't want to stay and play."

A door opened suddenly beside Volinette and she jumped to the side with a yelp. A Master stepped into the hall, his ornate robes, embroidered with his symbols of rank and station, swirling around his ankles.

"What's the meaning of all this ruckus?" he demanded, first looking at Volinette and then to the girls who were still standing outside the other classroom.

Volinette swallowed hard, trying to clear the lump from her throat. She turned so she could see the girls out of the corner of her eye. Halsie looked to Nixi, then to Syble. Neither of them said anything, they stood still and mute as statues. Halsie sighed, realizing that she wasn't going to get the support she wanted against the Master who was glowering at them.

"Nothing, Master. We were just leaving." Halsie's voice was sickeningly sweet, but the Master didn't seem to notice, or care.

"See to it that you do, then…and keep quiet about it."

Halsie and the others turned and disappeared down the corridor. With a last sour look at Volinette, the Master retreated into his classroom and slammed the door.

She took that as an opportunity to dash down the hallway as fast as she could go. There was no way she wanted to meet back up with the trio, and the sooner she got out of the classroom building and outside the Academy grounds, the sooner she'd feel safe from a chance encounter with them.

She dashed down the cobblestone path and past the North Gate, startling the guards who were lounging against the gate posts. Volinette called an apology over her shoulder, coming up short after she left the familiar territory of the Academy grounds. Being outside the walls of the Academy felt safer right now. In the city, she could escape from Janessa and her friends. Inside the school, there were only so many places she could hide, and those were often frequented by the other Apprentices, Acolytes, or Journeymen. Right now, she just wanted to be alone.

Volinette reached into her pocket, feeling the weight of the few Crowns she had there. The coins didn't amount to a fortune, but she'd earned enough doing odd jobs around the Academy for Master Casto that she was far from destitute. She could stop in an inn, tavern, or halfway house and get a good hot meal and something to drink if she so desired.

There was a narrow alcove in the wall that surrounded the Academy. She slipped into that alcove now, watching the bustle of people as they hurried on their duties around the city. She gnawed on her lower lip, trying to decide what she wanted to do. Curfew was the only thing that would drive her back to the dormitory. She'd have several hours before she had to deal with the other girls again. If she were lucky, maybe she could even make it to her room before the others noticed she was back.

Her hand went to the coins in her pocket again. She and Baris had just eaten, so a meal wasn't appealing in the slightest. Her best bet, as it often was, would probably just be spending the afternoon in the Great Library. It had never done her wrong before, and burying her thoughts in the stories and glories of the past was just the thing that might ease her nerves.

With a destination and a plan in mind, Volinette slipped from the alcove and set out for the huge stone building that housed an entire wealth of knowledge amassed by Quintessentialists since the Imperium had been founded.

Chapter Eight

When Volinette stepped out of the Great Library and onto the wide avenue that ran through Blackbeach, the streets were mostly deserted. The respectable folk of the city had retreated behind closed doors, leaving those few who were still out and about to wander at their peril. She wasn't sure how she'd lost track of the time, but it was the first time Volinette had been out past curfew. Her heart thundered against her ribs as she made her way back to the Academy. She dared not run, lest she attract too much attention, but she walked as fast as she could.

As she approached the entrance to the Academy grounds nearest to the dormitory, her heart sank. The heavy obsidian gates that separated the schools of magic from the rest of Blackbeach were closed. She could feel the guarding magic dancing along the glass bars as she approached. Volinette swallowed hard. Without the right spell or ritual, there was no way she was going to be able to get into the Academy until morning.

"Who goes there?"

Never before had Volinette been so happy to hear such a gruff voice. The guard that peered at her from the other side of the gate was a stocky man, wearing thick leather armor inset with obsidian details. He carried a heavy wooden staff that he could, she had no doubt, employ with deadly efficiency.

"My name is Volinette, Sir. I'm an Acolyte in the School of Sorcery."

"You're out after curfew, Acolyte. I'm not supposed to open the gate for anyone, for any reason."

"Please! This is only the first time I've missed curfew. Surely you missed curfew once or twice when you were being trained?"

There was a bark of laughter from beyond the gate, behind the wall where Volinette couldn't see. The guard glanced over his shoulder toward the sound and made a sour face.

"Quiet, you." He looked back at Volinette, his eyes scanning her from head to foot. "I guess I can make an exception this once."

He raised a hand and spoke a series of guttural words. The gates pulsed with a faint white glow, then retracted into the wall without making a sound. Volinette had squeezed through them before they were all the way open. She turned to the guard and bowed from the waist.

"Thank you! Thank you so much."

She heard another bark of laughter and looked up to see a man as thin and willowy as the other guard was stocky, leaning against the wall of the guard hut just inside the gate. He laid a finger aside of his nose and gave Volinette a conspiratorial nod.

The stock guard wagged a finger at her.

"Just remember that this was just this once. If you get caught outside after curfew again and I'm on duty, you're going to spend the night on the cobbles outside the gate. Understand?"

"Oh, yes, Sir. Thank you very much."

Volinette bowed again and hurried down the cobblestone path that led to the dormitory. Every step of the way, she thanked her good fortune that the house-mother for the girls' quarters was a notoriously heavy sleeper. She should be able to slip inside and get to her room without anyone else being the wiser.

She eased the dormitory door open, careful to slide it past the spot where it stuck and squealed in protest if moved with too much force. She flattened her stomach against the door, squeezing between it and the frame in as little space as she could manage. Once she was inside, she closed the door with as much care as she'd opened it. She pressed her back against the door and closed her eyes, finally able to take a full breath for the first time in what seemed like an eternity.

"Well, well, well, what *do* we have here?"

Volinette's eyes snapped open, though she didn't need them to know who was standing between her and her room. Sure enough, Janessa was standing there, along with Syble, Halsie, and Nixi. Any hope Volinette had of reaching her room without anyone else knowing she had broken curfew evaporated like breath on a winter morning.

"I can explain—" Volinette stammered, but Janessa and the others just laughed.

"You don't need to explain anything to *us*," Janessa said with a wave of her hand. "*We* sneak out after hours all the time. We're just a little, well, impressed that the perfect Acolyte, Volinette Terris, would be caught out after hours."

"You're impressed?"

"Of course," Janessa laughed. "We didn't know you had it in you, did we girls?" She waited just a moment for a murmur of assent from the others and then continued, "What were you doing out so late?"

"I was in the Great Library and lost track of time."

"Oh." Janessa's disappointment was palpable. "Well, I guess to each their own. We were just on our way out. You should come with us."

"Really?" Volinette's head spun. The change in Janessa's attitude was simply too extreme to credit, yet the others, whom she expected to protest, were nodding their heads with enthusiasm. Maybe it wouldn't hurt, just this once…and it would be nice to be included for a change. She'd spent so many nights alone in her room that the prospect of going out and getting into a little innocent mischief was very appealing.

"Yes, it's going to be a lot of fun." Janessa lowered her voice to the barest whisper and made a show of glancing around to ensure they were alone, even though the five of them were the only people in the narrow entrance hall to the dormitory. "We're going to the Hall of Wonders."

Volinette's heart skipped a beat. She'd dreamt of seeing the Hall of Wonders since she'd been a little girl. The Hall was where some of the most impressive magical artifacts in the Imperium were displayed. It was normally off-limits, only opened a few times a year for visiting dignitaries or study by exceptional students.

"Oh, I don't know."

"Come on," Syble said in her sing-song voice. "Don't you want to see? We've been there dozens of times. It's dead simple to get in and out. No one ever knows."

"It really isn't a problem," Janessa agreed. "Unless, of course, you're too scared to come."

"I'm not scared," Volinette protested. "I'm just, well…"

Janessa laughed and shook her head.

"She's too scared. Come on, girls."

Janessa stepped around Volinette and the trio followed, shaking their heads in much the same way as their leader. They eased the door open, and Volinette watched them disappear into the night.

Indecision gripped her. On one hand, she was terrified of being caught in the Hall of Wonders. She wondered what they did to students who they caught in restricted areas. Even so, she couldn't possibly be the first Acolyte to sneak into somewhere she shouldn't be. Syble said it was easy to get in and out. If they'd been in the Hall that many times, surely one more wouldn't hurt.

"Hey, wait for me," Volinette called quietly, stepping past the door and closing it behind her.

The four other girls were standing on the cobblestone path, as if they'd been waiting for her. Janessa grinned.

"I figured you wouldn't be able to resist the temptation. Come on!"

As they wandered down abandoned paths to the tall stone building that housed the Hall of Wonders, Volinette experienced a combination of feelings she'd never felt before. Her heart thundered against her ribs and her palms were slick with a sheen of sweat, but she felt more aware and alive than she'd ever felt in her life.

There were times when living at home that she'd snuck off into the woods to practice her magic. Forbidden as that was, it never filled her with the sense of danger and intrigue that she felt right now, sneaking along outside the edge of the building with Janessa and the other girls. They moved at a snail's pace, their backs pressed up against the cold stone wall.

They walked for what seemed to Volinette like hours before Janessa held out a hand and indicated for the rest of them to stop. Janessa spoke words of power, a cantrip of opening that Volinette and the others had practiced in class. To Volinette's amazement, a large stone slid out of the wall, opening a passage just big enough for the girls to squeeze through as long as they went one at a time.

Syble was the first in, followed by Nixie and Halsie. Volinette paused on the threshold, her nervous eyes darting between the pitch black opening and Janessa, who concentrated on keeping the entrance open.

"Go on," Janessa commanded, her voice made distant by her split attention between the physical and ethereal realms. "I can't hold this forever."

Well, Volinette thought, *in for a fraction, in for a Crown. I've come this far, might as well see it through.*

Volinette boosted herself into the hole, wiggled through the narrow space and dropped down to the cool stone floor on the other side. Janessa followed, nearly landing on Volinette as she dropped. Janessa whispered a few words and the wall sealed itself from the outside.

One of the other girls invoked a will-o-wisp, its pale white light illuminating what looked like a storeroom as far as Volinette could tell. There were crates piled up in the corners of the room and pieces of furniture scattered around like a child's jack-straws. A thick layer of dust coated the room, except for a narrow path between where they stood now and the door at the far wall. If nothing else, the girls' boast that they'd done this many times seemed to be an honest one.

In a perverse way, Volinette was comforted by that disturbance in the dust. If Janessa hadn't lied about that, perhaps the change in her attitude was something Volinette could count on. Growing up in the Terris family had left precious little time for making friends or nurturing friendships. Hours were spent in study and training, and those that weren't spent on instruction were spent on chores or tours. Volinette could count on one hand the number of friends she'd been able to maintain over the years, and Baris was the only one she had any contact with now. Having some girlfriends would be a welcome distraction from the stress of their studies.

Thinking of Baris gave her stomach a guilty lurch. When he found out that she'd seen the Hall of Wonders and hadn't brought him along, he was going to be furious with her. Especially after he'd spent so much time keeping her entertained when she didn't want to go back to the dormitory in fear of Janessa and the others being there.

She shook her head, trying to dispel the nagging feeling. He'd just have to get over it. She wasn't going to jeopardize her newfound kinship with her peers to make sure that he got a look at the treasures on display. Besides, Volinette knew where the secret stone was now. She was sure she could open the secret passage into the building and get Baris in on their own. She'd make sure he got a chance to see everything too.

Janessa was crouched by the door on the far wall, her ear pressed against it. The others stood still as statues, and Volinette did her best to do the same. She felt as if she were still fidgeting, even though she was trying to stand still. The excitement was overwhelming.

"Okay," Janessa whispered. "The corridor is empty. Let's go."

She eased the door open, revealing a passage lit with flickering yellow light. As the girls passed through the door and into the corridor, Volinette realized that the quality of the light was from the oil lamps that hung on lengths of chain that extended down the corridor. These weren't magic lanterns, they were filled with real oil and burned with a real flame. She was so consumed with wondering who would tend the lanterns in the hall that she didn't realize that Janessa and the others had gone off without her.

Volinette walked as fast as she could without making any noise. She caught up with Nixi, who was the last of the other girls, in short order. Nixi glanced at her over her shoulder, and Volinette thought she saw something there, an expression of disgust. The look was so fleeting and so soon replaced by a grin that she thought she must have been mistaken. She put it out of her mind and followed Nixi and the others down the corridor.

They arrived in front of a massive door, the likes of which Volinette had never seen. It was easily ten feet across and looked as if several trees had been uprooted, cut to size, and banded together with thick ribbons of obsidian. It sat in a massive obsidian frame, into which had been incised the sigils of every great Order in the Imperium. These icons glowed with subdued light, and Volinette could feel the power emanating from them, washing over her in waves.

"Isn't it great?" Janessa whispered in her ear, a wide grin across her face.

Volinette nodded, not trusting herself to speak.

"You haven't seen anything yet," Janessa said.

The older girl extended a hand and closed her eyes. Words of a spell that Volinette had never heard tumbled from her lips. The icons in the doorframe grew brighter, pulsing more quickly in response to the spell being cast in their presence. After a moment, Janessa fell silent and opened her eyes.

For a moment, Volinette thought that whatever spell Janessa had been attempting had failed. As they stood in the corridor outside the impressive door, nothing happened. Volinette wanted to ask what they were waiting for, but didn't want to appear the fool, so she waited along with the others.

After what seemed like minutes, the door swung open on silent hinges. The other girls stepped inside without any hesitation, leaving Volinette on the threshold. She looked from the doorframe to the open door, indecision flooding through every part of her. She felt guilty about sneaking into the Hall. She had no permission to be there, but so what if she didn't? This might be the only chance in her life she'd get to see the artifacts stored there. If she didn't do it now, then when?

Mastering her indecision, Volinette steeled her resolve and stepped through the door into the Hall of Wonders. The door swung shut behind her, latching with a series of clicks and clacks that seemed far more ominous than they probably should have. She looked over her shoulder at the door. It was there, closed. Volinette wasn't sure what she was expecting to happen. She put her apprehension out of her mind and turned her eyes toward the interior of the room.

"Oh my," Volinette whispered, her breath caught in her throat.

"I told you," Janessa laughed, no longer bothering to whisper. "It's something, isn't it?"

Chapter Nine

Magnificent was the only word Volinette could find to describe the resplendent beauty of the Hall of Wonders. A miniature sun was suspended from the ceiling thirty feet above, bathing the enormous room in light and warmth. Two to three dozen ornate display cases were laid out in concentric circles, beginning at the edge of the circular room and extending inward to a single large pedestal over which hovered a many-faceted crystal that caught the light from above and flashed every color imaginable.

Artifacts also hung on the walls. Weapons, tapestries, items that Volinette couldn't guess a use for, all were displayed on hooks or pegs that ranged the full height of the ceiling. She turned in a circle, forgetting that the other girls were there as well. There was just too much to see, too much to experience. Every item her eyes landed on was more interesting than the last. She rushed to a display case filled with rocks and crystals. Each had a hand-written card nearby stating what the item was and what importance it held for the Quintessentialists who had discovered it or brought it to the Hall.

Talismans and foci were the subject of the next case, with examples ranging from ancient wands to modern jewelry infused with the power of the Quintessential Sphere. Even separated from the treasures by panes of glass, Volinette could feel the items inside the cases thrumming with muted power, as if they were waiting for someone to come and wield them once again.

How long she spent dashing from one case to the next, Volinette would never be certain. What was plain when she returned to her senses, however, was that whatever brief reprieve she had earned with Janessa and the others had come to an end. Catching Janessa's eye, Volinette saw a malicious glint there that sent a chill up her spine. Her suspicions were confirmed when the girl spoke. Janessa's voice had returned to the cold, near hiss that she'd used with Volinette from the time that Tenika had died.

Too late, Volinette realized that she'd followed them into a trap, all unwitting. She wanted to scold herself for her foolishness, but not before she knew how bad things were going to get. She was outnumbered four to one, and she'd already experienced how cruel Janessa could be. Volinette had no reason to believe that the other girls would show any sort of mercy or restraint.

"Stupid girl," Janessa hissed at her, a malevolent smile spreading across her face. "Did you really think you were going to get off that easily? 'Oh, I understand, you killed my sister, but that's okay.' Honestly. How stupid are you?"

Volinette tried to find words, but her tongue seemed to be fused to the roof of her mouth. The hairs on the back of her neck stood on end and the only thing she could think about was running as fast and as far as her feet would carry her. The realization that she couldn't even do that settled like a cold fire in her belly. She had no idea how to open the door, or where to go after she managed that feat. She hadn't been paying attention to the route they'd taken from the storeroom to the Hall.

"So stupid she can't even talk," Syble crowed, slapping her hands against her thighs. "You were right. She took the whole thing, like a baby from a spoon. Unbelievable."

"She just wants to be accepted," Janessa said with mock sympathy. "Isn't that right, Volinette? Just want to be one of the girls? Not have to hide in your room night after night because of the murdering filth you are?"

Janessa took a step forward. Volinette took an involuntary step back. Still bereft of the power of speech, she knew enough that she needed to stay as far away from the other girls as the limited space in the room would allow. She backed into a display, the edge of the glass biting into the small of her back and making her yelp with surprise.

"Oh, look, she *can* talk, sort of," Nixi laughed.

The other girls had spread out behind Janessa, an impenetrable line of offense that Volinette couldn't hope to escape unscathed. The only hope she had was to make it to the door before they did something horrific. Digging deep, she found the strength to run.

Dodging the case behind her, Volinette ran for the huge door that secured the Hall of Wonders. She didn't need to turn to know that Janessa and the others were right behind her. They'd catch her by the time she reached the door, but maybe, just maybe, she could reach the corridor beyond. If she could reach the corridor, maybe she could call for help. Whatever punishment came from being in a restricted area was sure to be milder than whatever the girls had in store for her.

In the end, Volinette made it to the door. Her hand bushed the ancient wood before a powerful kick knocked her legs out from under her. She pitched forward, her face slamming into the door. She tasted copper and flicked out her tongue, giving the split lip a tentative prod. Blood was also streaming from her nose, painting her cheeks and chin crimson.

Volinette screamed, but Syble clamped a hand over her mouth before anyone could hear. Janessa was by her head, lifting her shoulders and dragging her back into the room, away from the door and any possible salvation Volinette had hoped to find there. Nixi and Halsie followed, a grim honor guard to the sinister scene playing out before them.

"Open her mouth," Janessa commanded.

Syble was quick to follow orders, digging her thumbs into the back of Volinette's jaw and forcing it open. Janessa took something from the pouch on her belt and forced it into Volinette's mouth. A nod from Janessa, and Syble forced her mouth closed, holding it shut with all her strength. Bitter flakes dissolved on Volinette's tongue as she tried to spit them out. Resistance was useless, Syble was just too strong.

A strange lethargy began to spread through Volinette's body. She noticed it first in her fingers and toes. Try as she might to move them, they just wouldn't respond. Next, her arms and legs became leaden. Full-fledged panic raced through her. Volinette was sure that she was going to die. The terrible stiffness spread into her chest, and she wasn't able to move at all. Only her eyes seemed to be unaffected by the poison. They darted in mute accusation from Janessa to Syble and back again.

"You can let her go," Janessa said to Syble, brushing her hands against the legs of her slacks.

Syble released her grip and peered at Volinette with undisguised curiosity.

"What'd you *do* to her?"

"Flakes of Lockroot," Janessa laughed. "She won't be going anywhere for a while. We'll have plenty of time to do what we need to do."

"We better get started," Halsie said from outside Volinette's field of vision. "The guard will be here soon, and we need to be gone before that happens."

Janessa nodded. "Did you bring everything we need?"

"We have everything," Syble said absently. She was prodding Volinette with an experimental finger.

"Then leave her there and let's get to work."

Syble frowned, as if she wasn't pleased to lose a prime opportunity. After a moment, she and Janessa disappeared from view.

Volinette could hear them moving around the chamber. They had moved some distance off and were speaking in the barest whisper, so she couldn't make out what they were saying. The blind panic of being frozen was beginning to wear off. Now that she knew that the poison wasn't going to kill her, Volinette was able to think with a clearer mind.

No matter how much she thought, Volinette couldn't come up with a way out of her predicament. Without her voice, or her hands, there was no way for her to invoke the power of the Quintessential Sphere. Cantrip, spell, and ritual, all were useless without the use of either her voice or her body. She was at the mercy of Janessa and the others, and that wasn't a place she wanted to be.

A blast of chilled air wafted over her and Volinette shuddered. A spark of hope flashed in the darkness of her despair. She tried to wiggle her fingers and toes. They moved! Not much, not enough to cast a spell, but a little. Perhaps the Lockroot wasn't as powerful as Janessa had expected. That could work to her advantage.

As hard as it was, Volinette forced herself to stay as still as she could. If she regained her movement before Janessa and the others finished whatever they were doing, she didn't want them to know about it. The element of surprise might be the only thing she had going for her. There was a shout of excitement from the girls, and Volinette tried without success to turn her head.

Volinette strained her ears, trying to glean any clues she could. Not being able to see what was going on was infuriating. There was a hushed argument, then footsteps. A moment later, a thud made the floor under her shoulders shake. She didn't hear anything else. At first, she thought the girls might be setting her up for another trick, but after a while, Volinette had to assume that they had really left the Hall of Wonders.

Minute after agonizing minute passed, but Volinette found she was able to move her fingers and toes. The cold ache that seemed to have invaded her body was receding. At long last, she managed to sit up, resting her back against the pedestal in the center of the Hall. She took a deep breath, trying to calm the trembling that shook her from head to foot. Whether it was fear, anxiety, or a side effect of the Lockroot, Volinette didn't know. What she did know was that she didn't trust herself to try to get to her feet just yet.

The tune came to her without warning and Volinette seized it as a drowning man would seize a rope thrown by a nearby ship. She hummed the tune under her breath, letting it carry her up out of the darkness that Janessa and the other girls had plunged her into. She whispered words of command, calling on the power of the Quintessential Sphere to infuse her with strength and warmth.

As she finished the spell, she felt as if she'd been dunked in a warm bath. The lethargy that had spread through her body after Janessa's betrayal began to ease. After a while, Volinette felt as if she could stand and managed to get to her feet. She braced herself against the pedestal, easing the worst of the shaking in legs that weren't ready for such exertion just yet.

Something was wrong. Volinette knew that. As she stood there, her hands braced on the edge of the pedestal, she knew that something important was eluding her, but she wasn't able to coax out the information she needed. It was as if the answer was right in front of her, but hidden by a veil of invisibility.

Volinette leaned against the pedestal until her legs steadied. She took a step backward and found that she was far less wobbly than she had been. As she looked out over the Hall of Wonders, the thing she'd been missing flashed into her mind like a lightning strike.

The huge multi-faceted crystal that had been suspended over the pedestal was gone. It was the same pedestal she'd been using to support her weight as she got to her feet, and she hadn't been able to see that it was gone. Maybe she was just too close for it to register.

No matter. It registered now. Janessa and the others had stolen the centerpiece artifact from the Hall of Wonders. Volinette wasn't sure what to do. She needed to tell someone, but who? Who could she go to? Who would believe her side of the story? She wasn't guilt free and she knew it, but there had to be someone who would at least give her the chance to explain what had happened.

Master Casto! The thought came in a flash, similar to the realization that the crystal was gone. Fulgent had always been a fair man, even to the point of overlooking some of Janessa's more obvious flaws, but at least he would listen to her side of it, Volinette was sure of it.

All she had to do now was get to him before Janessa and the others made use of the crystal. Volinette didn't even know what it was for, but she was sure Master Casto would know. Now, her only concern was getting to him and making her side of the story known.

Volinette took a few steps toward the door and remembered her previous encounter with it. She touched her face and dried blood flaked off, lingering on her fingertips. The worst of the damage was corrected by a swipe of her sleeve. The rest she could deal with later. Nothing was broken, though the lip would be sore for a couple days, she was sure.

Before she could move any further, the door swung open. Volinette was stuck to the spot as surely as if she'd been force-fed Lockroot for a second time. The sight of the Quintessentialist standing in the doorway was enough to freeze her where she stood. No spellcraft or herbalism was required.

The mage wore gray robes and a gray cloak, fastened at the throat by a golden brooch. The brooch was what Volinette's mind focused on. It was an eye within a hexagon, within a square. It was the symbol of the Inquisitors, the Quintessentialists who were tasked with the protection and preservation of magic and mages, and those who were called to mete out justice when the laws of the Grand Orders were broken.

The mage pushed back the hood of his cloak, exposing thick black hair shot through with streaks of gray. His blue eyes were frosted in ice as he gazed at Volinette and the pedestal that stood empty behind her. She felt as if his gaze could pierce her soul and see every transgression that she'd ever committed. Never before had she felt so naked and vulnerable.

The inquisitor spoke first, in a voice as cold as the ice reflected in his eyes.

"What is the meaning of this?"

"Wait," Volinette pleaded as the Inquisitor strode forward. "I can explain. Please! This isn't what it appears to be."

"I hope not," the mage said, taking her by the arm. Link-shock surged down her arm and into her chest, making her cry out. The Inquisitor paid no attention. "I hope not, for your sake."

Chapter Ten

Volinette sat squished all the way to one end of the narrow cot in her cell. Thick granite slabs surrounded her, embracing thick steel rods that completed the prison and made her head ache. No windows graced the room, which was no larger than her cubicle in the infirmary had been. Only a dim, flicking light from a torch in the hallway beyond lit the space.

Tremors wracked her thin frame, as much from the cold as from fear of the unknown. She'd never seen anyone as angry as the Inquisitor had been when he'd found her standing in the Hall of Wonders. She'd done her best to explain things on their way to the Great Tower. Her version of events and her pleading for mercy had both fallen on deaf ears. He'd propelled her through the corridors and courtyards with a vice-like grip on her arm. After a while, she gave up trying to defend herself and just went where she was guided.

After what seemed like both an eternity and a blink of an eye, he'd pushed her into the cell, slammed the door closed, and disappeared without another word. How long ago that had been, she could only guess. There weren't any clocks or hourglasses in the cell or near enough to see, and there were no windows for her to see the sky. She would be here until someone decided to let her out.

At least she wasn't alone. In the next cell over, there was a man with wild white hair that stuck out all over his head like a dandelion gone to seed. He hung from the bars as they entered the Inquisitor's dungeon, oblivious of the pain that the contact with the metal must be causing him. He howled and screeched at the Inquisitor, proclaiming loudly and repeatedly that 'they' were coming and that 'they' would kill everyone. The Inquisitor ignored the madman, locked Volinette in her cell, and left the dungeon.

With silent tears streaming down her face, Volinette hugged her knees to her chest and rocked back and forth. She'd done nothing wrong. No, she thought with an angry toss of her head, that wasn't true. She'd done a lot of things wrong. She'd trusted Janessa. That was wrong. She'd gone with the girls to the Hall. That was wrong. She had done many things she wasn't supposed to, but she didn't steal the artifact. They couldn't kick her out of the Academy for that, could they?

As if in answer to her unspoken question, there was a metallic squeal from the corridor. Soon after, she could hear two voices in conversation. They were both men, she could tell from this distance, but she couldn't make out what they were saying. She was almost positive that one of them was the Inquisitor who had put her in the cell.

"Every apprentice in the Academy has snuck into the Hall of Wonders at some point or another, Olin," the unknown voice was saying as it came nearer. "Need I remind you of your own exploits in places where you shouldn't have been?"

"That's not the point, Adamon, and you know it. Sneaking in for a look around is one thing. Theft, especially theft of such a powerful artifact, is something entirely different."

Their conversation stopped as they reached the door to Volinette's cell. They stared in at her like the caged animal she was. She was right. The taller of the men was the Inquisitor she'd had the misfortune of meeting earlier. The other was younger, thinner, and totally at odds with everything Volinette thought of when she thought of an Inquisitor.

His limp brown hair hung down, partially obscuring his storm-gray eyes from view. Instead of the traditional robes of the Order, he wore plain breeches and tunic, both in stone gray, cinched around his middle by a thick leather belt. From the belt hung some sort of contraption unlike anything Volinette had ever seen. There were small brass cylinders in a dozen leather loops that rolled over the surface of the belt like tiny waves. He wore a black traveler's cloak, fastened at the throat by his Inquisitor's brooch.

The younger Inquisitor extended a hand, flicking it to the side as he whispered a word of command. The cell door sprang open, banging into the stone wall with enough force that the sound made Volinette wince. The pain in her head worsened. Just that minor change in the proximity of the metal was enough to make her grind her teeth against the ache in her skull.

"What's your name, girl?"

"Volinette, Sir."

"You understand the depth of the hot water in which you find yourself, Volinette?"

"I do, Sir, but—"

He raised a hand, cutting off her explanation as effectively as the other Inquisitor had done before him.

Would she never get a chance to tell her side of the tale?

"Good. I am Grand Inquisitor Adamon Vendur, of the Order of Ivory Flame. I am the Head Master's right hand in all matters of crime and justice within the Imperium, do you understand?"

Volinette nodded, swallowing against the lump that had snuck into her throat. Even if she had tried to answer, she wasn't sure she'd have been able to produce more than a whisper. Adamon gestured to the older Inquisitor beside him.

"This is Olin Oldwell. I understand that he caught you in the Hall of Wonders when the Transcendental Prism went missing?"

She nodded again. Volinette had read dark tales of mages censured. Like many of the other things she'd heard of, she had gone to the library and found stories of the ghastly ritual and its outcome. Those stories usually ended with the mage dead by their own hand, or mad, roaming the world, forever severed from the rapture that came from their connection to the Quintessential Sphere. Is that why they were here, she wondered? To censure her?

"Very well. You're to come with us."

Adamon motioned for her to leave the cell while Olin looked on. He looked as if he'd just tasted something bitter, Volinette thought. Of the two of them, she decided that she'd take her chances with Adamon. At least he seemed to understand that there were differing degrees of guilty.

They led her from the dungeon and up through the tower. When she had arrived in Blackbeach, the Great Tower in all its obsidian glory had been a source of comfort. It seemed like the only place in the whole of Solendrea where she felt like she might belong. Now she felt none of that comfort. Instead, a sick feeling of fear and foreboding coiled around her stomach, squeezing it with its frozen tendrils.

The stairs leading up from the Inquisitors' level seemed to go on forever. They marched relentlessly upward, passing several other landings. One of which, Volinette remembered, led to the High Council's Concordance. It seemed like a lifetime ago that she'd been sitting at those tables, listening to the Head Master describe the journey she was about to undertake. So much had been different then.

They passed that level, continuing their way up through the tower, into the Grand Entrance Hall.

Under any other circumstances, Volinette would have been mesmerized by the beauty of the entry chamber. Tapestries depicting the rise of the Quintessentialists and their impact on the Imperium were hung from the walls. Displays were peppered around the space, much as they had been in the Hall of Wonders. These, however, didn't just hold ancient and powerful artifacts. They also held intricate urns, the mortal remains of some of the most powerful mages in Solendrea's history. Volinette hadn't noticed that detail the first time she'd been escorted through the chamber. She'd been too caught up in thoughts of what her life would be like once she had been accepted into the Academy. She'd come so far to fall so fast.

They crossed the emptiness to the far wall and stood before what appeared to be a huge brass cage set in the wall of the tower. Adamon yanked the grate open and motioned for her and Olin to proceed him. Once they were inside, Adamon entered and closed the grate. He pulled a few knobs and then yanked a lever.

Volinette couldn't help but shriek when she began to fall. Adamon and Olin exchanged a knowing glance but said nothing. It took her a moment to realize that she wasn't falling. Her feet were still firmly planted on the floor of the cage. It was the cage that was moving. She looked up and saw that they were attached to a pair of chains, each link as thick as a grown man's arm. An opening passed the front of the cage, and Volinette realized they were ascending higher into the tower.

At length, the cage came to a stop and Adamon opened the grate. Volinette and Olin followed him through a twisting maze of corridors, ending at a thick oak door. Adamon unlocked this with a key from his pocket and stepped inside without waiting for the others.

Adamon's office wasn't all that different from Master Casto's, Volinette thought as she entered. The main difference was the amount of clutter. Where Master Casto's office was a study in disorganization, it was clear that in Adamon's space, there was a place for everything and everything was in its place.

The younger Inquisitor took a seat at a wide desk, motioning for Volinette and Olin to seat themselves at a large square table. Adamon took a roll of parchment from the shelf beside his desk and plucked a quill pen from the inkwell on his desk. He wrote at a feverish pace for a few moments, the scratching of the feather across the parchment the only sound in the room. At the end of this burst of penmanship, he looked up at Olin.

"Well?" he prompted the older inquisitor.

"I didn't know you were ready."

"I am," Adamon said, indicating the parchment with the tip of the pen. "And you're wasting time."

"Fine," Olin huffed. "I found this girl, one Volinette Terris, in the Hall of Wonders without permission. The Transcendental Prism was gone when I found her there. I took her into custody and alerted you at once."

"Does she have the Prism in her possession?" Adamon asked, his head bowed toward his work.

"No."

"Did she ever have the Prism in her possession?"

"I…" Olin faltered. "What?"

Adamon sighed, looking up from the paper. He stabbed the feather end of the pen toward the older inquisitor.

"Did she ever have it in her possession, were there remnants or echoes of the Prism around her?"

Olin stammered and turned red. Volinette would have laughed had her situation not been so dire.

"I don't know," he finally admitted.

Adamon looked at Olin for a long time. He reached across his desk and deposited the quill in the well.

"Must I do everything myself?" he asked, but Volinette suspected that he wasn't expecting, nor wanted to receive, an answer.

Adamon extended a hand and commanded the Quintessential Sphere. Volinette felt queasy, as if her stomach had been picked up and tied in a knot. She closed her eyes and the feeling passed. When she opened them again, she couldn't believe what she was seeing.

They were standing in the Hall of Wonders. They were also still in Adamon's office. It was as if someone had sketched the Hall of Wonders over the physical realm. The lines of the walls, the displays, and the pedestal where the Prism had once been all glowed with faint luminescence.

Volinette watched in mute amazement as she saw Janessa, the other girls, and finally, herself, enter the chamber, all of them glowing echoes of their real selves. They moved around the room, just as Volinette remembered. Then they turned on her.

Now they'd understand, Volinette thought with relief. They'd be able to see for themselves that she hadn't had anything to do with the theft of the Prism. For all her bad judgment and admitted trespassing, she hadn't stolen anything.

Volinette rubbed her eyes with both hands. She couldn't believe what she was seeing. In the ethereal echo, Volinette's shade had attacked the girls, knocking them off their feet with spell after spell. After Janessa and the others had lost consciousness, Volinette dragged them out of the room. She reappeared then, glanced around the room, and lifted the Transcendental Prism from its pedestal. She shoved it into the fold of her tunic and with a furtive glance, dashed from the room.

There was another mild wave of nausea as the ethereal projection collapsed. This time, Volinette ignored the sensation altogether. The rage was enough to push it away without any effort on her part.

"That didn't happen!" she shouted, shooting to her feet so fast that the chair she'd been sitting on clattered over backward. "None of that ever happened!"

"Sit down," Adamon said, his voice cold and hard as ice.

Volinette struggled to set the chair on its legs before she sank into it, even more dejected than before.

"I think you better tell us exactly what you think happened," he said, once she'd seated herself.

"I don't *think* anything happened. I *know* what happened."

"Very well then," Adamon said with a sigh. He scrubbed his face with his hands. "Tell us what you know happened."

The entire story seemed to tumble from her in one long sentence. Once she got started, the words flowed like an avalanche, gaining speed and weight as they tumbled from her lips. When she got to the end of the retelling, the moment when Olin had entered the room, she felt as if she'd been running for days. She slouched down in the chair, spent.

Adamon peered at her, his fingers steepled under his chin, but he said nothing. He glanced at Olin, who gave an almost imperceptible shake of his head. Then the Grand Inquisitor looked back at her. He placed both palms on the surface of his desk and forced himself to his feet.

"You have a compelling story, Volinette Terris. However, the living memory of the Ethereal Realm tells another story. The problem is that the Ethereal Realm doesn't lie."

"I'm not lying." Volinette was so tired that the protest didn't even sound genuine to her own ears.

"For what it's worth, I don't believe you *think* you're lying. In any event, we're not going to sort through this tonight. You will stay here, in the tower, and we will see the Head Master in the morning. With her help and wisdom, we'll sort this out."

Volinette couldn't fight anymore. She just shrugged and nodded. They let her use the privy and freshen up. Then they took her to a small room with a single cot and a thin blanket, and they closed the door behind her. The simple click of the lock snapping into place hit her with the force of a landslide. At least it wasn't the dungeon, she thought miserably. That was something.

She climbed into the cot, pulling the blanket up around her chin. Volinette wept, and when she was too tired to cry anymore, she fell into a fitful sleep.

Chapter Eleven

Adamon slouched in a chair near the Head Master's desk. His elbow was planted on a small, cluttered table, and his head was resting in the palm of his hand. The boredom that oozed off the Grand Inquisitor was palpable.

"Why don't we just compel her to tell us where she hid the Prism," he asked, for no less than the third time in the hours they'd been questioning her.

Volinette's legs were numb. The chair she'd been told to sit in was hard, with no cushion or padding whatsoever. She'd been sitting there for hours. If asked, she couldn't say how long, but it had been long enough for the Head Master, Olin Oldwell, and Adamon Vendur to discuss the specifics of the case against her three times. In whole. No detail was spared, no piece of evidence cast aside.

Olin had, after the third retelling, excused himself to attend to his other duties. There was nothing more he could add to the conversation. Though he didn't seem to care for Adamon's personality, he seemed willing to let the other Inquisitor carry on the proceedings without him. That left Volinette with just the two of them, bickering back and forth.

Maera sat behind the desk, massaging her temples with long, slender fingers. Her eyes, the uncanny amber eyes that seemed to see straight into one's soul, were closed. For that, Volinette was grateful. It had been bad enough to see the disappointment in those eyes during the first retelling of her misadventure. It had only gotten worse the longer her interrogation ran.

"Asked and answered, Grand Inquisitor. The Order does not, has not, and will never condone the use of mind magic against a citizen of the Imperium. Was that not clear the first two times I said it?" Maera's voice boomed like thunder, seeming to fill the substantial office at the top of the tower. "Perhaps you need a change of pace? Reassignment to the Great Library as a researcher for several years?"

"Alright, alright," Adamon said, raising his hands in surrender. "We just aren't getting anywhere going in circles. Olin swears by what he saw, and Volinette swears that she wasn't involved."

"What about the Ethereal Memory?"

"Inconclusive," Adamon shrugged. "It appears to support Olin's assessment."

"But you're not convinced?" Maera asked, her eyes snapping open. She leaned forward over her desk, pinning Adamon with a hard stare.

"I have no opinion one way or the other. I haven't had time to investigate. We questioned the girl, then brought her directly here. Likewise, I haven't had an opportunity to question the other girls, either.

"Go to the Hall of Wonders and investigate thoroughly, Grand Inquisitor. Something about this doesn't seem right to me."

Adamon returned the Head Master's gaze, wagging a finger in warning. "I'm aware of your fondness for the girl, Head Master, but don't let that interfere with the appropriate dispensation of justice."

Maera tossed her head, casting an arch look at the inquisitor.

"Has it ever?"

"No," Adamon conceded as he got to his feet. He adjusted his cloak, letting it fall over the holster on his belt before he added, "But there's always a first time for everything."

He bowed from the waist, then turned and strode from the Head Master's office. Squealing metal echoed into the room from the antechamber, and Volinette listened to the muted rumble as the brass cage carried Adamon down from the highest level of the tower.

Once the roar of the descending carriage died away, Maera sighed and pushed herself to her feet. She turned, her purple robes swirling around her ankles, and walked out on the balcony that extended from the tower behind her impressive desk. Volinette was unsure what she should do. On one hand, the Head Master hadn't invited her out on the balcony. On the other, just sitting in front of the desk seemed like a waste of time.

Swallowing hard against the butterflies that seemed to have hatched in her stomach, Volinette eased herself out of the hard chair onto legs that had gone numb during her questioning. She pitched forward, only managing not to fall over by bracing herself against Maera's desk. Unfortunately for Volinette, the desk was stacked with parchment and papers, most of which slid off the sides when she caught herself.

Maera turned at the sound of shuffling papers and watched as the last few sheets slipped from the desk and wafted their way to the floor. Volinette wanted to say something, to apologize for her carelessness, but the words just wouldn't come at her command. She felt the flush creep up her neck into her cheeks and the prickle of tears at the corners of her eyes. The last thing she wanted to do in front of the Head Master was burst into tears.

Though they were unwelcome and unbidden, the tears came anyway. Volinette was well aware of how ridiculous she looked, and that only served to make her outburst that much more violent. She was standing in the Head Master's office, clinging to the desk, bawling her eyes out. At least the day couldn't possibly get any worse. Maera took one look at her and burst out laughing. *Okay,* Volinette thought, *maybe a little worse.*

"I'm sorry, Volinette," the Head Master said, regaining her composure after just a moment and rushing to her aid. Maera helped her steady herself, then guided her to an overstuffed armchair in the corner. With a gentle shove, Maera led her into the chair and pulled a stool over from a nearby worktable.

"I'm sorry. None of this is funny for you, but if you could have seen the look on your face." Maera motioned to the piles of paper that were now on the floor instead of the desk. "Don't worry about any of that. It is easily set right and no real harm was done."

Maera took a deep breath, casting an appraising eye over Volinette, who sat in sullen silence.

"You've had quite the couple days, haven't you?"

"I didn't do it," Volinette said, her voice flat and stubborn. "I don't know anything about the Prism, and I didn't take it."

Maera nodded.

"I didn't believe that you had," the Head Master said, raising her hand to forestall Volinette's objection. "There are certain protocols to be observed in the

Orders, as well as in the Great Tower, and to a lesser extent, the Academy. I'm not saying it is fair. I'm not saying that you deserved it. I'm just saying that there are certain ways that things are done and that we must follow them, regardless of what we know to be true."

"It's stupid." Volinette knew that it was neither a polite or tactful thing to say, but she was done with being polite and tactful. She was done with trying to get along. She'd tried to get along with Janessa and the others, and look where it had gotten her.

Maera shrugged.

"It may very well be stupid, as you say. However, it is our way…and for the time being, we must adhere to the protocols that are laid out for us. Did Olin or Adamon mistreat you in any way?"

"No," Volinette admitted grudgingly. "Except the cot was small and the blanket thin, I woke up with the worst crick in my neck."

"If that's the worst you come out of this misadventure with, Volinette, I'd suggest that you got off easy." Maera's smile faded a trifle. "Even though I don't believe you had anything to do with the theft of the Prism, you *were* out past curfew. You *did* break into the Hall of Wonders. We have rules for a reason."

Volinette hung her head. No matter how angry she was at the treatment she'd been subjected to, there was no fighting the Head Master on those points. If she'd just stayed in her room as she'd done so many other times since coming to the Academy, then maybe she wouldn't be in such an unenviable position.

Maera reached forward and patted her knee. It wasn't the first time that Volinette had wondered if the Head Master could read her mind.

"I know you've had a rough go of it. I also know exactly *how* bad things with Janessa had gotten. I respect Master Casto. I think he made a wise decision in allowing you to try and work things out on your own, but I think he may have let it go too far. He probably should have stepped in when it became apparent that Janessa wasn't going to let go of her resentment so easily. Perhaps that was our failing, and I'm sorry. Maybe we're both at fault here."

Maera looked as if she was going to say something else, but Volinette would never have a chance to find out what it was. A distinct rumble of stone against the thick glass of the tower walls announced the return of the elevator that brought visitors to the antechamber outside the Head Master's office. Volinette was mildly curious as to who was returning. Was it Olin, coming to fight for his observations of the crime? Or was it Adamon, who had completed his investigation of the Hall of Wonders and was returning with his findings?

The person who burst through the antechamber door and into Maera's personal office was the last person Volinette would have expected. Baris was gasping for breath, doubled over, and clawing at his chest.

"Head...Master...," he managed, between panting breaths. "Volinette...didn't...do...it."

"Sit down, young man," Maera commanded in a voice that tolerated no hesitation. She stabbed a finger at the hard chair that Volinette had so recently vacated.

Baris nodded, still trying to catch his breath, and slid into the chair. His doublet was open at the throat and sweat had turned his brown hair into a stringy mess pasted to his forehead. When Maera turned to the basin stand in the corner of the room, Baris flashed Volinette a thumbs up and a grin. By the time Maera handed him a glass of water she'd poured from the pitcher, Baris showed no sign of his support for Volinette. Instead, he took the glass and drained the liquid within in two huge gulps.

"Now, young man," Maera began, her voice stern. "You will tell me what is so important that you barge into my chambers uninvited and unannounced."

Baris took a deep breath and, for a moment, Volinette hoped that he'd change his mind. Maera surely couldn't know everything that she'd been subjected to at Janessa's whim, and she didn't want the Head Master to think less of her for being the butt of Janessa's jokes, or the victim of her cruel pranks. She breathed a sigh of relief when Baris began to speak, thankful that he, at least for the time being, was sticking to the most important facts.

"I'm sorry, Head Master. I just heard Volinette had been brought to you for questioning. Rumors spread like wildfire within the Academy walls. I ran here from the School of Sorcery, without stopping, because I thought you would want to know what really happened."

"And how, young Apprentice Jendrek, do you know exactly what happened?"

"Because I was there, Head Master." Baris had the good manners to shoot a sheepish grin at Volinette before he continued. "I saw Volinette meet up with Janessa and the others, and I figured that Janessa was up to her usual tricks, so I decided to follow them."

Maera's eyes flashed, as if she'd just spied weakness in her prey. Baris saw the look, and he gulped loudly.

"Pray tell, Apprentice Jendrek, how you followed them without being discovered?" Maera's voice was smooth and sweet, but Volinette knew a trap when she heard it. She was practically shouting at Baris in her head. *Shut up! You don't need to help me!* Unfortunately, Baris wasn't gifted with Maera's apparent gift of telepathy. He just blundered on, stumbling over his own words.

"I, uh…um…" Baris shook his head. He dug around in the pocket of his breeches and withdrew a small crystal cube. He lifted his chin and looked at the Head Master. "With this, Head Master. It's a Seer's Cube."

"I know what it is, Apprentice Jendrek."

Baris went red, but he didn't back down. "Well, then you know what it's good for. My dad gave it to me, and it's a good thing, too. Otherwise, Volinette might get the blame for what that awful Janessa did."

Maera put her forehead in her hand, massaging her temples with thumb and middle finger.

"Never let it be said, Volinette, that you don't have your defenders."

Volinette thought it would be wise if she said nothing, so she remained quiet. At length, the Head Master took her hand away from her head and peered at Baris.

"Okay, Baris, what did you see?"

His words tumbled out like a rockslide, but the basic information was the same as Volinette had said. They'd snuck to the Hall of Wonders, Janessa had opened a portal into the building, and they'd gone inside. They went to the relic room and Janessa attacked Volinette, leaving her to be caught for a crime she didn't commit. What came next in the story, Volinette had no way of knowing, but it ignited in her a hatred for Janessa that she hadn't had previously.

"Janessa did something to the memories in the relic room, Head Master. She mucked about with it, somehow. I didn't recognize the magic. I do know, though, that when she came out of the room with her harpies, they had the Prism with them. No matter what anyone says, Volinette didn't take that Prism. Janessa did."

The gaze that Maera directed on Baris would have made the most powerful mage go pale, but he stared back at her, unflinching. His eyes were bright, and Volinette could almost feel the pride swelling inside him. He'd brought them something they didn't know. Something that might clear Volinette's name.

"Are you saying, Apprentice Jendrek, that Janessa used spellcraft to alter the living memory inside the relic room at the Hall of Wonders?"

"That's exactly what he's saying, Maera," a new voice said from the direction of the doorway. Their heads whipped toward the door in unison. Adamon was standing there, his cloak pushed back away from the holster on his belt. "And she did a particularly crafty job of it. Not good enough to fool me, mind you, but enough that Olin wouldn't have given it a second thought."

Volinette felt as if she'd been dumped in a rushing river. The current was carrying her along, bouncing her off rocks before she could fully comprehend what was going on around her.

"I didn't do it," Volinette said again. It seemed to be the only thing her mind could process with any certainty.

"No," Adamon agreed. "You didn't. Now, thanks to my investigation and young Apprentice Jendrek here, we know conclusively who did."

"What happens now?" Volinette and Baris asked, almost in unison.

"Nothing for either of you." Adamon shot a knowing look at the Head Master. "I think it's time to recall Olin and the other Inquisitors. If she's willing to meddle with the fabric of the Ethereal Realm, I'm not sure we can trust her not to do something more dangerous."

Maera sighed.

"Send for the Inquisitors, Adamon. Find Janessa and bring her to me."

They were dismissed then, and Volinette and Baris shot from the room as if fired out of a cannon. They bypassed the lift entirely, instead pelting down the stairs as fast as their feet would carry them. It wasn't until they were outside the tower that Volinette turned on Baris, punching him lightly in the arm.

"If you saw everything, what took you so long to come find me?"

"What was I supposed to do?" Baris asked with a snort. "Break you out of the dungeon? Kick Adamon in the shins and steal you away? I thought Maera was the most likely person to see reason, so I bided my time."

"Well, I'm glad you did. Thank you."

Baris shrugged. "You'd have done the same. Come on, let's get out of here."

Chapter Twelve

A leaden sky hung over Blackbeach, as if it, too, was brooding over the events that had so recently transpired under its watchful gaze. Volinette shivered. She was wearing an undershirt, her tunic, and had her cloak cinched around her neck with the hood up. Even so, she was cold. Every time the wind whipped across the choppy waves, it pierced her like a dagger. As uncomfortable as it was on the breakwater, it would have been ten times as bad within the Academy walls. The Inquisitors were still looking for Janessa and the Prism, and Volinette didn't want to be anywhere nearby when they found her.

Glancing at Baris told her that he wasn't fairing their voluntary exile much better. His teeth were chattering and he looked as if he might freeze solid at any moment. He wore only a plain tunic. Volinette had offered him her cloak, but he'd brushed her off with an indignant eye. He was fine, he swore. He didn't need her mothering him.

"I'm f-f-f-f-ine!" he snapped.

"I didn't say anything," Volinette retorted. "And besides, if you can't say the word without stuttering, then you're not fine."

Baris launched himself off the breakwater, dropping with a certain boyish grace and landing on the balls of his feet. He extended his hand to Volinette with grave courtesy. She gave him an appraising look before she took his hand and dropped into the fine black sand below.

"What are we doing, Baris? I know that look in your eye. We don't need any more trouble right now. We've got trouble in droves."

"You worry too much," he said before dragging her along the wall. "We won't get in trouble, trust me."

Volinette had some choice words to say on that score, but she held her tongue. In truth, Baris was one of the few people she could count on to always put her wellbeing before his own. Well, if not before, at least alongside. He was a good friend. Volinette didn't know many, any actually, people who would have burst into the Head Master's office and declared her innocence. It was an act of either incredible bravery or incredible stupidity. Though she'd never tell him so, Volinette figured that it was probably equal parts of each.

They were both glad to reach the stone cobbles that made up Blackbeach's main streets and avenues. Trekking through the sand on the beach was exhausting, and the abrasive particles got everywhere and took forever to get rid of. They leaned on each other, taking turns knocking the worst of the sand from their breeches and from inside their boots.

"Where are we going?" Volinette asked, only to find her request again fall on deaf ears.

Baris led her through the alleys and back streets of Blackbeach as if he'd mapped them himself. "Just one quick stop first," he'd said, dragging her down a narrow fissure between two buildings that she wouldn't have gone down in broad daylight, much less this overcast day. And at night? Forget it. No chance.

Refuse was ankle deep, and more than once Volinette spied the beady eyes of a hungry rat appraising her before turning tail and fleeing out of sight.

"Gee, Baris, you sure know how to show a girl a good time."

"Grow a sense of adventure, Volinette. It's not like I'm leading you into the Warrens."

Volinette opened her mouth to reply and found that she had nothing witty to say. The last time she'd embraced her adventurous side, she'd ended up in the custody of the Grand Inquisitor and fighting for her future with the Head Master of the Six Orders. She closed her mouth and said nothing, following Baris in silence.

The door the boy stopped in front of was black with age. The iron banding that held the wood together was rusted lace. It looked as if a strong knock would bring the whole thing down, but that's exactly what Baris did. A moment later, the door opened a crack and a dirty face peered out. Eyes that reminded her of the rats darted from Baris to Volinette and back to Baris.

"Yeah?"

"I need one bag," Baris said, rummaging around in the front pocket of his breeches.

"Hold on."

The door closed and Volinette gave Baris a sharp look.

"I thought you said we weren't doing anything that would get us in trouble."

"Would you trust me?" he asked, looking pained. "Just a little? Sheesh."

A moment later, the door was opened a crack and a grubby hand thrust out. Baris dropped the Half-Crown coin he'd dug from his pocket in the dirty palm, which disappeared as if by magic. It reappeared with a small leather pouch, which Baris caught deftly as it dropped. The door snapped shut and they heard the sound of a heavy bar being dropped.

"What was that all about?" Volinette was feeling less and less comfortable about this adventure by the minute.

"Trust, remember? Come on."

It was hard for Volinette to trust anyone, but she decided that if there was anyone in Blackbeach who was unlikely to sell her out, it'd be Baris. After all, his record was exemplary when it came to standing by her side. She decided that it was okay to trust him and try to enjoy herself. After all, he wasn't Janessa.

More winding through hidden roads and back alleys led them somewhere Volinette recognized. They'd entered the courtyard of the Great Library through an almost hidden gate that she'd never noticed. The entry was so overgrown with hanging moss and ivy that it was almost like parting a curtain to gain access to the courtyard proper.

"See?" Baris asked with some exasperation. "Nowhere that you're going to get in trouble. Will you relax now?"

Volinette felt the blood rush to her cheeks. She ducked her head, unable to meet his challenging eyes. He was right, she knew, but it didn't feel good to be called out on it. Tears that she'd been fighting for days sprang to her eyes. She didn't cry, but the tears still made their escape down her cheeks.

"Aw, jeez. C'mon, Volinette." Baris shifted from one foot to the other. "Don't cry, I didn't mean it. I know it's been right shit the last couple days, but it'll be alright."

Awkward as it was, Volinette appreciated the pat on her shoulder that Baris managed to produce. It was hardly a natural action for him, but at least he was trying to make things better, which is what he always did. If nothing else, he always tried to make it better. She wiped the tears away with the back of her hands and looked up at him, even managing to summon a tentative smile.

"There you go!" he exclaimed, brightening. "Trust me, it'll be okay. Especially when you see what I've got to show you." He dangled the leather pouch in her line of sight. "C'mon…we need to go. Before he leaves."

"Before who leaves?"

"You'll see."

The Great Library always reminded Volinette of a sacred temple. Though she hadn't been to many clerical services when she'd been traveling with the family, there were the customary Spring Solstice and Yuletide rituals that most people in the Imperium attended. That same sort of hushed reverence is what Volinette felt when she walked into the towering stacks of volumes older than she was by hundreds or thousands of years.

Volinette took a deep breath, relishing in the smell of old paper and parchment. That was the smell of time's passage, a hundred-thousand lifetimes worth of knowledge and emotion frozen in time. Waiting, ready to be called upon at any moment, just by picking up the tome and flipping through the pages.

Baris groaned and grabbed her by the wrist, dragging her past the reference desk at the front of the ground floor and toward a staircase in the corner that curved skyward as far as the eye could see. They trudged up the stairs. Every time Volinette thought they'd finally reached their destination, they climbed ever upward.

They disembarked on the highest level of the library, and Baris led her down a narrow hall to a narrower door that looked older than the one they'd seen in the alley. He knocked once, a gentle rap of his knuckles, and then twisted the knob, pushing it open. Resigned to see this madness through to the end, Volinette followed.

The small office was unremarkable, save for the vast and impressive piles of paper, parchment, and writing implements that crowded every surface. Tall shelves were festooned in paper. Small cabinets seemed bursting with the stuff. A wide desk, standard issue for Quintessentialists in the Orders, was nearly buried under it.

Behind the desk, a wizened old man was nestled in a chair. His head was thrown back as far as his thin neck would allow. The snores that issued from his open mouth were at least twice as big as the man they came from. Baris shot Volinette an impish grin and rapped on the desk, hard, with his knuckles.

"What? Who?"

"Good afternoon, Master Archivist Jotun," Baris said loudly.

"No need to shout, you young scamp. I may be ancient, but there's nothing wrong with these." He tugged at the loose lobes below his ears so hard that for a moment, Volinette thought they might stretch like hot taffy. "Who is this that you've brought into my domain?"

Baris pushed the door shut with one hand and dumped a pile of paper onto the floor from a chair with the other. He plopped down in the newly vacant seat.

"This is Volinette."

"Oh?" Jotun's eyebrow went up, as if tugged by an invisible string. "I've heard about you, young one. You're the one with the voice like an angel." Volinette felt herself blush again as the archivist continued, "Angel or not, you lot aren't supposed to be here."

Her stomach flipped, and Baris held up a finger to forestall her panic.

"I'm sure you can make an exception, Master Jotun." Baris leaned forward in his chair, dropping the leather pouch on the desk and leaning back. The grin that spread across his face was infectious, and soon Volinette found that she was smiling, too.

"Hmph." That was all the Master Archivist said as he retrieved the offering. Fingers gnarled with more years than Volinette's entire family combined tugged at the silk thread that closed the pouch. She had to fight the urge to offer her assistance, almost sure that it would do nothing other than offend the old man.

At length, Jotun worked the neck of the pouch open and reached inside. He plucked a translucent yellow sphere about the size of a marble from the bag and held it up to the light. He turned it this way and that, admiring the myriad of small crystals that dotted its surface. Volinette had just begun to wonder what kind of stone it was when the old man popped it in his mouth and made an almost feline sound of delight.

"Deralt's?" the old man asked around the obstruction in his mouth. Baris nodded.

"Yes, Sir. Best lemon drops in the city."

Jotun nodded, slurping loudly.

"I taught you well, boy," he said, tucking the drop into his cheek, making it bulge. "So having been due and properly bribed, what do you want, scamp?"

"Can I take Volinette up in the tower?"

"Hmm," Jotun considered the request, weighing the pouch in his hand. "Seems your payment is a little light, youngster."

Baris's face fell. Volinette felt bad for him. This was clearly a well-rehearsed battle of wits. Somehow, Baris had been outsmarted.

"It's the same as every other time," Baris groused.

"Aye lad, but those times, you didn't bring your friend."

Volinette plunged her hands into her pockets, sensing an opportunity. "Please, Sir, perhaps I have something that can entice you…"

"Aye and you do, girl, but you won't find it in your pockets." Jotun leaned forward in a conspiratorial fashion and gave her a wink. "Sing me a song, and we'll call it even."

Volinette looked from Baris to Jotun, then back to Baris. He shrugged, but he was grinning from ear to ear. The little gremlin had known this was going to happen. He'd put her on the spot, knowing full well what the price of admission to his little show would be. She wanted to grab him by the neck and shake him.

"I, uh," Volinette struggled to adapt. "What should I sing?"

"Anything you like, dear," Jotun replied, using his finger to conduct an imaginary band.

She hugged herself, trying to think of what she could perform that would meet with the old man's approval. The black sand still stuck to her cloak was harsh against her fingers. Inspiration struck and she opened her mouth to sing.

What came out was an old, but popular, ballad from the fishing villages where her family would often stop to perform. It was the tale of a widow lamenting the loss of her husband to the ravenous sea and throwing herself into the waves.

> *Dear sea, sweet sea, how could you take my love*
> *from me?*
> *Days and nights, for weeks and weeks, my love*
> *came to you, far from me.*
> *Taking from thy heaving bosom, offering back his*
> *love and life.*
> *Now you've taken him forever, betrayal cuts*
> *through me like a knife.*
> *I cannot, will not, live without him, my life, my*
> *love, your trophy claimed.*
> *I commend myself now unto you, with his spirit, I*
> *will remain.*

As the last notes of the song died away, Volinette was surprised to see the Master Archivist dabbing at the corners of his eyes. Even more unexpected was the look of appreciation Baris turned on her. His mouth hung open, as if he was unable to credit what he'd heard.

"How do you do that?" Baris finally asked, managing to regain his composure.

"Do what?"

"Make it sound like you're singing with a host of angels?"

"Oh stop," she snapped at him. She didn't need his embellishments embarrassing her in front of Master Jotun. "I just sing. It's nothing special."

"On that score, dear girl, you are most decidedly wrong," Master Jotun said, getting to his shaky feet. "You are very special, indeed. Young Baris, I am indebted to you for bringing this girl to my attention. I suspect this will not be the last I hear of her."

"So we can go to the tower?"

"Aye lad," Jotun said with another wink. "I'd say you'd paid the admission in full. Come along. You know the drill."

Baris bounded to his feet and crossed the room to where Jotun was standing before a massive bookcase. Lending his young shoulder to Jotun's guidance, they pushed the furniture out of the way, revealing a tiny door behind it. Jotun took a key from his pocket and turned it in a little lock. The door sprang open.

"You know the rules, Baris. Half an hour, no more."

"Yes, Master Jotun, thank you." Baris crouched down and stepped through the tiny door, turning back to Volinette. He beckoned to her urgently. "Come on! We don't have much time."

Chapter Thirteen

"I don't understand what you hope to gather from this investigation," Olin said, rifling through a drawer of clothes. He picked up a few items, subjected them to a cursory inspection, and dropped them back, closing the drawer with a sigh.

"Which is why I am Grand Inquisitor, and you took the Fourth Level Inquisitor trials three times before you passed."

"Now listen here—"

"No," Adamon interrupted, his voice barely above a whisper. "*You* listen. We already suspect that Volinette is innocent of these crimes. We likewise suspect that Janessa, the daughter of two *highly* ranked Masters on the High Council, is guilty of stealing an artifact of immeasurable power. An artifact, I might add, that we have yet to recover.

"I intend to have every shred of evidence possible to possess before we take the girl into custody and return to the Head Master. Am I making myself plain?"

"What does it matter?" Olin shot back. "Why not censure them both and be done with it."

"And *that* is why you failed the trials. Sometimes the blade of justice should be a healer's blade, not the dull bludgeon of, well, whatever you are." Adamon's eyes lost the far-away, glassy look that indicated a mage split between the realms of the physical world and the Quintessential Sphere. "There's nothing to find here. To the other rooms."

The dormitory being empty assisted in their investigation. The apprentices were supposed to be in class, but Adamon doubted if Janessa and her ilk would have bothered with something as petty as class on the day after stealing the Prism of Transcendental. He would check with Master Casto later, but he suspected he already knew the answer to his inquiry.

Though Olin's mood was sour, no doubt due to Adamon's near constant needling, the man knew how to perform a thorough physical search. As a team, they made quick work of search the rooms of Volinette, Syble, Nixi, and Halsie. No trace of the Prism, either physical or ethereal, existed in any of their rooms. A short walk down the hall led them to the larger room that served as Janessa's quarters. The preferential assignment of room was, without question, attributable to the girl's parents.

Adamon could feel it before they even entered the room. The tingle of power that danced just over the surface of his skin, moving like an insect with a hundred thousand legs with a feather light touch. They'd find what they were looking for in Janessa's room. He was sure of it.

Olin entered first. He went stiff as the residual power of the Prism washed over him. He shook it off and moved further in. Adamon followed. He didn't even need to consult the living memory of the Quintessential Sphere. There was no doubt that the Prism had been here, but wasn't any longer.

Adamon slipped into sphere sight, cringing at the jumbled mass of mangled memories that confronted him. Whoever had tampered with the ethereal evidence in the Hall of Wonders had performed the same spellcraft here. Although the living memory of the Quintessential Sphere would reassert itself over time, it was a slow process. Adamon didn't want to wait.

Closing his eyes, he blocked out the intrusions of the physical world. He focused instead on the Quintessential Sphere and the wounds that had been inflicted on it. His fingers plucked at the edges of the memories like a phantasmal harp. Somewhere in the distance, he could hear Olin complaining that they didn't have time for this. Adamon shut him out, ignoring everything but the progress he was making setting things to rights within the sphere.

Each healed wound weakened the cohesive power of the spell used to scramble the memories, making each successive pass easier and faster. In less time than he would have imagined, Adamon had reconstructed the memories that Janessa had tried to obscure with her clumsy command of the Quintessential Sphere. It was Janessa who had tampered with the living memory of the sphere, and it was Janessa who had stolen the Prism and hid it here in her room, in the chest by the foot of her bed. Adamon opened his eyes, snapping back to the here and now, and facing Olin's impatient gaze.

"The Prism was here, but isn't any longer," Adamon said.

"I could have told you that," Olin replied at his driest. His gesture indicated a room that he'd turned inside out while Adamon was communing with the Quintessential Sphere.

"Perhaps, but now we have the evidence we need to take the girl into custody. Between what we've found and the witnesses, we can bring a solid case against Janessa and ensure that justice is done."

"You mean censure," Olin said.

Adamon shrugged.

"The sentence isn't for me to decide. I make my recommendations, and the High Council will have their say."

"How many times have they gone against you?" Olin snorted.

"Not many," Adamon conceded. "But how many times have we brought the daughter of two prominent Masters before them?"

"Fair point."

The men retraced their steps through the rooms, down the corridor, and out into the courtyard beyond. Long strides carried them with urgent purpose, so urgent that they nearly ran down the very girls they were searching for. Janessa stood before them, her fists jammed against her hips, her chin lifted at a haughty tilt.

"What in the nine hells is going on in here?"

"You have impeccable timing, Apprentice," Adamon said. "We were just coming to retrieve you."

"Retrieve me? For what? Do you have any idea who my parents are?" Janessa demanded.

"I do indeed, and I should think that they will be very curious why the daughter of two such powerful Quintessentialists, who sit on the High Council, could possibly be so stupid as to steal an artifact that she doesn't understand and can't hope to control from the Hall of Wonders."

"I stole nothing," she spat. "You can't prove it."

Nixi, Halsie, and Syble murmured their agreement. Adamon turned his glare on them and the girls quickly fell silent.

"I can," Adamon countered, taking Janessa by the arm. "And I will." He turned his gaze to the girls who were still hovering about. "The three of you leave, now. Before I decide to put you all in the dungeon and leave you there."

Without waiting for them to reply, Adamon guided Janessa along the path, toward the Great Tower. When the girl began to struggle, Olin stepped forward and took her by the other arm. Although he could have managed on his own, Adamon was thankful for the assistance. Olin may not have the skills that he had, but he was a good inquisitor, nonetheless. Perhaps even good enough to be spared the sharp edge of Adamon's tongue…at least for a time.

As they proceeded toward the tower, they crossed paths with a patrolling guard. Adamon stopped him with a word.

"Yes, Grand Inquisitor?"

"Please send a message to all the gate guards. I'm looking for an Apprentice and an Acolyte. They'll be outside the Academy grounds. When they return, I want them to report to the Great Tower at once. There is a matter of importance they must attend to."

"Of course, Master Vendur. Shall I have them escorted in?"

Adamon considered that. Volinette and the boy were young enough and unjaded by the power of prestige to be tempted to dawdle when summoned by the Grand Inquisitor. The fear of reprisal would be enough to keep them moving.

"No, that isn't necessary. Just pass along the message."

~~~

Dark, narrow, and rickety, the stairs leading up to the tower were barely wide enough for a grown man to climb. They spiraled up in darkness. Volinette would have thought twice about going if it weren't for the fact that Baris was ahead of her, urging her to hurry. He stopped short and she ran into him from behind.

"Hey!" she groused. "A little warning?"

"Sorry. Hold on."

There was a bang, a screech, and a groan as Baris did something she couldn't see. Then a flood of light poured down from above them, dazzling her eyes. Baris took her hand and led her up the last few steps and out onto a planked platform that was only just large enough for both of them to stand on.

Volinette had never felt particularly afraid of heights. In fact, she rather enjoyed the brief view of the city she'd gotten from the Head Master's office, but this was different. The tower was old and not well maintained. The thin railing that circled the four posts that held up the pyramid roof didn't look like it would withstand a strong wind, much less someone using it to keep from plummeting to their inevitable death in the courtyard below.

While it wasn't close to as high as the Great Tower, it was high enough to loom over every other building in the city and give an unrestricted view of the Academy grounds. Volinette could see the fountain in the courtyard where she liked to read. It looked like a craftsman's model, and she very much wished that she were perched on the edge of the fountain rather than standing where it felt like she might fall at any moment.

"It's pretty, Baris, but I want to go down," she said in a tight voice. She swallowed against the lump in her throat, determined not to glance down into the courtyard a second time.

"We can see what's going on at the Academy from up here. Don't you want to know if they find Janessa?"

"Can't we just do that with your cube?"

Baris ducked his head. "Naw, Adamon took it from me as soon as we left the Head Master's office. He said I'd get it back, but…"

He shrugged, indicating what Volinette already knew. There was no telling when Baris would get the bauble back. Adamon was going to be occupied for the foreseeable future.

"Hey, look," Baris grabbed her by the arm and dragged her far too near the railing for her peace of mind. As her eyes followed where he was pointing, her fear of being up in the tower evaporated.

It wasn't hard to decipher the scene that was taking place outside the girls' dormitory. Adamon in his traveling cloak and Olin in his robes were confronting Janessa and the girls. They were too high and too far away to hear what was being said, but Olin was visibly angry. He moved his arms in quick, short motions that conveyed his frustration, even over the great distance.

One Inquisitor took each of Janessa's arms and marched her, quite against her will by the way she was struggling, toward the tower. Still, as powerful and wily as Janessa was, she was no match for two fully grown men who had rid the Imperium of rogue mages and other threats to the Orders. They disappeared into the tower, and Volinette let out a breath she hadn't realized she'd been holding.

"Yeah," Baris agreed. "I wouldn't want to be her right now."

"What do you think is going to happen to her?" Volinette gnawed at her lower lip. Although she didn't want to take the blame for what Janessa did, she wasn't sure she wanted to think about what the consequences of those actions would be.

Baris rounded on her, his eyes wide.

"Are you kidding me? You're worried about what's going to happen to HER? SHE almost got you thrown out of the Academy, Volinette. What's wrong with you?"

"She hates me enough already," Volinette fired back, just as angry as Baris had been, if not more so. "Maybe I just don't want to add fuel to the fire!"

"Unbelievable," Baris muttered, turning back toward the tower. "You need to learn to stand up for yourself. No one else is going to."

"You did."

Baris sniffed, but said nothing. He continued to look out at the tower for several long minutes before he said anything else.

"I won't always be around. Besides, you're way more powerful than I am. You heard what Master Jotun said."

"That was just singing."

Baris glanced at her and shook his head. "That's just it, Vol. It *wasn't* just singing. Something happened to you. You changed. Your voice…the hair on the back of my neck was standing on end, and Master Jotun looked more alive than I've ever seen him. He's right when he says you're something special. I just don't know what."

"Well, I don't know either," she snapped, her exasperation with his fawning reaching its breaking point.

"Don't you want to find out?"

"Of course I do! I wouldn't be here if I didn't. I've only dreamed of becoming a Master for my entire life."

"Then don't let anyone else make that decision for you. Not Janessa or anybody. Not even me."

Baris was rarely this serious, and his demeanor was making Volinette more uncomfortable than what they'd seen. She wanted to get back to the dormitory. If she could just get one good night's sleep, maybe all of this would seem less dire.

"Okay. Can we go back down now?" She shivered as she spoke, her teeth knocking together. She couldn't understand how Baris wasn't frozen solid. "I'm cold and I want to go back to the Academy."

They descended from the tower, stopping only long enough for Baris to pull the trapdoor shut at the top, and move the bookcase back into place at the bottom. Master Jotun had abandoned his office, leaving them alone in the dimly lit space. Without his paternal presence, the room seemed much more foreign and cold.

Down the spiral staircase, through the library, and out into the city. Volinette didn't even register the change of scenery. Her focus was on getting back to the School of Sorcery and finding out what was going on with Janessa. Baris made a fair point about taking care of herself, but it just wasn't in her nature to not worry about the girl. Adamon and Olin had mentioned censure during their discussions about Volinette's involvement. She had a hard time believing that they wouldn't seek the same punishment for the girl who was actually responsible for the crime.

As they approached the obsidian gates outside the Academy grounds, the guard on duty trotted forward.

"Acolyte Terris? Apprentice Jendrek? Where have you been? The Grand Inquisitor has been searching all over for you. You're to go to the Great Tower immediately."

The lump in Volinette's throat grew and grew, threatening to choke her. When she spoke, the only thing that came out was the barest squeak. Baris glanced at her and shook his head.

"Do you know why they're looking for us?" he asked the guard, who shrugged.

"No idea. Master Vendur just asked that we relay the message if you were seen."

"Okay, then. Thanks."

Baris grabbed her arm and yanked her forward. It was probably best that he took the initiative. Otherwise, she might have stayed rooted to the spot forever. The young mage wasn't wasting any time in answering the summons. They were practically running through the courtyard. As they passed the dormitory, Volinette's eyes lingered on the door longingly. All she wanted was to go inside, crawl under her covers, and go to sleep. Alas, it didn't seem that sleep was in her near future.

Chapter Fourteen

Volinette and Baris skidded to a halt. The entrance hall of the Great Tower of High Magic was deserted, save for the now familiar form of the lanky Grand Inquisitor in his cloak. When Volinette was small, her grandmother had told her stories of winged demons, creatures with ink black skin, red eyes, and six arms that sought only to snatch away unsuspecting children and spirit them away to the Deep Void. Adamon, in his cloak, stirred memories of that not-so-distant fear in her breast. He might not be a demon, but he was every bit as dangerous in his own way.

"Come along, both of you," he said by way of a gruff greeting. "We are needed in the Head Master's chambers at once. I'd suspected that you'd have come along before now."

"I'm sorry," Volinette said, stepping toward the brass cage that had carried them to the top of the tower on their previous visit.

"No, not that way."

Adamon snapped his fingers to catch her attention and held out his hands. Baris seized the Inquisitor's hand almost immediately. Volinette took only a moment longer, but she imagined that he'd known her hesitation, that she could see it in his eyes. Adamon spoke a series of words, and the world inverted.

To Volinette, it seemed as if all of Solendrea was passing through her at once, compressed down into a sickening knot in her stomach. She didn't move. The world did. Different levels and rooms of the tower passed through her in an instant. Then they were standing in the Head Master's antechamber.

"Fight it, we don't have time for cleaning up," Adamon said. It seemed a silly thing to Volinette, until a wave of crushing dizziness and nausea drove her to her knees.

She pressed the back of her hand to her mouth, fighting back the gorge that rose in her throat. Beside her, Baris looked as miserable as she felt. He swallowed loudly, gulping air in a fashion that would have been comical under any other circumstances. It took a few minutes, but they were both able to fight down the sickness that had overcome them.

"What *was* that?" Volinette asked, when she felt that speaking wouldn't result in her lunch tumbling onto the smooth glass floor.

"Etherwalk," Adamon said with a dismissive gesture. "Something you won't be able to do until you're far more experienced. Enter the Quintessential Sphere in one location, exit in another, then pull your physical form through behind you."

"Does it always feel like that?" Baris asked.

"More or less. The more distance you cover, the worse it is. You *can* Etherwalk to any place on Solendrea, though I wouldn't recommend it."

There was a muted shout from behind the heavy curtains that had been drawn across the door to the Head Master's office. Volinette hadn't noticed the velvet partitions before, but then, they hadn't been closed on her first visit to Maera's domain.

"Our attendance is required. Come along."

Baris tried to protest that he needed another moment to settle his roiling stomach, but his plea fell on deaf ears. Adamon strode across the room and parted the curtains with one arm, ushering them through into a scene that Volinette would have been just as happy avoiding if she'd been given the opportunity.

Janessa sat in a solitary chair across from the Head Master's desk. Just behind her stood two Masters that Volinette had never met. From their sharp features and matching scowls, it wasn't difficult to guess that they were Janessa's parents.

"We demand evidence of these outrageous allegations, Head Master," Janessa's father said in a loud voice, as if he could redeem his daughter's transgression by volume alone. "Surely you are mistaken."

"The evidence has just arrived." Maera stood as Volinette entered with Adamon and Baris. "Grand Inquisitor Adamon Vendur, a witness to the crime, Baris Jendrek, and the victim, Volinette Terris."

Janessa's parents whirled to face the newcomers. They went pale as Adamon's name was mentioned, and Volinette knew that she wasn't the only one who felt fear in the pit of her stomach when faced by the formidable mage. Their respect for Adamon soon curdled as their eyes slid across Volinette and Baris.

"We demand evidence and you give us children. Is this some sort of joke?"

"Children and a Grand Inquisitor of the Orders," Adamon replied, his voice cold. "I assure you that no one here considers the crimes of which your daughter is accused the slightest bit amusing."

"Then present your evidence at once, Inquisitor." The tone of Janessa's mother's voice told Volinette all she needed to know about the daughter's attitude. It was unlikely that Janessa had ever had to work for anything in her life. Her parents issued commands and they expected those commands to be carried out without delay.

Adamon stared at the pair of them for so long that Volinette was convinced he was making a point. No matter what demands Janessa's parents might believe they were entitled to, Adamon was still the Grand Inquisitor, and his authority over matters of law within the Orders was paramount. Even Maera, as Head Master, could not directly countermand the Grand Inquisitor on points of law. She would have to convene the High Council of Masters to review his decision.

"You are in no position to demand anything," Adamon said, apparently satisfied that he'd made them wait long enough. "Your daughter is the accused. The evidence will be presented, and I will render my judgment."

Adamon waved his hand, muttering under his breath. Volinette knew that Inquisitors were notorious for their secrecy, possessing spells unknown outside their circles, but she'd never realized that their secrecy extended to the execution of their spellcraft.

Her curiosity about his methods evaporated as the memory of what had happened in the Hall of Wonders shimmered into view over the Head Master's desk. Miniature images of Volinette and the other girls moved about in the replica, just as they had on the night the prism was stolen. Janessa shot to her feet as the events played out. She swiped a hand through the facsimile, but failed to disperse it or even disrupt it in any way.

"This is a lie!" she blurted, turning to her parents with wide, wild eyes. It was the first time Volinette had seen the girl touched by genuine fear. It was infectious. Volinette felt her stomach clench in sympathy. No matter what Janessa had done, and she'd done plenty, no one deserved to be that afraid. She wasn't even that afraid of her own parents. What kind of people were Janessa's parents to instill that kind of fear in their own kin?

"Silence, child," Janessa's father demanded, his voice eerily similar to Adamon's earlier tone.

They watched the events in the Hall of Wonders play out, and the echo of the memory ended in the scrambled mess that Janessa had made of the Ethereal Realm while trying to cover her tracks. Janessa's mother sank into the chair that Janessa had vacated, holding her face in her hands. Her father turned to Adamon, Volinette, and Baris.

"You swear on your lives that these are the events as they transpired?"

Volinette nodded. Out of the corner of her eye, she saw Baris doing the same.

"You've seen the living memory of the Quintessential Sphere," Adamon said. "As a Master of the Orders, do you deny the power or revelations of the Ethereal Realm?"

"You know I can't, and won't."

"Then your question is null and void. You saw the events as they transpired, as our world and the spirits beyond remember it. No swearing by mere mortals is required."

The color drained from Janessa's father's face. He scrubbed his face with both hands. Maera rose from the chair behind her desk, smoothing down the royal purple robes she wore, as if she was reminding everyone of her role in the proceedings. Though her eyes were troubled, her voice was steady and even when she spoke.

"The weight and severity of these crimes cannot be overlooked. Justice must be done. However, I'm sure that the Grand Inquisitor could be swayed toward leniency if only the item were returned. If Janessa would be willing to return the Transcendental Prism..."

"I can't *return* what I don't *have*," Janessa spat.

"Then I'm sure Master Vendur could be convinced to lessen the punishment required," Maera continued, ignoring the girl's heated outburst.

Volinette thought that Adamon looked as if he had no intention of reducing the consequences of Janessa's actions, but she kept her mouth shut. If discretion were the better part of valor, she'd have earned a medal by the time the night was through. She saw Baris open his mouth and kicked him soundly in the shin. Baris wouldn't be earning any medals.

Janessa's father changed tack, sailing into previously explored waters of courtesy.

"Head Master," he said, inclining his head. "Might we speak to our daughter in private?"

"Of course, Master Navita," Maera motioned to the curtain separating the main office from the chamber beyond. "My antechamber should suffice."

Janessa's parents escorted the protesting girl through the curtain. Olin, who had been observing the proceedings with a stony detachment, came to life and moved to stand by the partition separating the rooms.

The Head Master's office was dead quiet. Even so, it was impossible to hear the conversation that Janessa and her parents were having beyond the curtain. Except for a few muted outbursts by the girl, they might as well have disappeared from the tower. Volinette shifted from foot to foot. She wanted to be back in her room with the door closed, the light out, and snuggled under her blanket until all of this had blown over.

"What happens now?" she blurted when she couldn't take the silence any longer. Maera and Adamon exchanged a knowing glance. The Inquisitor shook his head.

"If she continues to claim ignorance of the crime or the whereabouts of the Prism, I'll have no choice, Head Master." Adamon shrugged.

"Surely there must be another way, Adamon. She's still a girl." Maera's eyes searched the Inquisitor's face before she turned away, toward the window.

"She has shown a flagrant disregard for our laws, our ways, our heritage, and other mages. She's a danger to herself and every other Quintessentialist in the Imperium. Censure is the only way."

Censure. The word echoed through Volinette's mind like a pebble dropped down a deep well. Each time the pebble bounced off a wall, the word seemed to get louder and louder. It landed in her stomach like a block of lead, making her feel sick and cold.

The horrors of censure were legend among the people of the Imperium. Tales of mages who went rogue and were caught or who were censured for their crimes, were often told around campfires and tavern tables. Each tale would be worse than the last. Stories of men who lost their minds and went feral, or worse, became homicidal madmen who could no longer stand the company of other people, because the pain of what they had lost was just too great. Entire volumes in the Great Library were dedicated to these tales. Volinette had devoured them with a voracious appetite she didn't quite understand.

She wanted to plead for Janessa. Surely censure wasn't the only option, but she found her mouth had gone very dry. No matter how she worked her tongue, she couldn't manage more than a whisper. That was probably best, she decided, as Adamon didn't look as if he was in any mood to barter any favors.

Olin stepped away from the curtain, flashing a hand signal to Adamon, who nodded and turned to face the entrance. Maera turned as well, and they all focused their attention on the velvet partition as it was pushed aside.

Janessa's father entered first. His jaw was tight and his eyes were fixed straight ahead. He acknowledged no one else in the room as he entered and waited for his daughter and wife to follow. Janessa came next, her chin raised in her typical haughty manner. The most significant change was in Janessa's mother. While she had left as a hard, cold woman, she returned with red, swollen eyes that betrayed her tears. Her shoulders were stooped. She was a woman who had admitted defeat. Volinette had seen that look before in many singing competitions. This time, though, the consequences of failure were much direr.

Adamon addressed Master Navita as soon as they had all entered the Head Master's office.

"You've had your time to confer, Master Navita. Your daughter stands accused of these crimes, witness has been brought, but yet she denies the claims. Further, she will not return the stolen artifact. Have you been able to convince your daughter to cooperate?"

At Adamon's question, Janessa's mother burst into fresh tears. Janessa's shoulders jerked a little straighter. Volinette winced in sympathy. The brave front Janessa was putting on was just that, a front. Janessa's father worked his jaw for a moment, then lowered his face to the floor.

"No, Grand Inquisitor, despite our pleas, she maintains her innocence."

"Very well. Janessa Navita, I find you guilty of crimes against the Imperium and the Orders. I sentence you to censure. You will be remanded into custody until such time as the Rite of Censure can be scheduled."

Janessa's mother rushed to Maera's side. She clutched the royal purple robes, bunching them between her bony fingers.

"Please, Head Master, please convene the High Council of Masters. I beg you, let me make my appeal."

"The High Council of Masters shall be called. I trust Adamon will ensure that Janessa is kept comfortably until such a matter can be resolved."

The Grand Inquisitor nodded. He motioned to Olin, who stepped to one side of Janessa. Adamon went to the other. They marched her from the room in much the same way that Volinette and Baris had seen her escorted from the dormitory to the tower.

Janessa's parents followed the Inquisitors through the curtain, and the muted rumble of the elevator beyond filled the otherwise quiet room. For the first time since Janessa and her parents had reentered the Head Master's office, Volinette dared to look at Baris.

He looked back at her and shrugged. His eyes were as dark as she felt. They'd witnessed one of their peers being sentenced to censure. Volinette couldn't remember ever hearing of the ritual being performed on someone so young.

"You've witnessed something traumatic in its own right here today," Maera said, her voice quiet yet still thundering in the stillness. "The decision to cut a Quintessentialist off from the resonance of the Quintessential Sphere is never one to be taken lightly. I trust Adamon and his decision, though I don't like it."

"What about the High Council of Masters?"

Maera shook her head, her eyes sad.

"While many of the Masters may see the merit in offering a lesser penalty considering Janessa's age, her attitude will almost certainly seal her fate. Once they witness her crimes as they were committed, she will have few friends within the tower, much less on the High Council."

Maera turned her back on them then, looking out the window over the darkened city.

"It's getting late. I thank you for your service. Both of you. I'm sorry you had to be involved with this so young and so early in your time at the Academy. I hope tomorrow is brighter for you."

Volinette knew a dismissal when she heard one. She reached down and took Baris's hand, unsurprised to find it trembling. Her hands were no steadier. The link-shock that danced between them was a welcome reminder that they were still connected to the Quintessential Sphere. They followed the accused and the Inquisitors. They reached the shaft for the cage and rang the bell to call the strange and wonderful carriage.

When they parted ways in the courtyard to go to their respective dormitories, Volinette had never felt more alone.

Chapter Fifteen

The next morning brought a return to class and with it, Volinette had hoped, some normalcy. Any desire for things to be more normal evaporated like fog in the sun as soon as she walked into the classroom. Most of the apprentices whispered to each other behind cupped hands. Syble, Nixi, and Halsie were less sneaky about their feelings. Violinette's table was conspicuously empty. Poor Baris was obviously getting the dirty end of the stick. He and Syble were as far apart from each other as the length of the table would allow, and they both looked as if that wasn't half long enough for either of them.

"Class, come to order," Fulgent Casto said as he stalked into the classroom. His usual cheerful demeanor was nowhere to be found, and there were dark bags under his eyes. Volinette suspected that she wasn't the only one who had suffered through a sleepless night.

Under the watchful eye of Master Casto, the girls couldn't really make a move against Baris or Volinette. She suspected that they lacked the bravery and innate sense of entitlement that made Janessa so formidable. However, that didn't stop them from cornering Volinette and her friend after class let out.

Volinette caught Baris's eye as Master Casto dismissed the class. She wanted to be out of the room before the harpies had a chance to regroup. Why she thought her luck should be any different today, she didn't know. From the time that Master Casto left the room, Syble was just steps behind Baris. Nixi and Halsie closed in on Volinette, blocking her escape.

"You didn't think you were going to get away with it, did you?" Nixi demanded, taking nominal leadership of the group in Janessa's absence. "The High Council will never rule against Janessa. Her parents are too well known and too powerful for that to happen."

"That's not what the Head Master says!" Baris exclaimed. Volinette glanced at him. His hands were balled into fists by his side.

"Baris!" she snapped, hoping to quell some of the madness before it began in earnest.

"And how would a farm boy like you know what the Head Master says?" Syble demanded.

"We were there. We saw everything." Baris's eyes took on a hard gleam, something Volinette had never seen before. "Janessa wasn't so tough when the Grand Inquisitor sentenced her to censure!"

The harpies gave a collective gasp and a quick smile flashed across the boy's face before he regained his composure.

"Oh? Didn't know about that, did you?" Baris gave them a wicked grin. "You only have half the information. Yeah, they're calling a High Council of Masters to decide Janessa's fate…but it isn't to decide if she's guilty or innocent. Adamon already declared her guilty. It's done. Janessa's mother pleaded for the Council, begged the Head Master for it, to try and pull Janessa's bacon out of the fire!"

Volinette couldn't help but to commiserate with Baris. He'd put up with so much at the hands of the girls that it was only natural for him to want to take his pound of flesh. She just wished he'd done it in a more public place, or at least when they weren't outnumbered three-to-two.

The harpies recovered from the shock of Baris's revelation with relative ease. Nixi stepped forward, her eyes flashing with menace.

"Janessa's parents won't let anything happen to her, High Council of Masters or not. They certainly aren't going to let that…that outlander allow the Grand Inquisitor to censure her. They'll cause a revolt first. They have considerable power, you know."

Volinette couldn't believe her ears. Nixi's epithet, though technically true, was a vile accusation against the Head Master. Maera wasn't, strictly speaking, human, but her people, the Theid, were close enough to human that it shouldn't matter. Her retort was just as heated as Nixi's had been.

"I think you vastly overestimate the amount of sway they have, Nixi." Though she'd scolded Baris just moments before for wading into the fray, here she was doing the same thing. "My family probably has more influence than the Navitas."

As soon as she'd uttered the words, Volinette couldn't believe what she'd said. Her family stature had never entered into her life in the Academy. In fact, until it was proved otherwise by Janessa and her ilk, Volinette had always assumed that one's rank or standing outside the Academy or Great Tower had no bearing on the treatment one received once they had been welcomed into that hallowed institution. How wrong she had been. Now she knew better. Maybe if she'd pulled rank from the beginning, she wouldn't be in this mess now. That's not how she had wanted it to be, though. She'd wanted to stand on her own merit, for all the good it had done her.

"Yeah!" Baris agreed, taking up the baton and running with it. "Who's ever heard of a Navita outside the Academy or Blackbeach? Nobody. That's who. Everyone's heard of the Terris Singers. You can't swing a dead cat without hitting someone singing or humming one of their songs. What's that one you sang for Master Jotun earlier, Vol?"

Volinette was beginning to think that with friends like Baris, she didn't need enemies. Still, she knew he was just trying to help in his own way. Even if that way was as likely to get them killed as not.

"It was nothing," she said, trying to downplay Baris's enthusiasm. "Just an old fishing ballad."

"*You're* a Terris? As in, the traveling family minstrels?" Halsie barked, laughing. "Right. And I'm Queen of the Pheen."

"You're damn right she's a Terris, your *Majesty*," Baris countered. "She can prove it too. Can't you, Vol? Weren't you on the training ground, Halsie? Don't you remember what she did to that elemental? With her *voice*?"

Halsie exchanged glances with Nixi and Syble. For the first time since they'd started this confrontation, they looked as if they might be having second thoughts. Syble was behind the other two girls and was working her way toward the door.

Nixi struck first, but Baris was waiting. Nixi had only spoken a few words of her cantrip when Baris finished his spell. It was a simple magic missile, a bolt of white light that streaked from his outstretched fingers and slammed into Nixi's face. Her head snapped back on her neck. The girl's cry of rage and pain assured Volinette that the girl wasn't dead, and allowed her to turn her attention on Halsie, who was following up on Nixi's spell with one of her own.

Baris dodged Halsie's bolt easily, and fired back one of his own. It went wide and hit a chair, tossing it across the room with a clatter. Volinette took a deep breath from her belly, and it rushed out in a pure, clear note. Taking advantage of her instinct, she slipped into the Quintessential Sphere. The silver-gray living memory of the Ethereal Realm intruded on her vision. Nixi and Halsie were easy to see, their darker gray shadows dominating her view. Syble's shade was a lighter gray and further off. She wasn't as much of a threat as she'd have liked everyone, especially Baris, to believe.

Focusing on memories of storms, thunder, and violent winds, Volinette summoned forth the memories of ancient skies gone dark. She sang words of power that she'd never heard before and had never read in any book. These were the songs of the wind, whispering their names in her ear just ahead of the words tumbling from her lips.

The impact of slipping back into the physical realm made her rock back on her feet, but she managed to keep her balance. Volinette blinked, unable to accept what she saw with her own eyes. A tempest raged around her fingertips. Dark clouds rumbled with muted thunder, fighting for attention from the miniature gale that pushed and pulled the clouds in every direction imaginable. Flashes of white lit the room as tiny bolts of lightning danced from cloud to cloud.

By the time Halsie realized the danger she was in, it was too late. The melody Volinette was singing came to a crashing crescendo and the storm in her hands raced forward in a blue-gray blur. It slammed into Halsie chest high and expanded, lifting both Halsie and Nixi off the ground and launching them toward Syble who scrambled toward the door.

The three of them landed in a sprawling heap of arms and legs that stuck out in every direction. For a few moments, they fought against each other before realizing that neither Volinette nor Baris were in their pile of flailing limbs. They managed to get to their feet and looked back at the prey who had become the predators. Nixi looked as if she wanted to press the fight and continue a counterattack, but Syble and Halsie each grabbed an arm and dragged her out the door and into the hallway beyond.

It took some time for the residual power that Volinette had called from the Quintessential Sphere to dissipate. The hair on her arms and head stood straight out. She ran her fingers through the crackling strands, trying to get them to lay down as they should. She turned to look at Baris, whose face was split by a wide grin.

"Did ya see that?" he crowed, clapping with delight. "You bowled them right over! I bet that's the last time they try and pull rank on you."

"This isn't funny, Baris." Volinette felt unsteady on her feet and sank into one of the chairs by the nearest table.

"Like hell it's not," Baris snorted. "They finally got the smallest taste of what they've got coming to them. I'm glad you gave it to them, too. You have no idea how long I've waited for that to happen. You were incredible. How'd you do that?"

"How did I do what?"

"*How'd I do what?*" Baris tossed up his hands in exasperation. "Oh, I dunno, maybe summon a miniature hurricane in the middle of a classroom and use it to throw your enemies across the room?"

"I didn't."

Baris gaped at her. He waved his hands in a gesture that Volinette couldn't decipher while his mouth opened and closed like a landed fish.

"You...*didn't?*" he sputtered, finally finding his voice. "I think if you ask any of those girls, they're going to tell you otherwise. You whomped them but good."

"You helped," she said by way of weak protest.

"Oh, yeah, my piddly magic missile was the thing that turned the tide in that whole battle. I'll admit, though, that I gave Nixi a pretty good black eye." He paused a moment, rubbing his chin with one hand. "What did you mean when you said 'I didn't,' when I asked you how you'd done it?"

"I meant that I didn't do it," Volinette snapped, her voice raising to a near shout. "I didn't cast any spell. I slipped into the Quintessential Sphere and—"

She broke off. Baris was her closest friend in the Academy, but she wasn't sure she wanted him to know what had happened. She'd never heard of any Quintessentialist being able to cast spells without knowing them beforehand. She was enough of an outcast already. She didn't need to make matters any worse.

"And what?" Baris prompted, still stroking his chin.

It was obvious that he wasn't just going to let this go. She might be able to wiggle out of explaining it now, but eventually he would wear her down and Volinette would end up telling him. Might as well just get it over with now, she thought.

"You're going to think I'm crazy," she said, her shoulders sagging.

"Try me." Baris hopped up on the table next to her and let his legs dangle off the side. "We live in a pretty unique place."

"The sphere sang to me," she blurted, deciding that getting it all out at once was best. "It was like I could hear the words in my head a second before they came out of my mouth. I'd never heard those words before, not in a spell, not in a song. Somehow, though, I sang them. The Sphere told me what to sing and I sang it."

To his credit, Baris didn't laugh at her, which is what Volinette had expected him to do. Instead, he sat on the table and stroked his chin, swinging his legs back and forth and staring into space.

"Well?" she demanded.

"Well what?"

"Well tell me what you're thinking! I just told you that I'm probably a monster or a freak. You think I'm crazy, right? There's no way that could actually have happened. I don't even believe it, and I'm the one it happened to!"

"I don't think you're crazy." He was dead serious. Something that was such a rarity for Baris that it scared Volinette more than what she'd just done. "I was just thinking about what Master Jotun said, about you being special. I think he's right. I think you're something that nobody's ever seen before."

Before she could stop herself, Volinette leapt to her feet and threw her arms around him. She kissed Baris on the cheek.

"Hey!" he exclaimed, pulling away. "What'd you do that for?"

"Because you're amazing."

"Well, that much is true." His grin faded a trifle. "I think we ought to see Master Jotun and tell him what you did."

A tight knot of fear tied itself around Volinette's stomach. She swallowed, the sound much louder than it should have been in the quiet classroom.

"I'll get in trouble," she whispered.

Baris laughed.

"I doubt it. Master Jotun was Head Master of the Academy for sixty years. He's seen every form of mischief and merry-making known to man. More importantly, he bears no particular love for the Navita family. They're the ones who ousted him, you know?"

"Really?"

Baris nodded. "Yep. Convinced a bunch of the Masters that he was too old to continue his duties. They had him shunted off to the Great Library for his trouble. Janessa's dad thought he'd just slide into the Head Master's office, but Master Jotun got him good."

"How?"

"Master Jotun's clever," Baris said, his eyes twinkling. "He put in a word with Master Indra and Lacrymosa and they worked their gift of gab on a few of the more influential Masters. Things sort of snowballed from there. They elected Maera as Head

Master by one of the largest margins in history. Master Jotun says the Navitas were furious."

"Sounds like someone who I can trust with my unique…er…problem."

"Not much of a problem, if you ask me. Saved our butts today, didn't it?"

Baris grinned at her and hopped off the table. He extended his hand, waggling it at her until she took it, experiencing the customary tingle.

"Come on, I'm starving. Let's go get something to eat, then we can see about talking to Master Jotun."

"I'm not hungry."

"You will be, though. You did some pretty hefty magic there, whether you know how you did it or not."

As if agreeing with Baris, her stomach rumbled loudly.

"Alright! Alright!" she cried, laughing.

Hand in hand, they left the classroom. As they entered the hallway, the entire building shook, the ground beneath their feet heaving so violently that they had to clutch the wall to keep from falling. Baris turned to Volinette.

"What the hell was that?"

Chapter Sixteen

Violent shaking heaved the earth up and down beneath their feet, tossing Volinette and Baris against the walls of the corridor. They sank to the floor, clutching each other as much to keep from being separated by the upheaval as for emotional support. A fine sifting of dust slipped from the joints in the walls and ceiling, floating to the ground with a peacefulness in stark contrast to the savagery of the shaking.

After a minute that seemed like an hour, the disturbance passed. Confused students appeared in the corridor, looking around for an explanation for the unexpected assault. Volinette pushed herself to her feet first. She extended her hand to Baris, giving him a little yank and getting him back to his feet again. He glanced around with a shrug.

"Well, that was interesting."

The crowd parted as Master Casto came striding down the hall, his long robes swirling around his ankles. He stopped here and there for a word with a Master or with a student. His bushy eyebrows went up when he came across Volinette and her companion.

"Still here? I'd have thought you'd be enjoying your midday break. Is something wrong?"

"Nothing Volinette couldn't handle," Baris quipped. She punched him in the arm and scowled in his direction, hoping he'd get the message and shut his mouth.

"What was that tremor, Master Casto?" Volinette asked loudly, drowning out Baris's cry of pain and protest.

Master Casto frowned and shook his head.

"I don't know. I'm actually on my way to find Master Vendur so that I can ask him that very question." He cast a sharp look at Baris. "Have either of you seen him?"

"Not today," Baris replied before Volinette could get a word in edgewise.

Fulgent's eyes lingered on the young man's face a moment longer, just long enough to be disconcerting. Then he nodded.

"If you do, please tell him that I'm looking for him. I'll see you both for second session this afternoon."

After Master Casto had moved down the hall, Baris rounded on Volinette.

"Hey! What'd you do that for?"

"Not everyone in the Academy needs to know about the kind of mess we're in, Baris. I know you think it's all just a big adventure, but I'm thinking about our future here."

"Worrying about it, you mean," Baris replied with a sour face. "It doesn't hurt for anyone to know what's going to happen to Janessa. She's got it coming. Besides, the rumor is going to spread with or without our help."

"Still, we don't need to be throwing fuel on the fire."

Baris shrugged. "Alright. Whatever you say."

The students who had been milling about in the corridor were being herded back into their respective classrooms by the Masters overseeing their instruction.

There really wasn't any reason to hang about in the school wing, other than the fact that Volinette was worried about meeting up with the harpies in the cafeteria.

"I wonder what's for lunch today," Baris mused, turning toward the end of the corridor that was nearest to the courtyard across from the cafeteria. It was as if he could read Volinette's mind. He made a face. "It better not be pickled sea snake again. I don't know what it is about these people, but their fondness for weird sea creatures as food takes some getting used to."

He reached down and took her by the hand. She ignored the faint pain of link-shock as it danced between them.

"C'mon," he said. "Nixi isn't likely to show her face in public until that shiner I gave her goes down a little."

Volinette gave him a tolerant smile and followed him to the door at the end of the corridor. He took entirely too much joy in the damage he'd done to the girl. Not that she didn't deserve it, but it wasn't a proper thing to gloat about.

They turned onto the wide lane leading up to the Great Tower. A low stone wall separated the walkway from the well-manicured grass just beyond. The grounds of the Academy of Arcane Arts and Sciences were renowned across the Imperium for the wide variety of exotic species of plants and flowers that grew there. A little magical intervention helped some of the specimens thrive, even though they were so very far from home. Volinette loved to look at the flowers on her way to and from the various buildings in the complex.

One of her favorites was the Etherlily, a flowering bush that responded to subtle variations in the Quintessential Sphere. As they passed it, Volinette succumbed to habit and glanced over at it. What she saw took her breath away. The blooms, usually vibrant with bright whites, yellows, and pinks, were dark blue and black. The green fronds at the base of the plant reached out toward the girls' dormitory, as if they were trying to draw the building closer.

"Baris," Volinette gasped. "Look at that!"

"Yeah, it's pretty. Can we go? I'm hungry."

Volinette wanted to explain how significant the change in the flower was, that there was definitely something wrong for it to be behaving so strangely. She tried to find the words to voice her concern, but it was too late.

Dark clouds were forming over the girls' dorm. Billows of black and violet seemed to engulf the building. Flashes of purple light danced within the clouds, accompanied by the sound of tortured howls that made the hair on the back of Volinette's neck stand on end.

"Okay," Baris said, backing away from the wall. "I'm not hungry anymore, but I *really* want to go now."

"I think you're right, but where? I guess seeing Master Jotun will have to wait."

A rage-filled bellow came from inside the cloud surrounding the dormitory. The bellow was answered by a series of high, shrill screams. A few girls bolted out of the swirling mist, shooting off in every direction, as they got clear of whatever was happening inside.

"Into the tower, both of you, now!" a familiar voice yelled from behind them. Volinette tossed a look over her shoulder and saw Olin Oldwell. He was ushering a handful of other apprentices toward the tower. As soon as the majority of them had disappeared up the path toward the tower, Olin leapt the wall and raced toward the enshrouded dorm.

Olin had nearly reached the wall of shadow when the most horrific thing Volinette had ever seen jumped out of the darkness and landed with a howl on the green grass of the courtyard. It towered over Olin and was a giant compared to the girls who hadn't managed to escape before it arrived. It stood half-again as tall as the tallest man Volinette had ever seen.

Its six legs were roped with bunches of glistening black muscle and supported a fat, squat body. Atop the front part of the body, a huge horned head perched, swiveling to and fro as if searching for prey with its six crimson eyes, one for each leg. Rows upon rows of sharp fangs made up the lower part of the head and oozed with milky white secretions. It was something Volinette never could have imagined, not even in her worst nightmares.

"Inside," Volinette managed to say, stumbling backward away from the wall as Baris had done moments earlier. "We need to get inside, Baris. Now!"

Baris didn't answer. He seemed to be rooted to the spot. His eyes were following the massive thing as it stalked Olin. The Inquisitor had stopped just beyond the reach of the predator staring down at him. Olin shouted the words of a spell, made unintelligible by the distance between them. The air in front of the Inquisitor shimmered, blurring the clouds and the dormitory building beyond.

With a scream that made Volinette's blood run cold, the thing wound down into a crouch, the powerful leg muscles bunching with straining effort. It sprang forward. A moment later it folded in on itself as it collided with the barrier Olin had erected. The force of the impact rocked the Inquisitor back on his heels. He managed to keep his footing, but he was dangerously off balance.

Volinette was torn between the tower and the courtyard. One offered the safety of being amongst the most powerful mages in the Imperium. The other offered a fight that she wasn't sure Olin could win on his own. There was no one else who could help the Inquisitor. No one except herself and Baris.

"Come on," she said, putting her palm against the base of Baris's neck. She was counting on link-shock being enough to knock the boy out of his paralysis. It worked. Baris jumped, batting her hand away. He rounded on her, eyes blazing with power he'd drawn from the Quintessential Sphere.

"Volinette." He seemed to recognize her from across a vast distance. Part of him was still in the sphere. "We've got to help. Nobody else will make it in time."

"I know." She shot a quick look out across the courtyard. The monster was slamming its forelegs into Olin's barrier, forcing him backward toward the tower. When she looked back, Baris was already over the wall and rushing toward Olin.

Baris was hurling spears of white light as he ran. The projectiles were brighter and more powerful than any Volinette had seen him cast before. Most of them went wide, missing his target by several feet or more.

Those that did make contact ripped shallow furrows in the ink-black flesh, spraying green ichor from the wounds.

The thing stopped advancing on Olin and turned to face the new threat. Wavering on unsteady legs, it swayed back and forth, as if weighing its options in what to attack first. Apparently deciding that Baris was the more vulnerable prey, it turned on the young Quintessentialist and scurried forward with surprising speed.

Volinette slipped into the Quintessential Sphere and the world took on the strange silver-gray cast that stemmed from sphere sight. Focusing with all her will, she summoned forth memories of flame. Through the Sphere, she brought forward the echo of every hunter's campfire, of lanterns hung over dinner tables, and of a hundred million candles that had been burning in the timelessness of the Sphere for thousands of years. These memories she channeled into the palm of her hand. She felt the flames spring to life, hovering just above her skin, bathing her in their warmth.

She tried to hurl the ball of flame at the beast advancing on Baris, but something stopped her. No matter how hard she tried to direct the projectile, her hand stayed frozen out in front of her. Master Jotun's words echoed down the tunnel of her mind. She couldn't block them out. Something special, something special, something special. The words throbbed in her head like a heartbeat, added to by the same words repeated by Baris later. Two simple words that became a chorus, blocking out everything else, even the ability to save her best friend from certain death.

"I don't know what you want from me!" she cried, but instead of coming from her throat, the words in her head sliced through the cacophony like a blade.

The answer came not in the form of words, but in a strange tickle in her chest. She took a deep breath, trying to ease the strange feeling. Her diaphragm moved down, sustaining the inhalation, and Volinette realized what the Sphere wanted her to do. Closing her eyes, she blocked out the last vestiges of the physical world. Volinette sang, beginning with a single clarion note and waiting for the words to come.

Come they did, unbidden, as if whispered to her on the back of a roaring wind. She sang the words as quickly as they tumbled through her head. The flames still burned in one hand, but in the other, she felt the power of the Sphere coalescing. Volinette screwed her eyes shut tight, determined not to break her commune with the Ethereal Realm until it had finished speaking, or singing, through her. As the last note passed her parched lips, her eyes sprang open and she marveled at the blue-white globe of energy that hovered above her other hand.

It pulsed gently, thrumming with a faint echo of the words she had just sung. Baris's scream of fear brought her back into the moment, and she looked up to see the creature on top of the boy. Baris had been knocked to the ground and the thing was standing over him, reared up on its middle and rear legs. The forelegs were drawn up, preparing to strike a killing blow. There was no time to waste.

As series of brilliant yellow globes smashed into the monster's head from the side, bright flashes of light exploding around it. Olin's offense pushed it off to one side, giving Baris just enough time to roll from under the descending legs. He wouldn't last very long unless the battle was ended and soon.

Pain seared through Volinette's head and chest, feedback from the power of the Sphere she'd held for what seemed like hours. If she didn't release it, she knew the psychic backlash of the dissipating spell might kill her. She looked out across the courtyard, trained her mind's eye on the massive monster's head, and extended her hands.

As she released her hold on the orbs, they streaked across the open area between Volinette and her foe. Baris, just getting to his feet, threw himself back to the ground to avoid being hit by her missiles. The ball of flame hit first, exploding into a wreath of flame that encircled the beast's head, making it roar in anger and pain. The other sphere, the one of blue-white magic summoned through her song, hit a second later, and Volinette watched what happened next with amazement.

The flames, which had been confined to the great head, multiplied, rippling down the lines and curves of the body. Living snakes of flame entwined the beast, growing, spreading, and covering it until the entire body was a mass of magic fire. The flames began to pulse in the same way the Sphere had done. With each new flash of fire, the thing screamed louder. It pulsed faster and faster, until the brightness of the fire was so great that Volinette had to shield her eyes from the conflagration. It exploded, raining smoldering flesh and ichor down over the courtyard. Volinette escaped most of the gore, but poor Baris was covered in it.

Volinette's heart fell. Blackness still covered the girls' dormitory. The thing they had killed hadn't been the cause, or killing it hadn't been enough to release the building from the evil that gripped it.

Olin and Baris, who had recovered his feet for the second time, were rushing toward her from across the courtyard. Sudden pain ripped through her body, setting her aflame from the inside out. She burned from tips of her toes to the top of her head. An anguished wail escaped her lips, burning her throat as it passed from deep within her soul, out into the world.

Volinette saw the looks on Olin and Baris's face change as they ran toward her. Olin's was a look of horrified realization. Baris's was pure, unfettered panic. She didn't have more than a few seconds to consider either expression before she tumbled into the darkness between the realms.

Chapter Seventeen

It seemed to Volinette as if she were stumbling down a long, dark tunnel. She could see nothing, and her grasping fingers met only a spongy resistance. Something like thick carpet was underfoot, flexible and not feeling sturdy at all to stand on. Droning, like the distant hum of a thousand bees, filled her ears and made it impossible to think with any clarity, much less call on the power of the Quintessential Sphere.

"I told you it was dangerous," a voice echoed through the void. Her father's voice. "I told you it was dangerous and you weren't likely to survive."

Volinette ignored him. Wherever she was, it was comforting to know that her father's arguments were the same predictable, paranoid drivel they'd always been.

"Look what you've done to your grandfather's lute!" her mother screeched. "Ruined! Just like you've ruined your life and career. Just like you'll ruin this family!"

Other voices rang out through the darkness. Her brother. Her sisters. A dozen people from Dragonfell who had told her that hiding her magical ability was the only sensible thing to do. She was born into one of the most prestigious entertaining families in the whole Imperium. What did she need with magic anyway?

"The Head Master believes in me," Volinette said. "Master Jotun thinks I'm special. Baris believes in me too."

"You'll never be a Master," a voice sneered. That one was easy to recognize as well. That was Janessa's voice. "You'll never be as important as I am."

Volinette stopped her aimless wandering. She wasn't getting anywhere anyway. She thought about the words that the non-Janessa had spoken. It surprised her that she didn't feel badly about it. Those words summed up the greatest fears she'd arrived at the tower with. Since then, she'd faced far more insidious words, said by far more insidious people. Somehow, hearing that she might never be a certain rank didn't hurt as much as they might have before.

"I'll be what I am meant to be," Volinette said, feeling the weight of the words as she said them. "If what I'm meant to be is something other than what I've dreamed of, then so be it. I'll adapt. I'll grow. I'll learn. That's what I'm meant to do. Anything else that happens is a gift."

It took a moment for her to realize that the far off droning had stopped. Though just as dark, the quiet of the void seemed more welcoming. The ground underfoot now seemed to support her instead of impeding her. Her steps no longer stumbled when she tried to walk.

"Volinette?" Baris's voice wasn't the directionless voice of the void. In seemed to be coming from far up ahead. She stretched her arms out in front of her, though she saw nothing, and walked toward the sound.

"Baris?"

"Volinette!" Baris sounded scared. "Wake up!"

"I'm awake," she protested, still plodding toward his voice. "I'm here."

"Then open your eyes! We need to go."

Light flooded her vision. She raised a weak hand to block out the offending brightness and realized how badly she hurt all over. Her head pounded as if there were someone inside it, beating on the biggest drum in the world. Her arms and legs were leaden and burned with the slightest movement. Her chest hurt worst of all, a deep burning ache that seemed to be lodged under her breastbone and wrapped around to her spine.

When she was finally able to focus her eyes, Volinette saw Baris and Olin crouched over her. Ignoring the screaming of the muscles in her arms, she managed to sit up. The world swam and she groaned, shaking her head to try and clear away the worst of the fog.

"Are you okay?" Olin asked her in a more solicitous tone than she'd ever heard from him. "We need to get you to the tower. There seems to be more portals opening."

"I'll manage," she said through gritted teeth. She forced herself up onto her knees, then onto unsteady feet. She swayed from side to side, in danger of losing her balance, before Baris put one of her arms across his shoulders and Olin did the same on the other side.

What should have been a mild tingle of link-shock, instead tore through her already weakened frame like wildfire. She cried out and went rigid, but Olin ordered Baris to keep moving.

"She overtaxed herself with that amazing piece of spellcraft," the Inquisitor said. "Her system is raw, and any magical stimulation is going to be quite painful for some time. It will pass."

As Baris and Olin carried her into the lower floor of the Great Tower of High Magic, Volinette saw that she was in much better shape than some. The entrance hall had been converted into a temporary triage ward. Injured students and Masters alike were laid out where there was space, or propped up against walls and made as comfortable as possible. From what she could see, there were far too many patients and far too few healers and clerics scurrying back and forth between their charges.

"I need to leave you here, I'm sorry." Olin lowered her to the floor and rushed off, calling to another mage who was passing through the entrance hall.

"How long was I out?" she asked Baris, who looked adrift in a sea of memory.

"Not long," he replied, snapping out of his reverie. "A couple of minutes, maybe. You gave Olin a right scare. He wasn't sure you were coming back."

"And you knew I'd be fine, right?"

"Of course," he said with a grin. "It'll take more than some fancy spell to knock you out of the game. I'd ask you how you did it, but I've got a feeling I already know the answer."

"It just came to me."

Baris grinned. "'Course it did. Cause you're Volinette Terris, super mage."

"Cut it out," she snapped, feeling her cheeks burning.

"I told you that Master Jotun was right." He looked out past the entrance, beyond the Academy walls. "I hope he's okay. How are you feeling?"

"Like someone took me apart and put me back together wrong. I'll live. Think there's anything we can do to help?"

"Dunno, but I guess it doesn't hurt to ask."

Getting on her feet took longer than expected. They had to find someone who wasn't busy with the injured and avoid the Masters who were gathering. They stumbled, quite literally, over Master Casto, who was sitting up against the wall, holding a pad of folded cloth to a nasty gash on his forehead.

"Master Casto!" Volinette dropped to one knee beside him. "Are you alright? Did you find Adamon?"

"I did. How do you think I got this?" Fulgent peeled back the bandage to show that, while the wound bled freely, it was shallow. "I'm glad that both of you are safe. I was worried since you were still in the School of Sorcery when the attack began."

"What's going on? Where did these things come from?"

"I wish I knew what was going on, dear girl. I can tell you with certainty that there are demons from the Deep Void loose on the Academy grounds, and I'd give anything to know how that happened."

Baris and Volinette exchanged worried looks. She couldn't be sure that her theory was right, but it was obvious that Baris was thinking the same thing, or close enough not to matter very much.

"Master Casto," she asked through lips that didn't want to move. "Could the Transcendental Prism be used to open portals to the Deep Void?"

Fulgent gave her a startled look and her heart sank. She couldn't shake the feeling that she knew exactly how the demons had gotten loose in the Academy. If she was right, Baris had been spot on when he said that Nixi wouldn't show her face in public. She hadn't. She had done something much worse.

"I suppose, in theory, yes, the Prism could be used to pierce the Meridian and open a gate to the Deep Void. Why?"

"Janessa stole the Prism from the Hall of Wonders," Volinette said. Ignoring the shock in the old Master's face, she continued, "Even under the threat of censure, she wouldn't reveal where it was hidden, but I bet that Nixi, Syble, and Halsie knew exactly where to find it."

Master Casto shook his head and sighed. "No, I don't think that a single, inexperienced Quintessentialist could open a portal to the Deep Void. Not even with the focus of the Prism."

"What about the three of them working together?" Volinette asked, her eyes begging him to deny that it was even a possibility.

Fulgent lowered his bandage and laid it in his lap. He bowed his head, as if the blood-stained cloth held the answers to the mysteries of the universe. He stayed that way for so long that Volinette thought he might have fallen asleep. When he looked up at last, the look she saw in his eyes made her wish that he had.

"The three of them working together? Yes, I believe they could. The demons of the Deep Void will exploit any weakness they perceive. If the girls managed to even come close to finishing a portal ritual to the Deep Void, I'm sure there was something on the other side just waiting to help them open the door."

"Those things are intelligent?" Baris asked in disbelief.

"Not all of them," Fulgent said with a sigh. "Some of them? Absolutely. Intelligent enough to keep the Pheen busy with a war that's been raging for millennia."

"The Pheen!" Volinette seized Master Casto's words as if they held the key to stopping the madness going on around them. "Can't we ask Lacrymosa for help?"

Fulgent shook his head slowly, his eyes sad. "Once Pheen leave the Meridian, they're stripped of most of their powers. Lacrymosa would be in great danger, for reasons I don't have time to explain. As soon as I knew there were demons on the Academy grounds, I banished her. I sent her to Master Jotun in the library."

"What chance do we have against them?" Baris slumped over, the picture of defeat. "If the Pheen have been battling them for hundreds of years, what are we going to do? Make them a welcome banquet?"

"This is no time to be flippant, young man. As luck would have it, the demons, much like the Pheen, are weaker the farther away from their native plane they travel. It's not going to be easy, but we should be able to drive them back."

"Where do we start?" Volinette asked. Despite the pain still wracking her body, she'd do whatever she could to ensure the safety of Blackbeach and the people who lived there. Master Casto raised a hand, arresting her enthusiasm.

"I appreciate your willingness to help, Volinette, and no one disputes your strength or the power you've already demonstrated, but this is a matter for the Masters to deal with. The best thing you can do is stay out of the way and let those more powerful do what they need to do."

Before Volinette could object, Maera, Adamon, and Olin arrived. Under normal circumstances, she would have been sobered by the arrival of some of the most powerful Quintessentialists in the Imperium. Instead, she was annoyed that their presence meant that she would be excluded from seeing the incursion through until its end. Those more powerful, indeed. If it hadn't been for her abilities, both Olin and Baris would be in much worse shape than they were now.

"Master Casto," Maera said without even acknowledging that Volinette and Baris were standing there. "If you're well enough, we need you in the Council Chamber at once."

"Of course, Head Master."

As soon as Fulgent stood, he, Adamon, and Maera strode across the chamber toward the corridor that would lead to the Council room. Olin, to his credit, hung back.

"The two of you should go up to the third floor. The rest of the apprentices and Acolytes are gathering there. It will be safe until we get things under control."

"We can help," Volinette said, but Olin shook his head.

"No, the best thing for you and Baris to do now is stay with the others. You've got a story to tell. A lot of the younger apprentices are saying that the demons can't be defeated. The two of you know better, don't you? Share your experience."

"I guess," Baris said, but it was clear that he'd rather be in the thick of things.

"You'll get your chance when you're older." Olin gave Baris a light punch in the shoulder. "You'd make a good Inquisitor."

Olin excused himself and hurried after the Head Master and the others. Baris looked at her, and Volinette shrugged. The decision had been made for them. Looking around the room, she saw a few of the older journeymen escorting the younger students through the triage area and into the lift that would take them to the higher levels.

"I guess we might as well go up. I don't think there's much we can do down here." Volinette rubbed her temples with her palms. The ache was maddening, but it was starting to subside. She'd take what she could get. "I could use the rest, to be honest."

Baris's eyes lingered on the corridor where the Masters had gone. He looked as if he wanted to protest, but he shrugged with a sigh.

"Alright. I suppose we'd better. No sense in making more of a mess of things down here." He brightened. "Besides, the Masters wouldn't like it if you made them look bad with your tricks."

"I didn't do anything," she countered, somewhat heatedly.

"Maybe not, but you had the good sense not to fight it. How many of these people do you think could do that? Can you just imagine Janessa giving up control and letting the power of the Quintessential Sphere guide her? Not bloody likely. You're special. All the important people think so. Just deal with it."

Volinette was very quiet as they followed the steady stream of students. The queue outside the lift dock was thick with bodies, enough to convince them to take the curving stairs that led up through the interior of the tower. As they stepped out onto the wide landing two stories up, a journeyman greeted them and ushered them into a large storage room that had been cleared for their use.

A few tables and lots of chairs were scattered about. A group of journeymen was moving cots into the room and arranging them along the walls. Soon, there would be enough accommodations to turn the room into a makeshift dormitory.

Judging by the tear-streaked faces of some of the younger apprentices, she knew that Olin had been correct in his assessment of the emotional toll being taken.

Baris leaned in close so he could whisper in her ear without anyone else hearing.

"Did you notice who isn't here?"

She had, but her stomach still gave a lurch when he mentioned it. Halsie, Nixi, and Syble were nowhere to be found. Deep in hear heart, she knew the girls were responsible for the chaos that was unraveling around them.

For the better part of an hour, Volinette and Baris toured the room. They spoke to members of their School, as well as apprentices from the School of Summoning, and the School of Enchantment. A few of the children were so rattled by the experience that Volinette wondered if they'd be able to continue their education.

With nothing better to do, Volinette flopped onto a cot and laid back. Everything hurt. Sitting hurt. Standing hurt. Laying down hurt. As promised, the pain was beginning to fade, but it was going much slower than she would have liked.

Baris dragged a chair over and dropped into it, propping his feet on the edge of her cot.

"I wonder what the Masters are doing. Think they're done with the Council meeting by now?"

"I hope so," Volinette said, aghast. "If not, how many of those things do you think would be rampaging around the Academy?"

"Dunno, but I wish we could be out there instead of cooped up in here. We can't even see what is going on."

A shudder ran up Volinette's spine as she remembered how ugly and terrifying the creature they'd fought had been. She wasn't sure she needed to see any more of them. As if reading her thoughts, Baris sat bolt upright.

"Hey!" he said, dropping his feet from her cot. "I've got an idea."

Volinette sat up, eyeing him warily. When Baris used that particular tone of voice, he was scheming. Sometimes his plans worked out perfectly. More often than not, however, they ended up going all sorts of wrong.

"What?"

"Come on," he said, grabbing her hand and ignoring her yelp of pain. "I need to talk to that girl from the School of Summoning. You know, the one with the long black hair."

"The one you were making eyes at?"

Baris clutched his chest and pantomimed pulling a dagger out of his heart. Volinette gave him a weak laugh.

"I was not…but I totally will if she can do what I want her to do."

It didn't take very long for them to find the girl with the long, silky black tresses.

"You're back," she said with a smile as Baris approached. Volinette nudged him in the ribs, and he pointedly ignored her.

"I am. You said you are an Acolyte in the School of Summoning, right?"

"Yes." The girl's smile faded a trifle and her eyes narrowed. "Why?"

"Well, since we're stuck here for the time being, I wondered if you could summon something for me. I can tell you exactly where it is."

"Baris," Volinette interrupted. "What are you doing?"

"Trust me. I just want my cube back." To the girl, he added, "I left my Seer's Cube somewhere. If you can summon it, we can see what's going on outside."

"Oh. Sure. I can do that easy."

As Volinette listened to Baris describe Adamon's office and desk in vivid detail, she wondered if the girl would have been so eager to help if she knew that the item she was summoning was on the Grand Inquisitor's desk.

The dark-haired girl sat down on the floor, folding one leg over the other. She turned her palms skyward, closed her eyes, and said words of power, enticing the Quintessential Sphere to allow Baris's crystal cube to traverse the boundaries of time and space.

A soft pop, like a stopper being pulled from a bottle, was the only indication that the spell had been completed successfully. Looking down, Volinette saw the Seer's Cube resting in the palm of the girl's hand.

Baris took it, offering his profuse thanks and swearing to return the favor in the future. He tossed it back and forth from one hand to the other as he grinned at Volinette.

"Alright, let's see what we can see."

Chapter Eighteen

Channeling her essence through the Seer's Cube was unlike anything Volinette had ever experienced. Where normal sphere sight washed the color out of the physical realm, leaving it a pale, washed out echo, the Seer's Cube showed them the world as their eyes would see it. In fact, she'd almost panicked when Baris had cast the spell. Seeing herself sitting cross-legged across from Baris was disorienting.

"You're sure I can return to my body?" she asked for the third time.

"Oh for crying out loud," he said. "Just try it already. Concentrate on being back in your body and open your eyes."

She did as she was told and found that she was, indeed, back in her body, sitting cross-legged on the floor across from Baris, who still had his eyes closed.

"Okay, so how do I get back in?"

"Close your eyes and concentrate on the cube, I'll do the rest."

Volinette did as she was told. She closed her eyes and concentrated on the cube, waiting for something to happen. Baris muttered something under his breath, and suddenly she was hovering over her body again. It was still weird, but having rejoined her body and come back into the cube, she felt better about it.

"Can we go now?"

"If you tell me how. You've done this before, Baris. I haven't."

"Okay, okay. It's dead easy. Just think what you want to do. Think forward, float forward. Think backward, float backward. Think about your body and you can hear what's going on around you. Think about your…uh…spirit, for lack of a better word, and you'll hear what's going on around your spirit."

"I can hear you and I wasn't thinking about hearing you."

"We're both inside the cube, silly. Of course we can hear each other."

"Oh." His matter of fact tone of voice told her she was worrying too much, so she quashed the voice in the back of her head that wanted to ask more questions.

"Come on."

Baris's spirit floated across the room, passing through chairs, tables, and a group of students who appeared to be none the wiser. He passed the journeymen who were standing guard at the door and stopped on the landing, waiting for her to catch up. Volinette thought of following Baris and her spirit body followed the same path he'd taken, passing through the same objects and people that he'd passed through.

"See? I told you. Simple. If you can kill a demon, you can master the Seer's Cube."

"I guess."

"Well, it beats sitting around not doing anything. At least this way we can see what's going on."

"And nobody can see us?"

"Ugh! Stop worrying! There are demons on the loose. Do you really think the Masters are going to be looking for a couple kids using a harmless bauble to see outside the room they're trapped in? Let it go, Volinette."

"Alright. Alright."

"Besides, we're not doing anything wrong. The cube is mine. Adamon just hadn't gotten around to returning it yet. I did him a favor by getting it myself. I didn't even go in his office."

Volinette wasn't sure that Adamon would see it that way when he found out, but she wasn't going to argue about it. By the time things were returned to normal on the Academy grounds, maybe he'd be too tired to be upset at Baris. Though, he didn't seem like someone who would take too kindly to having things removed from his space. Not even if the item in question did, in fact, belong to someone else.

Gliding toward the stairs, Volinette heard Baris laugh.

"What are you doing?"

"Going downstairs. I want to see what's happening in the entrance hall."

"Just think where you want to go. You can go anywhere you've been before. Sometimes you can even think yourself some place you've never been, if you get a good enough description that the Seer's Cube can figure it out. Otherwise, you just end up in a void."

"That doesn't sound like fun."

"It's no big deal. You just think yourself back to your body and try again."

"Can you get trapped outside your body?"

"Nah. It's just a projection. You're still you, you're just looking at the world through spirit eyes. It takes some getting used to. Fun once you get hang of it, though."

Volinette wasn't sure she'd ever get the hang of it. It felt weird and it made her uncomfortable on a level she couldn't quite explain. It wasn't just the uneasiness of the Baris's sly appropriation of the cube. It was something deeper. Something about the process itself. As uneasy as it made her, it was the only way they'd see what was going on outside their room, so she'd deal with it.

Taking Baris's advice, she thought of the spot in the entrance hall where they'd been standing earlier. It was just across from the big double doors that led out onto the path. Without warning, she was there, hovering inches over the floor. Baris arrived a moment later.

"Well, you're getting the hang of it," he said, spinning in a slow circle to take in the entirety of the room. "Guess they've moved the wounded to somewhere better."

She'd been too involved with her own discomfort to notice that the scurrying healers, clerics, and their patients were gone. Litter was strewn about the normally pristine hall. Jugs of water, discarded bandages, and pieces of healer equipment were scattered about. They'd apparently left in a hurry, not willing to stop to pick up after themselves. That alone was enough to send a chill up her spine.

If that wasn't enough, Volinette caught movement out of the corner of her eye. When she turned to get a better look, she screamed. There was a demon coming through the doors. Its shape was roughly that of a man standing between seven and eight feet tall. Three legs, each ending in a pod that secreted green mucus as it walked, moved it forward. The trunk was humanoid, but four arms sprouted from the sides where two were the standard. A misshapen head topped off the monstrosity, a mouthful of rotting yellow teeth that jutted from between twisted lips. Huge, fiery orange eyes that took up more than half the face swiveled to and fro in their sockets, taking measure of the entrance hall.

Then she was back in the temporary dorm, Baris's hand clapped over her mouth. She ignored the pain that coursed through her from that simple touch, more concerned by the look in her friend's eyes.

"Quiet!" He glanced over to the journeymen by the door who were watching them. He nodded to them and took his hand away from her mouth. "It's in the tower. I saw it too. The last thing you need to do is touch off a panic with your screaming."

"You're right. It just surprised me."

"You and me both, but we need to go get a better look."

She shuddered again.

"Why? And do we have to? And why?"

"We need to know where it's going. If it's coming up here, we need to tell the journeymen, and we all need to get out of here."

"Okay. Hurry."

Baris spoke the words of the spell so quickly that Volinette could only just make out his intonation. She floated free of her body once again. This time, she ignored the discomfort altogether. There was too much at stake. She willed herself to be in the entrance hall and appeared there a split-second later.

The demon was still there. She fought against the irrational urge to start laughing. There was a demon in the Great Tower, and the only thing she could think was how happy she was that it hadn't moved. Baris's spirit form appeared beside her.

"Good. It doesn't seem to be interested in the higher floors. At least, not yet."

As they watched, the demon settled back onto its legs, planting the mucus pods on floor. Each huge hand moved in the air, tracing intricate symbols that glowed with faint emerald luminescence. The ragged lips and jagged yellow teeth parted, allowing the thing's long black tongue to snake out of the maw as if it had a life of its own. The sounds it produced couldn't be called speech by any definition Volinette had ever heard. It was a series of grunts, screeches, and howls that sounded as inhuman as it looked.

No matter how it sounded, it was clear that the demon was calling on the power of the Quintessential Sphere. A purple and black mass began to swirl into existence on the floor of the chamber. It faded in from the edges of reality, spreading until it was almost twenty feet across.

"What is that?" she whispered to Baris, aware that they were still safe in the Seer's Cube and waiting for his snide remark.

"No idea," he whispered back. "But there's no way it's good."

Baris was right. It wasn't good. As they watched, a flood of smaller demons climbed, slithered, and flew through the open portal. Each one was more horrific than the last. Volinette had thought that the things they'd seen had been the worst, but she'd been mistaken. The monsters that were pouring into the tower were almost indescribable masses of fangs, claws, and appendages. Some of them went out the doors, some fell down the lift shaft that led to the bottom floors of the tower, and still more sought out the stairs, moving their way upward.

"Baris," she hissed, realizing that they were out of time.

No answer.

"Baris!" she said louder.

No answer.

"BARIS!" she shouted, snapping them both out of commune with the Seer's Cube.

He looked back at her, his eyes wide and haunted.

"I know. We need to tell them, now."

Baris snatched the cube off the floor between them and leapt to his feet. Volinette was only a moment behind. Most of the room was looking at them since they hadn't been subtle about their outburst. It didn't matter. Right now, the only thing that mattered was warning the journeymen that they were about to come under siege. It wouldn't take long for the second floor of the tower to be overrun. They'd seen no sign of the Masters during their exploration, but there was little hope that they were all waiting just one floor below. They were probably still investigating the first portal, not realizing what was happening inside the tower.

"What are the two of you going on about?" one of the journeyman, an older boy with a swarthy complexion, demanded as they ran up.

"There are demons in the tower," Volinette blurted, her heart pounding frantically against her ribs. "They're coming and will be here any minute."

"Demons inside the tower?" the young man barked laughter. "You must be mistaken."

Baris thrust his hand under the journeyman's nose, the cube sitting on his palm.

"Know what this is? Seer's Cube. We saw them. The demons are coming, and coming fast."

Two things happened almost simultaneously. First, the look on the journeyman's face changed from disbelief to fear. Second, a small, winged demon with a wedge-shaped black body and glowing green eyes streaked into the corridor from the direction of the stairs.

The other journeyman standing by the door reacted to the threat quicker than the one who'd been talking to Volinette and Baris. He rattled of a string of words that Volinette only vaguely identified as magic. A howling gale filled the corridor, dagger sharp shards of ice formed in mid-air and shredded the flying demon. Its scream of pain echoed into the room and touched off a panic among the apprentices like lightning to dry grassland.

Mortally wounded, the demon flopped to the floor of the corridor, a pulpy mass of blood and tissue. A number of calls from further down the hall told them that the flying sentry had been the least of their concerns.

The second journeyman committed to his role as guardian. He pushed Volinette and Baris away from the door.

"Get back, both of you." To the room, he yelled, "Everyone stay back away from the door. Prepare your spells and cantrips if you know them, and if you can control them well enough to only kill the demons and not your fellow students."

Volinette switched into sphere sight, casting down along the hall to the stairs where a handful of pitch black shapes were clawing their way toward them. Sphere sight was the most basic of all spellcraft. It wasn't even a cantrip, rather it was an innate ability for all Quintessentialists. That innate ability made her head feel as if it was going to split down the center. She couldn't imagine how painful it would be to actually use real, destructive magic.

Dropping out of the Sphere, she looked at Baris. His eyes glowed white with harnessed power. His fingers twitched, holding tight to bolts of energy he'd summoned. Magic missiles were his weapon of choice and these were a class above and beyond even what he'd used in the courtyard. He was learning through experience, that much was certain.

"Ready?" he asked, his voice throbbing with the strange vibration that accompanied the power of the sphere.

"No, but I'll do the best I can."

She called on the power of the Quintessential Sphere, coaxing memories of fire and destruction, of savage winds and lightning. No single element would save them from the onslaught of darkness that was about to sweep down upon them like a storm-tossed wave.

No matter how much it hurt, she would channel the primal forces of magic until the pain was so great she could no longer hold on to the tenuous link between her soul and the Ethereal Realm. She took a deep breath to calm her nerves and felt the power of the Sphere react to that instinct. It wanted her to sing again. She would sing, she promised, but not yet. Not until they were joined in battle against the foes that were probably, even now, still pouring into the tower from the portal below.

Bolts of white streaked past her. Baris had thrown his first missiles into the corridor, sending them racing toward targets that either deflected them with dark magic of their own or roared in pain as they were hit. The journeyman unleashed their spells next, filling the corridor with summoned ice and magical fire. Electricity crackled in the air. She could feel it dancing on her skin. Several Acolytes stepped forward, adding their own spells to the tumult. One of the demons fell and the others scrambled over it, ignoring its death throes.

A writhing green missile, a mutated mimic of the same spell Baris was using, split the air, shooting into the room and hitting the dark-haired girl who had summoned the cube for them squarely in the chest. Her anguished cry turned into a sickly burble as her skin bubbled, the flesh and muscle melting away from gore stained bones, which collapsed in a haphazard pile.

Full blooded panic swept through the room like a dark tide, and Volinette waded into the fray.

Chapter Nineteen

"Look out!"

Volinette's shout only just kept Baris from being skewered by the razor sharp claws of the demon that towered over him. Baris brought both his hands together, as if he were applauding their performance. Instead, the magic missiles he had summoned merged with each other, becoming a single massive bolt. He twisted his hands and thrust them forward. The missile flew straight and true, slamming into the demon waist high. It burned a hole through flesh and bone, letting them see straight through to the battle raging on the other side.

Bodies littered the floor. Half a dozen apprentices had fallen to claw, fang, or spell. In places, the floor was slick with blood, and they had to be careful not to slip, lest the demons take advantage of the temporary weakness. Though they'd lost a few of their force, Volinette was impressed with how well the students were working together against a threat that never seemed to ease.

The apprentices who couldn't concentrate enough to cast, or who didn't have the confidence to add their spellcraft to the battle, had been shoving cots, tables, and chairs up to the doorway, creating a waist high barricade that the demons were throwing themselves against with undiminished fervor.

Volinette and Baris crouched down behind the barricade now. She squeezed her eyes shut, trying to will away the pain that burned in her chest and made her head feel like it was going to explode. She'd taken a nasty knock to the ribs while the barricade was going up, and that made it hard to inhale, much less sustain a proper note. Still, the Quintessential Sphere was singing through her, and as long as it continued to whisper the words, she would give them a voice.

"You alright?" Baris spared her a quick glance, but his attention was on the barrier and the journeymen standing guard. There had been a few of these brief lulls in the battle, just enough time for them to catch their breath. Baris had guessed that it was the time it took for another wave of demons to come through the portal. That, or the growing pile of otherworldly bodies stacking up outside the barricade had given the demons cause to think twice.

"I'll be fine. How is it out there?"

"Juicy. We're gonna need to find a way to close that portal. I don't think we can wait for the Masters to rescue us. I think they've got their hands full."

"What about the cube? Maybe we can figure out how long it'll be before we can count on reinforcements."

Baris rummaged around in his pocket and tossed her the Seer's Cube.

"You heard the cantrip it requires, it's pretty simple. Don't be long though. We really need you here fighting."

"You're not coming with me?"

He ducked suddenly as something struck the other side of the makeshift barricade. Wood splintered. Baris shook his head.

"Can't. Both of us can't go. Hurry."

He gave her a little shove, pushing her deeper into the room and away from the barricade. No part of the room was particularly safe, but at least being further away from the door would minimize the risk of being hit by a rogue spell. She half-ran, half-crawled to the back wall, hunkering down over the cube and whispering the words of command. A moment later, she was hovering above herself, seeing the carnage from a new angle.

Through force of will, she appeared in the entrance hall of the Great Tower. The arch demon was gone, but his summoned portal was there, disgorging more of his minions. At the rate they were arriving, the students on the third floor would be fighting forever. She wondered if there was anyone still alive on the second floor. There almost had to be, because they alone couldn't be fighting off the sheer numbers coming through the portal. In fact, all the levels of the tower must have been coming under siege. After all, the curved stairs ran the entire height and depth of the tower, from the top floor down to the Inquisitors' cells.

The Inquisitors' cells! Janessa was still locked away down there, waiting for Adamon or Olin to return. If the incursion from the Deep Void had reached the lower floors of the tower, she'd be completely at the mercy of the demons, and they'd shown precious little mercy. She'd be slaughtered, unable to defend herself.

Volinette was torn. Her goal was to find out how long it would be before reinforcements would arrive, but she needed to know if Janessa was still alive. If she was, they had to find a way to get her out of the cells. That was no way for anyone to die. She was penned up like an animal, waiting for slaughter.

A moment's more hesitation and Volinette made up her mind. She popped onto the landing outside the Inquisitor's level. It was the only place she knew well enough that she wouldn't end up adrift in the void. Not that she couldn't get back, but there wasn't any time to waste. She chose one of the three hallways at random and set off. Gliding out into the corridor, she was struck by how quiet and still it was. No bodies were scattered along the hall, no echoing roar of demon or shouted spell. Maybe they hadn't penetrated this far into the depths of the tower. Maybe there was still time.

Every minute she spent searching the Inquisitors' level was one that she wasn't helping to keep them safe. She could hear the faint sound of the battle raging around her physical form and knew that the demons were making another push. She made a wrong turn into a storeroom, then into a privy. She was just about to give up when she noticed a stairwell leading deeper into the earth under the tower. The door was banded in iron, its bars and hardware polished steel. That was the door to the dungeon. She recognized it from her very brief passage when Olin and Adamon brought her before the Head Master.

She glided through the door into a stone corridor. It was forty feet long, with four cells on each side. The first two were empty, as were the next two. One of the third set had a cot in it, on which the man with the long white beard was curled and covered with a thin blanket. Consistent with her luck, the very last cell on the right was the one where Janessa was held. Her ankles and wrists were bound with iron manacles, and she hunched in the far corner, half hidden in shadow.

Volinette had seen what she needed to see. She focused her will and popped from the dungeon out into the courtyard by the fountain. It was the one place of all the grounds that made up the Academy that she would be able to find without any effort. She'd spent so much time there that it was ingrained in her memory.

The fountain was broken, the pool shattered on one side, spilling water out onto the cobblestones of the courtyard. Rubble littered the paths. The Academy of Arcane Arts and Sciences looked like a war had taken place. Was taking place, she hurriedly corrected herself. She looked out toward the gate and saw Olin there, standing with Casto, Janessa's mother, and a handful of mages she didn't know. They were ranged in a loose circle, performing a ritual. Their hand gestures were complex, the words of power nearly unpronounceable. Volinette felt the Quintessential Sphere tremor, even though her body was in the tower and these Quintessentialists were so far away.

Something tickled her senses and she looked skyward, seeing a familiar blur that extended from the tip of the tower to the outside walls of the Academy. The Masters had assembled a barrier, much like the one that had been used in her trial. This shield seemed to be much thicker. Where the one at the Trial had been nearly transparent, now she could only just make out the fuzzy shapes of buildings beyond the walls. The Great Library, the nearest building to the grounds, was just a blurry shadow.

As she watched, a demon bounded out from behind the administration building and loped toward the far gate, unguarded by the Masters who were clustered near the broken fountain. It hit the barrier at a run, its head lowered as a battering ram. Volinette heard the crack from where she was hovering. Its neck broken, the demon collapsed, twitching on the path. Whatever happened now, at least Blackbeach would be spared from the invasion. The Quintessentialists would have to face the demons on their own.

"Volinette! We need you!"

Snapping back into her body like a taut bowstring, Volinette blinked and looked up at Baris. His face was a mask of panic, features contorted by fear.

"I'm here," she said, shaking her head to clear the last of the cube's fog from her mind. She realized she still had the cube in her hand and handed it to Baris. "How can I help?"

"You were supposed to be finding reinforcements." Baris looked pained.

"I did, but it's not good news. They've got their hands full. The portals are still open and Olin and Fulgent were just out by the West Gate."

"Why?"

"They put a shield over the Academy grounds. Like at the Trial, only a lot more powerful."

Baris looked crestfallen, his eyes taking on a haunted darkness that hurt her heart.

"They sealed us in. We're going to die in here."

"They saved the city," she said firmly, hoping to quell his panic. "We'll make it out of this. We just need to figure out how to close those portals."

"How are we gonna do that when the demons just keep coming? The bodies are probably waist deep out there."

"Wait a minute," Volinette said suddenly. "Hear that?"

"Hear what?"

"That's my point. It's quiet. It hasn't been this quiet since we got here."

The apprentices were a huddled mass against the far curve of the wall. The journeymen were crouched by the barricade, their faces drawn and haggard. Every now and then, they'd peek over the edge and then hunker back down. The howls and screams of the assaulting demons were gone. Uneasy silence had settled over the tower like a musty blanket.

"I never thought the quiet would creep me out," Baris said, shifting from one foot to the other.

"Check the entry hall."

"Now? Really?"

"Hurry up, or let me do it. Who knows how long it'll be before they're back. Better to know, right? We can't stay here forever."

Baris clutched the cube so hard his fingers turned white and passed into his spirit form. A moment later, he opened his eyes and a wide grin spread across his face.

"Adamon's here! Olin too. They're in the entrance hall. The portal is gone."

"Okay, we need to get out of here. We're safer with Adamon and Olin. Come on."

She trotted back to the barricade. The journeymen looked dead on their feet. Volinette had wondered earlier about the apprentices being able to continue with their education. Now, looking at the journeymen, she doubted any of them would ever fully recover from what they'd been through.

"We need to tear down the barricade and get downstairs," she said to the older journeyman. "Adamon and Olin are down there."

"How do you know?"

Baris held out hand, displaying the cube. "We've been keeping an eye on things between waves. We need to get out of here now. If we don't do it now, we might not be able to later."

"We were told to stay here."

Volinette cast an appraising eye at the journeyman. He was only a couple years older than she was, and he wasn't nearly as confident as he let on. She left Baris arguing with their appointed guardians. She trotted over to the cowering apprentices.

"The Inquisitors are in the entrance hall. You all want to get out of this room, right?"

There were nods and murmurs of assent.

"Okay, then we need to go now…and we need to be quick and quiet. Can all of you do that for me?"

The idea of getting out of the room they'd been trapped in appealed to most of the apprentices. They followed Volinette willingly to the barricade, where Baris was still arguing with their protectors.

"Listen," she interrupted. "We're leaving. Come with us, or don't, I don't care. If you want to stay here, I wish you luck, but we're going. Two of the most powerful Inquisitors in the realm are two floors down, and they can protect us better than we can protect ourselves."

A moment later, she'd summoned the power of a gale and directed it at the already battered barricade. It tumbled aside like so many matchsticks. Getting past the bodies of the demons they had killed was far more complicated. It was slow going, but Volinette managed to lead the apprentices to the landing. She listened at the lift shaft, then at the head of each set of stairs, and heard nothing that sounded the return of the rampaging horde of demons. Baris brought up the rear of the column of students, with the journeymen tagging along behind him.

Reminding them to be as quiet as they could, they worked their way down the stairs. A few dead demons lay across the stairs. It took time to get around the massive hulks of the bodies after she'd made sure they were dead. The landing of the second floor looked as if a wholesale massacre had taken place. There were many more dead Quintessentialists among the dead demons here, and Volinette urged everyone not to look at the carnage as they passed.

They moved into the next stairwell, the one that would lead them to the entrance hall and would determine whether the risk of their move was a gamble that would pay off. The last few steps seemed to be more imposing than she remembered. As her foot touched the smooth glass floor of the entry hall, she looked out and saw Olin and Adamon still standing there. She'd never been so relieved to see anyone in her entire life.

Volinette led the apprentices, Baris, and the journeymen across the room to where the Inquisitors were standing. Adamon and Olin turned to face them with their weapons drawn. The bore of Adamon's hand cannon seemed enormous so close up. Olin's staff wasn't as impressive, but she was glad he was armed as well.

"I'm sorry," she blurted as she stopped just short of the pair of Inquisitors. "We couldn't stay up on the third floor any longer. There were too many dead demons and no one else up there."

"You did the right thing, Volinette," Olin said. "The other Masters have cleared and secured the admin building. We'll get all of you over there. It'll be much safer, and you won't have to fight."

"We've already been doing that," Baris snorted with something near his normal lack of tact.

"No doubt," Adamon said drily. "I trust this also explains why you're holding something that should be on my desk?"

"We can discuss that later," Olin said quickly. "For now, let's get them to the admin building."

Adamon looked at Baris until the young man lowered his head. Then the Inquisitor shrugged and led the way out of the tower.

Chapter Twenty

Volinette had thought she'd seen chaos in the tower during the first wave of attacks. She'd been wrong. The wholesale evacuation of the tower had caused a commotion unlike anything she'd ever seen. Everyone who had been able to move on their own and some who had to be carried, had been relocated to the administration building on the far side of the Academy grounds. Though ample room for offices and archives, the choice of locale left much to be desired as a storehouse for all the living people within the barricade.

As Masters worked to close demonic portals and moved people into the safety of the admin building, things got very cramped. Volinette and Baris kept moving into offices further and further away from the main entrance, trying to escape the crowd that seemed to grow by the minute and showed no signs of stopping. Volinette had never fully appreciated how many people lived and worked within the Academy. She did now. Adamon said that this wasn't even half the number of people who would eventually be crammed inside, and Volinette wasn't sure she wanted to see that.

Olin found them sitting on a desk in one of the unused offices. He stepped inside and closed the door behind him. He flopped into a chair and leaned his head back, staring at the ceiling with bloodshot eyes. The Inquisitor didn't say anything, and they weren't inclined to interfere with his moment of respite.

Besides, they knew how he felt. They'd all been fighting for hours. Volinette felt as if she'd been picked up and twisted until everything that defined who she was had been rung out. She existed, and that was as much as she could muster.

"You two certainly know how to ferret out the quiet spots, don't you?" Olin asked, wearily raising his head.

"I needed somewhere that I could hear myself think," Volinette said with a shrug. "I've never been particularly bothered by crowds. I mean, I sang in front of thousands of people, but this is different."

Olin nodded.

"Different when you're down amongst the huddled masses."

Volinette peered at him, wondering if he realized how much his words stung. He must have seen the look in her eyes, because he raised his hands in entreaty, shaking his head.

"That's not what I meant, Volinette. I'm sorry. I meant no offense. I just meant that it's different when you have bodies pressing in on you on every side."

"Especially when some of them are none too fresh," Baris said, waving his hand in front of his nose. "You always hear people talking about the stink of fear. Phaugh. I know what they mean now."

"They've got good reason to be afraid, Apprentice Jendrek." Olin looked through the wall, toward the main entrance of the building. "Word is spreading that we sealed off the Academy grounds and that decision isn't proving to be a popular one. Maera will have a lot of explaining to do if we all come out of this alive. At least we saved the city. That's something. Can you imagine those things rampaging around Blackbeach?"

Silence settled over them. Pain and exhaustion were taking their toll. Volinette almost felt as if it would be worth it to turn the tower over to the demons if it meant that she could curl up in a ball and get a couple solid hours of sleep. The thought of curling up put her in mind of the old man in the Inquisitors' dungeon, which in turn led her thoughts to Janessa in the half shadows of her cell.

"What's going to happen to Janessa?" she asked suddenly.

Olin scrubbed his face, refusing to meet her eye to eye. He waited a long moment, as if hoping that she might retract the question. When he finally looked at her, he heaved a sigh and shrugged.

"I don't know. There are some Inquisitors sweeping the tower, but reported back that there were too many portals to close. It seems like for every portal we close, two more open. The small ones aren't too bad. The big ones, like the one in the tower, require a considerable amount of power to close, and we're running thin on both Masters and stamina."

"Then my question remains, what's going to happen to Janessa?"

"She'll probably die there."

"Good riddance," Baris said. Volinette rounded on him.

"That's not right, Baris. She was supposed to go before the High Council of Masters. They might have granted her appeal. We can't just leave her there to die. What if it were one of us?"

"We wouldn't be down there," he returned, just as heatedly. "Need I remind you that Janessa's friends are the ones who did this in the first place? If it weren't for her taking something that didn't belong to her, people wouldn't be dying."

"You can't believe that she told Nixi, Halsie, and Syble to summon demons on purpose."

"I don't know what to believe, but I'm not about to give them the benefit of the doubt."

"Did they?" she demanded of Olin. "Did you find them, or the Prism?"

Olin shook his head again.

"No. Adamon and I got as near to the girls' dormitory as we could, but we weren't close enough to either find the girls or locate the Prism."

"Do you think they did this intentionally?"

"What difference does it make?" Baris asked, and Volinette held up a hand to shush him.

"It makes a huge difference, Baris. Olin, do you think they did this intentionally?"

"No…and for what it's worth, which is precious little at the moment, Adamon doesn't either. He may be a first rate pain in the ass and about as social as an angry hornet, but he is very good at what he does. He didn't get to be Grand Inquisitor by being everyone's friend. He got there by doing the jobs that no one else wanted to do. Or couldn't do, for that matter."

"So if Adamon doesn't think they did it intentionally, doesn't it stand to reason that they shouldn't just be left to die? We're better than that."

"There's a fine line between a live hero and a dead lunatic, Volinette." Olin pinned her with his gaze. "The tower is infested with portals to the Deep Void that are still spewing demons into our realm. We barely made it out the first time. Going back now would be suicide."

"So the tower is lost? We're going to, what, let the demons take up residence while we cower in this building?"

Olin shot to his feet, his face suffused with rage.

"Good men are dying out there, Volinette! We're doing the best we can to save as many people as we can. You weren't there! You don't know…"

He trailed off, realizing what he'd said. He closed his mouth with a snap and sank back into the chair.

"I *was* there, Olin," she said softly. "I do know. I know that many of us are dying to those things. I also know that some of those who survive will never be the same. The bodies of the demons we killed on the third floor of the tower were waist high around the storeroom. If it's that bad everywhere, we may have already lost…and if we lose here, Blackbeach will fall. Once Blackbeach falls…"

"Then the rest of the Imperium," Olin finished for her. "You've thought it through, I grant you that. But there are only so many Masters who can fight. The apprentices don't have the power or the stamina to make a difference in a fight. They just haven't built up enough magic…muscle, for lack of a better term. We're spread thin. Until we find the Prism, wherever it is, we stand a very real chance of losing this fight. With the Prism, we can reverse the magic and close all the portals at once. Without it, we're fighting uphill."

Olin sighed and silence overtook them once again. Volinette didn't like Olin's answer, but she had to admit that it made sense. After all, how long had it taken for the Inquisitors to reach them in the tower?

Even after they'd arrived, it had taken Volinette's initiative to get them all down from the third floor. Who knew how long it would have taken for them to get around to checking on the students huddled in the converted storeroom.

The tense silence hung over them like a storm cloud until Olin got to his feet with a groan.

"We're doing the best we can," he said, his voice rough with exhaustion. "If we can get to Janessa, I promise we'll try."

"I don't even know why they'd try," Baris said after he'd left the room. He shrank back under the look Volinette gave him. "Well, I don't. I think we'd all be better off if we just left her down there."

"If you can leave someone to die just because they were mean to you…to us…then you're not who I thought you were, Baris. I can't just let her die. I won't. She's been a world class bitch to me. You're right…but she doesn't deserve to die for it."

"Alright, alright." Baris held up his hands in surrender. "It probably doesn't matter anyway. By the time the Masters find the Prism, it might be too late for her."

"Which is why we're going to go get her."

"Okay, that…Wait, what?"

"We're going to get Janessa from the Inquisitors' dungeon. Olin just said they're not going to make it a priority, so it's up to us."

"Volinette…it's great that you want to help people. It really is. But I think this is a bad idea. We could die out there. I don't want to die…and I really don't want to die for Janessa. She may not deserve to die either, but she doesn't deserve us dying to save her."

"Do what you need to do, Baris. I'm doing this with you or without you. I could really use your help, but if you feel that strongly about it, I understand. I won't ask you to go with me."

"Damn it!" Baris pounded balled fists against his thighs. "Fine, I'll go with you, but if we die, I swear I'll never forgive you."

"Deal."

"So how are we going to do this?"

"I'm not sure yet." She paused, giving him a half smile. "I was hoping that you'd know some secret way out of here."

Baris snorted.

"We don't need a secret way out. Half the first floor offices have windows. We can let ourselves out. It's going to be getting back in that's the trick."

"Well, that part we can worry about when we get there."

"Yeah," Baris agreed, his tone grave. "We might be dead long before we need to worry about that."

"Think positive, Baris."

"I am. I'm positive we're going to die."

"Baris!"

"Alright!"

"Can I borrow your cube again?" Volinette asked. Baris's trinket had become invaluable for checking things out before they stumbled across them all unwitting.

"Sure, but it's looking kind of gray. Might not hold out much longer." He reached into his pocket and withdrew the cube. When he handed it to her, she noticed what he meant. Where the cube had been nearly clear when she'd first seen it, it had progressed through a muddled translucence and was now a dingy gray.

Clasping the cube in her hands, she closed her eyes and spoke the words of power. Volinette thought she felt…something, but then it was gone. Opening her eyes, she looked at the cube, or rather, what was left of it. It had crumbled into dull, waxy shards. She opened her hands and showed it to Baris.

"Yep. So much for that, then."

"You're not upset?"

"Nah. My dad can make me another one. He was top of his class in the School of Enchantment. He was a bit disappointed when I opted for sorcery…but I like blowing things up."

"You'll probably get your chance. Okay then, let's figure out how we're going to get to the tower."

It took them some time to find a window that was on the tower facing side of the building and wasn't directly in the line of sight of the Masters who were guarding all of the entrances. As Baris had suspected, getting out of the admin building wasn't a problem. They dropped from the window onto the soft earth below. As soon as her feet touched the ground, Volinette had a flash of doubt. What if Baris was right? What if she was leading them into their own slaughter?

There was still a chance to go back. If they went to the main entrance of the admin building, they could slip inside as more people came to seek refuge from the demons. No one would probably notice. Still, doing that meant leaving Janessa at the mercy of the demons running rampant through the tower, and that was just something she couldn't allow. Deep inside, a little voice told her that there was another reason Janessa was so important. She'd been the one to take the Prism. She'd know where to start looking for it. She might even be able to feel its echo.

"Alright," she whispered. "Let's go."

The Academy grounds between the admin building and the Great Tower were, thankfully, lush with plants and trees. They moved from one bit of cover to the next. Hiding behind a bush here and a thick tree trunk there. Between them, Baris and Volinette pointed out hazards to each other. Once Baris pulled her back just before a towering demon, slithering on a single monopod, crossed in front of them. Another time, Volinette dragged Baris down behind a tree as a pair of Masters she didn't know cut through the wooded grounds on patrol.

Although it took them a long time to get there, they reached the tower entrance without further incident. Volinette slipped into sphere sight and peered inside. There were no shadows that would indicate lurking demons, no bright sparks that would be Masters seeking to drive the demons from the tower. It seemed to be abandoned. She motioned to Baris and they walked inside.

Though the building was no emptier than when they'd left, it seemed much more desolate now. Somewhere high above them, a rage-fueled howl echoed through the tower. A chill ran down Volinette's spine and she glanced at Baris. He looked back at her, his brown eyes dark. He shrugged.

"I told you," he whispered.

"That was above, hopefully below will be better." She crept toward the stairs leading down from the entrance level.

"Yeah, because things always get better the further underground you go."

Volinette wanted to scold him, but in truth, she couldn't blame him for his pessimism, or even argue with it. There were bodies, both human and demon, on the stairs leading down into the bowels of the tower. She did her best not to look at them, but she noticed that Baris studied each one, his eyes lingering until they'd passed them by.

"Why do you look at them?" she asked softly as they neared the landing to the inquisitor's level.

"Because I want to know what we're up against. The ones who died by claw or fang don't scare me much. It's the one who've been obviously killed by magic that scare me. I don't want to run up against anything that's more skilled than I am. I've seen how that game ends."

Volinette saw the haunted look in his eyes and wondered if he was thinking of the dark-haired girl from their time in the makeshift dormitory. Her death had been gruesome, and if that was weighing heavily on Baris's mind, it might explain the morose turn he'd taken. That, or the fact that there was a very real possibility that they might die down here.

"Down!" Baris shoved her out of the way just ahead of the claws that rang against the cold glass of the wall beside her.

Sharp claws raked deep furrows in the magical glass, and Volinette knew she'd have been dead from that initial blow if Baris hadn't been with her. He summoned and fired his missiles, the gleaming light flying straight and true into the humanoid form in front of them. She slipped into the Sphere just long enough to gather the memories of forgotten flames and cast a fireball of her own. The demon's roar died aborning as the fire engulfed it.

"Thanks," she said to Baris as they stepped around the charred corpse.

"Don't mention it."

Then they stepped onto the landing on the Inquisitors' level, and into hell.

Chapter Twenty-One

Slick with blood, the obsidian floor of the landing was almost like walking on ice. Raw, red chunks of meat were scattered around. They might have once been human, but Volinette didn't want to know. Even Baris kept his eyes trained straight ahead as they carefully navigated across the carnage. Working their way over to the wall, they followed the curve of the tower, leaning on it as much for support as for the knowledge that they hadn't actually departed Solendrea for a darker, twisted realm, something more a part of the Deep Void.

Though human corpses were plentiful, there were very few demon bodies amongst them. The walls were scored and cracked by claws, but there was little indication that much magic was used. Whatever had happened here, had happened quickly and without warning. It also meant that there might be more waiting for them down here than Janessa and the old man in the cell nearby.

Slipping into sphere sight had given her an instant headache. The jumbled mess of living memories was too much for her to sort out. She'd fallen out of concentration almost as soon as she switched. It would take days, maybe even weeks, for the psychic imprint of the events that had happened here to calm to the point where sense could be made of things. In any event, it wasn't going to do them any good now.

Without being able to rely on sphere sight to alert them to any hidden dangers, and the Seer's Cube a broken memory, they'd have to explore things the hard way. With their eyes and minds, and without the aid of clever magic to help them along.

"What a mess," Baris hissed. Volinette wondered if he meant the floor or the Sphere, but decided not to ask for clarification. She didn't want to know.

Three long corridors set out from the landing. Volinette knew that the middle corridor was the one that had the door to the dungeon at its terminus. One of the other two led to offices, the storeroom, and privy she'd discovered earlier. She assumed that the other led to similar offices, but she couldn't know for sure. That lack of knowledge set her teeth on edge. There was no telling what they'd find down that corridor, or what might be waiting there for them to pass by on the way to their final destination.

"Middle corridor, all the way at the end, there's a door," she whispered, pointing to the hallway in question. Baris just nodded. His eyes had taken on a dull glow. He'd called on the power of the Quintessential Sphere and was holding it in reserve. It wasn't much, but it might be enough to give them the edge if they came across something unexpected. Concentrating on the power of the Sphere, she summoned her own memories of light and fire and held them in abeyance.

They stood at the open end of the corridor and looked down it. It might only have been about sixty feet long, but it seemed like it went on for miles. Every doorway was a gaping maw, waiting to slash them with razor sharp teeth as they passed. Volinette took Baris's hand and they crept down the corridor. They picked up their feet and put them down with such care that they didn't make a sound. It was an agonizingly slow process, only allowing them to move a couple feet per minute. Beads of sweat stood out on Baris's forehead, which was furrowed with his effort.

Screaming echoed off the walls of the corridor and seemed to slam into them from all sides. It was a hideous sound that sent them both into a wild panic, pelting toward the end of the hall. Almost to the end, Volinette remembered what she'd seen in the Seer's Cube. There was so much iron and steel that neither of them would be able to cast. They'd be trapped up against the door with no way to defend themselves. Neither one of them had a knife hanging on their belt.

Volinette grabbed Baris by the collar, hauling him back with all her strength. He stumbled backward, knocking her off balance and sending them both sprawling on the cool glass floor. Heavy footfalls slapped toward them from the far end of the corridor, and Volinette's head snapped up to face the demon bearing down on them.

Vaguely shaped like a woman, it had two heads atop a pair of stunted necks. Wrinkled breasts lay flat against its chest like empty flour sacks. Its dusky gray skin was drawn drum tight across its bones, making the ribs and joints stand out in stark relief against the lights in the corridor. All four of its eyes were locked on them. It seemed to recognize that they were vulnerable.

Opening both mouths, the hideous creature screamed again. A tidal wave of sound barreled toward them. The wave lifted Baris and Volinette inches off the ground and threw them back, closer to the door at the end of the hall. She could feel the pain of the steel lancing into her chest, as if a white hot needle pushed through her breastbone. The pain in her head was different, a dull ache with an almost subliminal hum that made it hard to think.

As soon as the banshee stopped to draw breath, Volinette scrambled forward, sparing only a moment to check over her shoulder to see if Baris was following. He was, but he'd gotten a late start. She was out in front of him by several feet. Every fiber of her being protested moving toward the thing that glared at them with menacing eyes. She wanted to turn and run the other way, but she knew that wasn't an option. It was kill, or be killed.

A bolt of light streaked past her. Baris might have been farther behind, but he wasn't wasting any time going on the offensive. The banshee dodged to one side, neatly avoiding the projectile, but it was enough time for Volinette to do what she needed. She slipped into the Sphere, slowing the world around her. Summoning the living memories of geysers and whirlwinds, she waited for the sphere-song.

"Sing through me," she said in the timeless void of the Ethereal Realm, and the Quintessential Sphere answered.

The notes that left her were as pure and true as any she'd ever sung. The memories and magic flowed out of her, merging with the melody that burst from her lips. Tendrils of blue-white light encircled the banshee, trapping it in a cage of ethereal energy, singing in harmony to the words coming from the sphere. It screamed a third time, but this time the sound seemed muted, as if coming from a great distance.

As Volinette's song reached its crescendo, the writhing tendrils of magical music snapped up, slamming the banshee into the ceiling of the corridor. Its necks snapped like brittle twigs, the body compressing down to a fraction of its former height as blood and gore spurted from splits in the flesh. As the magic dissipated, the corpse fell to the floor with a wet smack and was still.

Baris walked up beside her. He looked at the corpse, then to Volinette, and back again.

"Remind me never to make you mad."

She glanced at him sideways. "Aren't you glad you decided to come with me?"

"Oh, yes." He said drily. "Thrilled. Especially since you left out the part about the door that wants to kill us as well as keep us out."

"Isn't getting Janessa back worth a little pain?"

"No."

Volinette sighed. "There's still time for you to go back."

"No, thank you. I think I'll stay with the scary Quintessentialist who kills things with her jaunty tunes."

"Then stop complaining, and let's get Janessa and get out of here."

The closer they got to the door, the worse the pain became. By the time they were ready to open it, it was all they could do to remain on their feet. The agony was so intense, it threatened to drive them to their knees.

"Open…it…already…" Baris grunted, his eyes narrowed slits against the pain.

Volinette braced herself for the jolt to come and grabbed the handle of the door. Fire flashed up her arm, burying itself in her chest. She screamed, and yanked as hard as she could.

Nothing happened. No matter how hard she pulled, the door wouldn't come open. She let go of the handle that seemed to be searing itself into her flesh and bounded back away from the door. Far enough that she could think. She watched Baris try the door himself, crying out in much the same way she had. He, too, admitted defeat and retreated to a safe distance.

"All this way and the damn door is locked?" Baris kicked the wall of the corridor, then swore and grabbed his foot. He hopped around cursing for a full minute. In any other situation, Volinette would have found his antics hysterical. Now, she was furious with him.

"Stop it! Do you want to have every demon in the tower down here on top of us?"

Her harshly hissed reprimand sobered him abruptly. He stopped jumping about and stood still, his head cocked to one side, listening. She listened too, but heard nothing. It seemed that they weren't in danger of any threat in the immediate area.

"Adamon's office," she said, thinking aloud. "There must be a key in Adamon's office."

"Oh. Hell. No." Baris shook his head wildly. "We're not going back up to Adamon's office and then coming back here. That's not happening. So you summon up thoughts of butterflies and fairy farts, or whatever it is you do to make the Sphere sing to you, and you open that damn door."

"I can't break down the door! Adamon will—"

"Will what? Blame you for something the demons are going to do anyway?" Baris lost what control of his temper he had left. "OPEN THE DAMN DOOR!"

"Well you don't have to be rude," she snapped. She turned back to the face the door and slipped into the Sphere. Wind and waves seemed most appropriate, forces that pushed and moved inexorably forward. The song was brief, not even a song so much as a melodic phrase, but it did the job. When she opened her eyes, the door lay splintered in pieces no larger than a toothpick. The metal banding was twisted and thrown into the corridor beyond, and the fittings were tossed around like a child's discarded toys.

"Now," Baris said striding forward, "let's get Janessa and get the hell out of here."

They ran down the corridor, ignoring the pain that lashed at them each time they passed a cell or got too near the railings that ran down the walls. As they got near to the end of the hallway, Volinette raised her hand.

"Slow down, I want to check on the old man who was here. We should rescue him too. He was raving when they brought me in, but no one deserves to die down here. Not even a madman."

They approached the cell slowly, but they needn't have worried. It was still locked tight, as were all the cells. The demons hadn't cared enough with what was beyond the door to penetrate it, so things were as they had been when she'd last seen them. Well, almost.

The old man who had been huddled with his blankets when Volinette had seen him last, now lay on his back, staring up at the ceiling. His eyes were dull and glazed. Never again would he be troubled by anything in the physical realm. His loss stung Volinette deeply, though she couldn't say why. Tears sprung to her eyes and she swiped them away with the back of her hand. She'd made the right decision, coming down here. No one deserved to die this way, not Janessa, not anyone. Baris glanced at her, but said nothing.

They moved to the last set of cells and Volinette peered through the bars. Janessa still sat against the far wall, mostly hidden by shadow. For a brief, horrifying moment, Volinette thought she might be dead too, but then she saw the girl's leg move. The chain attached to the leg dragged across the floor, the metallic ring seeming far too loud in such a confined space.

"Get her and let's go," Baris whispered under his breath. He glanced over his shoulder toward the door, and it wasn't difficult for Volinette to guess his worry.

"Hello?" Janessa said, her voice small and timid. In fact, she didn't sound like Janessa at all. She sounded like a scared little girl. "Is someone there?"

Volinette looked at Baris and he looked back at her. Somehow, she hadn't planned for this part. Why was she so certain that Janessa would even accept her help? What if she told them that she wanted to stay in the dungeon and take her chances, what then? The entire ordeal now seemed to be as foolish as Baris had made it out to be from the start. A lump in her throat made it hard to swallow. She wasn't sure how she was going to speak around it. She cleared her throat.

"Um, Janessa? It's Volinette and Baris. We're...uh...here to help you."

Silence. The only sound in the dungeon was the grating of Janessa's chains sliding across the floor as she got to her feet. Now the girl was entirely hidden in shadow. Volinette had a vision of a demon in the darkness. A demon that had torn off the girl's legs and was speaking with her voice. Volinette put the thought out of her head, forcing the fear that was welling up inside her down deep into her belly. There would be plenty of time to be afraid later. Now, she had to finish this.

Janessa stepped into the pale light cast by the torch bracketed in the corridor. Her hair was askew, unkempt, and greasy. Her eyes were haunted, deep pools of darkness surrounded by swollen, dark skin. She'd been crying. A lot, by the looks of things. She walked to the limit of the chain, close enough to the bars of the cell that she could grab them with both hands. Aside from a little wince, there was no indication that she felt the pain of the metal against her flesh at all.

"No one's been here for a long time," Janessa said absently, as if she were only half paying attention to the words she was saying. "There was a fight, I think. Something happened. There was shouting. A lot of shouting. Then there was screaming. There was so much screaming that I thought it might never end, but then it did…and the quiet was worse. Then I wished that the screaming would come back."

Janessa looked at Volinette, or rather, seemed to look through her, to some distant point on the horizon. Her head swiveled and she looked at Baris, then she looked back at Volinette.

"Volinette," she said, tears beginning to stream down her face as sobs wracked her lithe frame. "Please help me."

Chapter Twenty-Two

Baris was shaking his head again. Volinette wondered if it was the incessant buzz of the steel around them, or his disbelief in Janessa's apparent change.

"Don't let her fool you," he said, stabbing an accusing finger at the girl behind the bars. "She only wants your help because no one else is here to help her. As soon as you let her out, she's going to be back to her old tricks, mark my words."

"I won't," Janessa said in a weak voice. "I've learned my lesson, I swear. I'll perform the Rite of Fealty if you let me out. Whatever it takes for you to help me."

Baris whistled under his breath. Volinette raised an eyebrow.

"What's the Rite of Fealty?"

"Those who don't study history, Volinette, are doomed to repeat it," Baris chided her. "The Rite of Fealty is a spell they used in the olden days when there were few Masters and even fewer apprentices. A Master would have his apprentice cast it to ensure their loyalty, to keep their secrets secret. It's an archaic practice, but it proves that she's willing to put her life in your hands. Once she completes the spell, she will be subject to your every request. Refusing you would cause her considerable pain, maybe even death."

"That's awful," Volinette said with a gasp.

"It was different in the olden days," Baris said with a shrug. "Besides, what better way to know that she's turned over a new leaf? She'd be your personal slave until you release her from the rite."

Every wicked thing that Janessa had done to her flickered through her head, and for a moment, Volinette considered using their situation to exact revenge on the girl for everything she'd done. Just as quickly as the thought entered her head, it was gone. Janessa needed her help. Just because she'd done some awful things to Volinette didn't mean that she couldn't change. If Volinette were to take advantage of her imprisonment in any way, that would make her no better than Janessa. She deserved a second chance. Everyone did.

"No, that won't be necessary," she said decisively. "Everyone deserves a second chance, Baris."

Baris opened his mouth, about to protest, then closed it and shrugged.

"Just don't say I didn't warn you," he said. "How are we going to get her out?"

"Magic won't work," Volinette mused. "That's the whole purpose of this place. One of us has to go to Adamon's office and look for keys."

"One of us?" Baris cocked his head at her. "You realize there are demons out there, right?"

"I remember. One of us has to stay here. We can't just leave her."

She could feel his disbelief. He wanted to argue the point, but evidently decided that even his best laid argument wasn't going to sway her from her decision. He shrugged with a sigh.

"Fine," he snapped. "But if I die, I'm coming back to haunt you. You'll never get a full night's sleep again for as long as you live. I promise you."

Volinette watched Baris trot down the corridor leading from the dungeon. Then he went up the stairs and was gone. She shivered. Without him near, the dungeon seemed far colder. It felt danker, darker, and more hopeless. She stole a glance at Janessa who hadn't moved from the bars, though the pain it was bringing her had to be intense.

"You should let go of the bars, Janessa. The pain isn't doing you any good."

The girl looked down at her hands and took them off the cold metal. She folded her arms over her chest and shivered. She looked down at her feet.

"Did you mean what you said about everyone deserving a second chance?" she asked, her voice the barest whisper.

"I did. We don't always make the right decisions the first time around."

"And after everything I've done to you, you'd give me a second chance?"

"I would. I will. That's why Baris is out there right now risking his life to get the keys that will set you free."

"I'm not sure I'd do the same," Janessa said candidly. "My parents always taught us, me and my sister I mean, that 'people do to you, unless you do to them first.' That's how they handle things. That's how they've gotten to be so powerful. They're always the first to pounce on any weakness..."

Janessa trailed off and Volinette looked at her. The girl's head was still bowed, looking at her shackled feet. A few tears fell on the dusty floor, leaving little splash marks.

"Even ours," Janessa sobbed. "We weren't allowed to show any weakness. We were Navitas. We were supposed to do to others, not allow them to do to us. Do you know what my father told me when we were in the Head Master's office? That I had to pay for the disgrace I brought to the family. That no matter if I wanted to return the Prism or not, I had to pay."

Volinette wasn't sure what to say, so she said nothing. It seemed to be helpful to Janessa just to talk about it, and Volinette was happy to let her unburden herself, but she wished that Baris would hurry up. She missed his ability to make her smile, despite the circumstances. It felt as if he'd been gone for hours. Janessa drew a shuddering breath.

"Tenika was the only person I could really talk to. When she died, it was like I'd been set adrift. I didn't have anyone I could talk to. Not really. Syble and Nixi…Halsie too, all they wanted was the prestige and fame that went with running in the same circles as I did. They weren't real friends. Tenika was my only real friend…and now she's gone."

The girl looked up at Volinette, the tears still fresh on her cheeks.

"I did it. I murdered my own sister. I was the one who summoned the water and the elemental. We practiced it, how she'd survive the flood. Our parents told us if we weren't accepted into the Academy, we wouldn't be welcome at home. I know it wasn't your fault. It was just easier to take it out on you than to deal with what I'd done. I'm sorry."

"I want to believe you," Volinette said with a little shake of her head. "But I believed you once before, and look where it got us."

"I know." Janessa sighed. "I'll try to fix it. I swear."

They lapsed into silence and Volinette wondered again where Baris was. She was starting to get worried. She hadn't heard anything from the end of the hall. His footsteps would be a great source of comfort right now, but all was quiet and still.

"What happened to them?" Janessa asked suddenly.

"Who?"

"The girls. Halsie, Nixi, and Syble."

"I don't know. We think they used the Prism to try and get back at Baris and me for getting you thrown down here. No one's seen them since the portals opened, but the first portal opened in the girls' dorm. Did they know where the Prism was?"

"Yes," Janessa whispered, her eyes haunted. "Do you think they're...?"

It wasn't hard to piece together the rest of Janessa's question. As conniving and cold as the girl was, Volinette didn't believe that she'd wanted to kill anyone. Thinking about it, even threatening it, was one thing. Actually having the wherewithal to go through with it and deal with the aftermath was another matter altogether.

"I hope not," Volinette answered honestly. "But it doesn't look good."

Janessa started to speak, but Volinette shushed her with a savage hiss. Something was moving in the darkness at the end of the hall. Whatever it was moved like an animal, close to the ground, darting from shadow to shadow as if the light would banish it from existence. Volinette tried to shut out the incessant buzzing of the metal surrounding them, just enough to concentrate for a single spell, but it was impossible. She should have been at the other end of the corridor. Now it was too late.

Fortunately, it was only Baris that burst from the shadow and pelted down the corridor, a large ring of keys clutched in his hand. Volinette blew out a sigh of relief that could have moved a sailing ship. She'd never been so happy to see anyone in all her life. She threw herself at him, ignoring the shock that jumped between them, crushing him with the strongest hug she could muster.

"Enough," he panted, wriggling free of her grasp and running to the cell door. "You can throw yourself at me later. Right now we need to get out of here." He was trying keys in the cell lock, fumbling a bit more with each successive try. "There's stuff moving around out there, and I'm pretty sure they're getting closer. It doesn't sound like we're alone."

There was a metallic click and the door swung inward. Baris looked at Janessa, then back at Volinette. He paused on the threshold, still outside the reach of the girl in chains. "You're sure you want to do this?"

Volinette nodded, not trusting herself to speak. If she was wrong again, if Janessa was just using her to get free of her confinement...

Baris closed the remaining distance to Janessa and grabbed the manacle clasped around her wrist. He grunted, shaking his head as if he could dispel the pain. The restraints were a simpler mechanism than the cell door and all opened with a single key. It didn't take him very long to figure out which key was the right one and free Janessa from her confinement. She stepped away from chains, rubbing her wrists as she went.

As quietly as they could, the trio slipped down the hall toward the small set of stairs that would lead them back into the tower proper. The farther they went, the more normal Volinette felt. As they entered the upper corridor, the droning of the dungeon left them altogether, and her connection to the Quintessential Sphere came flooding back.

Janessa gasped. She must have felt it too. Janessa turned and Volinette saw the luminous sparkle in her eye, the telltale glow of power drawn from the Ethereal Realm. This was it, Volinette thought, she'd made the wrong decision one too many times and now Janessa was going to kill her for her folly. Instead, the girl reached up and fisted a bunch of hairs, yanking them from her head with a grimace and yelp of pain. She twisted them in a crude ring, tying the ends together with a delicate knot that belied her weary appearance. Janessa placed the ring of hair in one palm and hovered her other palm over it, speaking words of power. Golden sparkles floated down from the upper palm, seeking out the hair and being absorbed into it. Once the spell was complete, the ring pulsed once with a golden glow, then faded to its natural spun straw color.

With a timid smile, Janessa offered it to Volinette. Baris stood to the side, shaking his head.

"What is this?" Volinette asked, taking the offering between thumb and forefinger, as if it might explode at any moment. Given what she knew of Janessa, she wasn't so sure it wouldn't.

"It's a Token of Fealty." Baris said wearily. "Wear it on one of your fingers, and she'll be compelled to do your bidding. Whatever you command, she'll do to the best of her ability, or die trying."

Volinette eyed the ring of hair, twisting it back and forth between her fingers. It had a light, almost airy quality to it. All magic carried an echo of the forces used to create it and this didn't feel dark or brooding. Maybe there was some truth to what Janessa had said. Maybe she really was ready to turn toward the light. Volinette slipped the ring into the pocket of her tunic, tucking it down deep to make sure she didn't lose it.

"What are you doing?" Baris asked in disbelief. "Put that on and let's get out of here."

"We're going," Volinette said, giving Janessa the same timid smile the girl had given her moments before. "I have the ring if we need it, but I don't think we will."

"Thank you," Janessa said quietly.

"Oh, for crying out loud!" Baris stomped up to Volinette and poked her in the shoulder. "Have you forgotten everything she's done?" He stabbed a finger at Janessa before poking Volinette again. "She's the entire reason we're in the mess we're in. If it weren't for her—"

Baris stopped short as Volinette took a sudden step forward. He cringed as if she was going to strike him, but she took him by the shoulders and kissed the tip of his nose. He blinked, and then sneezed as the link-shock made his nose twitch.

"Second chances, Baris. Everyone deserves one. Even surly old curmudgeons crammed into young men's bodies. We have the ring if we need it. I don't think we will, and we have work to do. You promised to help me. Are you going to live up to that promise?"

Baris blinked, then found an important reason to look at the tips of his boots. He scuffed them against the smooth glass of the corridor floor, as if he were trying to dig a hole that he could disappear into. "Haven't I always?"

"You have," she agreed. "You're my best friend, and I'm lucky to have you with me."

The moment of peace was shattered by an unearthly howl. It came from the direction of the landing and shook the walls around them with its awesome fury. The three of them turned toward the sound, then looked at each other. They were all very pale. Heavy footsteps echoed down the hall. It sounded as if a giant were stomping around on the landing of the Inquisitors' level. There was no way out but through that level, Volinette knew. Her fingers lingered above the pocket that held Janessa's hair. She was inclined to trust the girl, and if she didn't believe in her own intuition, what else did she have?

Almost as if she were reading Volinette's mind, Janessa slid to the floor. She crossed her long legs, folding them in toward herself. She laid her hands on her knees, palms up, and closed her eyes. She whispered to the Quintessential Sphere and a silvery-white ambient light blossomed up around her like a spring rose. The more she spoke, the brighter the light became.

"We don't have time for this!" Baris hissed. "We need to figure out a way to get past whatever is on the landing and get out of this tower before we're buried here."

Janessa paused in her incantation, her hair standing out like an aura around her. "I can help. I just need you to be patient."

Baris glanced at the young woman, then down the hall. "I'll be patient. I don't think *it* will be patient."

"Just let her finish, Baris. What can it hurt?" Volinette took him by the hand, squeezing it, trying to impart her worry and strength to him in a single motion.

Janessa slipped back into the spell as easily as a fine ship cutting through smooth seas. The words she spoke were pretty, almost lyrical, and Volinette caught herself composing an accompanying melody on the fly. This wasn't the harsh, guttural tongue that Janessa had used against them. This was something else entirely. Something more pure.

A flash of light dazzled their vision. Janessa spoke a single firm word, and the light faded. Volinette was the first to recover. She looked at the girl on the floor in front of them and tried to find words that had suddenly and completely abandoned her.

Nestled in the crook of Janessa's crossed legs was a perfectly faceted crystal column. She'd summoned the Transcendental Prism.

Chapter Twenty-Three

A towering mass of black flesh stood in the center of the landing on the Inquisitors' level. Volinette had seen it before. It was the arch demon she'd seen in the entrance hall, opening portals for more of its diseased brethren to crawl through, further infecting the Great Tower of High Magic and the Academy. The monstrous construct paced the open space between the two curving stairways that let up out of the tower, and to salvation. The oily sheen on its skin rippled in a disgusting rainbow as it passed the lanterns hanging from the ceiling. It swayed back and forth on its massive trunk legs, as if searching for something.

With each pass, the demon got closer and closer to their hiding place behind a pile of mangled corpses. Janessa had balked at the proximity of the bodies at first, paling even more than she already had at the sight of so much blood and offal, but it was the only place that offered them a clear line of sight to the stairway while also allowing them to see where the demon was. Unfortunately, the demon seemed to be taking undue interest in them. Baris's hands were clenched so tightly that his knuckles stood out, pale ghosts in the dim light.

"It senses us," he whispered. "What are we going to do now?"

"Only two options I can see," Volinette said, her eyes never leaving the beast towering over them. "Fight or run. If we run, I'm not sure we can make it to the stairs in time."

"I don't think we'll survive a fight," Janessa whispered. "Not even with this." She hefted the Prism.

Whether it was the sudden motion of the crystal, a glint of light from one of the lanterns, or the latent power in the artifact, they'd never know, but it drew the arch demon to them like a month to a flame.

"Look out!" Baris managed to shout before a massive arm slammed into the pile of bodies they were hiding behind.

The force of the blow sent them flying in all directions. Volinette slammed against the corridor wall and knocked her teeth together so hard that it sent a jolt of pain through her skull. She saw Baris slide out onto the landing, spun by the unexpected attack. Janessa fared no better than Volinette had, also hitting a wall and only barely able to keep hold of the Prism, which she cradled to her chest. They were separated now and vulnerable. Volinette scrambled to her feet, only just avoiding a massive hand that slammed into the wall where she had been, sending a crack through the magically infused obsidian. She'd never heard of anything powerful enough to break the walls of the tower. The tower was supposed to be indestructible. It was the pinnacle of achievement for the greatest Quintessential craftsmen. As she watched the crack race up the wall, she felt her stomach tumble. So much for indestructible.

There was no time to worry about the state of the tower. The arch demon was lumbering toward a dazed Janessa, who hadn't moved from where she'd ended up after the initial attack. Volinette darted between the massive legs, took hold of Janessa's arm, and yanked her to safety a split second before six-inch long claws raked across the floor where the girl had been. It was fast for something so huge. Fast and dangerous. Volinette gave Janessa a shove toward the landing where Baris was just picking himself up off the floor.

"Go! Get to the stairs!"

Janessa ran and Volinette followed a half-step behind. With the arch demon in the corridor, they had a clear shot across the landing to the stairs. Baris saw them coming and turned to match their direction. Janessa's foot touched the bottom step, and Volinette heaved a sigh of relief. A sigh that twisted and transformed itself into a scream as the room seemed to fold in on itself. Invisible hands tore at them, dragging them away from the stairs and toward the open maw of the demon that had made its plodding way back to the center of the landing. As it drew them in, it spoke in a harsh, guttural language unlike anything Volinette had ever heard.

The words it spoke were a series of anguished screams, a thousand damned souls crying out for succor and finding no peace. Nightmares were more comforting than the voice of the demon that was drawing them inexorably toward their deaths. Baris managed to fight against the spectral restraints enough to toss a magic missile. It struck the demon square in the chest, kicking up a thin mist of the oil that coated the thing's skin, but nothing more. A short, staccato screaming came from the demon, and it took Volinette a moment to realize that it was laughing at them.

"Fire, wind, ice, earth," Volinette chanted as she slipped into sphere sight, trying to summon any ancient memory that might help them against the danger drawing them ever closer. The mantra didn't help. The sharp teeth and claws that were looming ever closer dominated her mental vision. A brilliant flash caught her attention and drew her to Janessa, who still clutched the Prism. She slipped out of the Sphere.

Baris was holding another missile, charging it before he unleashed it toward the demon. If she broke his concentration, he might lose control of the spell altogether. She'd have to risk it. No time for a different plan.

"Baris! Use the Prism!"

His eyes widened and he tossed his head from side to side. He looked to Janessa, then to the hulk of the demon who nearly had them. Baris squinted at the crystal. His face contorted in the epitome of concentration. A roar escaped from Baris that could almost rival the demon's voice. He held his hand out toward the Prism, and Janessa thrust it out in front of her like a shield. The missile flew straight and true, and the Prism absorbed it. Janessa's arms wavered, and for a single, terrifying moment, Volinette thought she might drop the crystal. Janessa recovered a moment later, grasping the Prism even tighter than before.

White light pulsed in the center of the Prism, making it look like a giant heart. They were almost within reach of the demon. If they were dragged within striking distance, it was over. There wasn't anything they could do to escape at that point. The Prism didn't seem to be inclined to help, though Baris still had his eyes shut tight and was mouthing words that Volinette couldn't hear.

Three things happened at once, and so quickly that it took Volinette a moment to realize what happened. Light so brilliant that she could feel its warmth flashed out of the Prism, the drag of the invisible hands ceased, dropping them on the floor with a thud. The demon howled in rage and pain. Volinette blinked a few times to clear the dazzle from her eyes. The demon had retreated to the far side of the room, leaving its severed leg in the middle of the landing. She watched with a certain horrified fascination as the mangled stump began to regenerate, growing a new leg to replace the one that had been lost.

"Move! Now!" Baris barked. He was already on his feet and running for the stairs. Volinette and Janessa followed his lead. The demon tottered forward on two legs, maintaining its balance in an ungainly waddle. It was able to move, but without the terrible speed that had been such an advantage before. It began to chant again, beginning another invocation, but this time they rounded the curve of the stairs, breaking line of sight, and making it more difficult for the demon to reach them with its spellcraft. Not impossible, though, so Volinette had no intention of slowing down.

Never before had a few flights of stairs seemed so impossibly long. They ran as fast as their feet would carry them up the never-ending staircase. They rounded corners without slowing, their feet sliding dangerously on the smooth glass stairs. Stumbles threatened them all with death, so they pressed forward, even when they were out of control. At long last, they burst into the entrance hall of the Great Tower, sprinted across its open expanse, and out through the doors that still stood open.

Baris was first out the door. He skidded to a stop, rocking back on his heels at the pandemonium that greeted them. Volinette and Janessa only avoided crashing into him by the narrowest margin. What they saw was almost beyond belief.

The grounds of the Academy of Arcane Arts and Sciences were frantic with battle. Buildings were aflame, belching dark clouds of smoke that gathered at the top of the force dome. A dozen different types of demons skittered, leapt, and oozed toward Quintessentialists that were scattered around. Spells were flying in every direction, including into other unsuspecting mages. Unless the chaos was quelled, and fast, they were going to lose everything. Where the hell was Adamon, Volinette wondered. Then she saw him out of the corner of her eye. Olin was sprawled on the ground behind Adamon and another mage lay not too far off. Adamon was holding three demons at bay with inhuman speed. As soon as one spell landed, he'd flick another at one of the demons bearing down on him.

"Look!" Volinette pointed at Adamon. Baris was off running before she could say another word. Janessa saw the Inquisitor and her eyes narrowed almost imperceptibly. For a moment, Volinette thought this might be the girl's breaking point, when she went back to the Janessa she had been before the dungeon. Janessa said nothing, but ran after Baris, leaping over walls, hedges, and the occasional errant spell, to catch up.

Nothing left to do but to join in, Volinette thought and she followed. By the time she reached Baris and Janessa, Baris was already charging the Prism. Volinette closed her eyes, summoned the power of the flame, and let the Sphere sing through her. She concentrated on the Prism, willing its glowing, shimmering form in the Ethereal Realm to absorb both the power and the melody. Volinette thought of the dozen demons she had seen and envisioned them burning in purifying flame.

"Janessa..." Volinette's voice seemed so far away from her body.

"I know. I'm ready."

The last note of her melody faded away, and the light within the Prism had taken on a life of its own. Flames jumped and flickered, licking at the crystalline walls within. Orange, red, and yellow motes of light danced on the surface of the Prism. Volinette could feel its power, building, folding, compressing down upon itself and then growing again. Adamon was running out of time. She wished the Prism would do what it needed to do.

Janessa screamed. Her weapon blossomed like a miniature sun. It engulfed them in its fire, but it wasn't the intensity of the heat that burned the worst, it was the awesome power of the Quintessential Sphere riding the waves of magical fire that disgorged from the facets of the crystal-like tiny phoenixes. They streaked across the courtyard, slamming into demons and setting them ablaze. Flames raced across demonflesh, consuming all they came into contact with. Screams of agony were abruptly censored as the demons crumbled into ash. Adamon's battle was cut short as the three demons he was fighting erupted into flame at the same time, then exploded into cascades of fading sparks.

Sudden silence fell over the Academy, and that was almost as unnerving as the sounds of battle had been. There were some moans and cries of pain from those who had been injured during the battle, but the raucous, ear-splitting shrieks of the demons had been silenced. Volinette turned to look at the girls' dormitory, hoping that somehow they'd closed the portal that had allowed the invasion. Her heart dropped into her stomach. It was still there, and still growing.

"The three of you have a considerable amount of explaining to do," Adamon said without a hint of a smile. His hand cannon was on the ground by his feet. The Inquisitor picked it up, loaded fresh rounds into the chambers, and tossed his cloak aside to drop it in the holster hanging from his belt. "I trust there's a reason for the prisoner to be out of her cell?"

Baris seemed uninclined to fight for Janessa, but Volinette stepped forward.

"We weren't going to leave her to die. She's changed, and she wants to return the Prism. We just needed to use it first."

"Then return it. Now."

His tone allowed for no argument or reasoning, so Janessa offered the Prism and Adamon took it. He turned it over in his hands, as if seeking out some damage or flaw he could blame on their handling of the artifact.

"We were careful," Volinette said, somewhat defensively.

"You were lucky." Adamon leveled his gaze at each of them in turn. "Did the fate of the three who came before you teach you nothing? Meddling in magic you don't understand can get you killed, or worse. The Academy would survive without your impetuousness…but what of the others you might have put in harm's way?"

Volinette felt Baris's eyes burning holes in her back, but she couldn't look at him. Janessa was giving Adamon a curious look, her head cocked to one side, as if he were just as alien as the demons had been. Janessa drew a deep breath, and Volinette closed her eyes with a sigh. She'd had experience with that particular mannerism and knew what was coming. A harangue about who she was and who her parents were would place Janessa in prime position to destroy any progress she'd made with Volinette.

"You are, of course, correct, Grand Inquisitor," Janessa said in a soft, respectful voice. "In this particular case, might not the ends justify the means? I will gladly submit myself again for your discipline after this crisis is over, but haven't we three proven, beyond doubt, that we can handle ourselves and help to push this menace back?"

"She has you there, Adamon." A new voice joined the conversation. Olin was sitting up. He'd drawn his legs up to his chest and was flexing his muscles one by one, as if assessing the damage done. "And well and politely spoken, at that."

Whatever retort Adamon would have made was obliterated by the side of the Great Tower exploding into shards of deadly glass. Baris and Adamon threw themselves to the ground. Volinette grabbed Janessa around the waist and dragged her down. Ribbons of pain lanced through her arms and legs as the flying shards cut shallow furrows.

No time to recover. No time to think. The arch demon had burst through the wall and was coming down on them, fast.

Chapter Twenty-Four

Adamon's hand cannon was a miniature dragon, roaring and spitting fire. Unfortunately for all of them, the projectiles did nothing to harm the huge demon closing in on them. Puffs of oily residue blossomed where the bullets hit, but they didn't penetrate the ink black demonflesh. Spells glanced off the thick hide. Nothing seemed capable of stopping the monstrosity intent on destroying them. Olin, who had recovered and was back in the fight, summoned massive vines from the earth. Thick green tendrils shot out from between the cobblestone pavers and wrapped themselves around the demon's legs, arresting it mid-step and causing it to shriek in frustration.

It didn't take very long for it to tear through the vines with the wicked claws that tipped each finger. Even so, that didn't stop Olin from doing it again and again, effectively holding the demon off from reaching them. The other Masters in the courtyard had gathered behind Adamon and Olin. A few of them tried their hand at defeating the creature, but nothing they tried seemed to work. Even Maera had shown up, her ornate black cloak tattered and singed, her silver hair disheveled from combat in her own corner of the grounds.

"Well Adamon," Olin said with a grunt as he twisted his hands to control the vines he'd summoned.

"If you have any ideas, I'm sure we'd all love to hear them."

"We need to draw it back to the portal," Adamon declared. "If we can't destroy it, we can at least push it back through to the other side."

A series of pops and snaps echoed across the courtyard, and the demon was free once again. Olin began to cast his spell once more, but Volinette interrupted him.

"In the tower, it was drawn to the Prism. If we take it back to the girls' dorm…"

"Perhaps it will follow," Adamon finished for her. "Clever, and worth a shot."

As one, the Masters moved toward the swirling vortex of darkness that had almost entirely engulfed the building where the girls' dormitory had been. Creeping tendrils of shadow snaked out, as if seeking for more life to devour and destroy. The closer they got to the building, the harder it was to think, to concentrate. There was a sort of psychic feedback, and it reminded Volinette of being in the dungeon under the tower. Unlike being surrounded by iron and steel, she found that if she tried to close out everything else, she was able to maintain her connection to the Quintessential Sphere.

The hair on Volinette's neck stood on end. She hadn't seen it until just now, but they'd managed to put themselves in a precarious position. While trying to lure the arch demon back to the portal, they'd put an opening to the Deep Void at their backs. The demon was still in front of them. It would be just as easy for the demon to drive them through the portal, as it would be for them to try to push it back to its native realm.

"This was a bad idea," Adamon said, glancing over his shoulder as they moved closer to the swirling blackness of the portal. Volinette took very little solace in the fact that the Grand Inquisitor had reached the same conclusion she had.

"Hold it off, Olin," Adamon said. "I'm going to try to close the portal."

Hoisting the Transcendental Prism over his head, Adamon invoked the Quintessential Sphere, speaking ancient words of power and imploring the forces of magic and nature to close the rift between the realms. A dim pulse in the crystal was echoed by the vortex. The edges of the portal blurred, then drew back toward the center of the portal. Though it had shrunk some, the portal was in no danger of being closed permanently.

Adamon stumbled, his reserves of will and strength overtaxed by the massive expenditure of magical energy trying to close the portal.

"I don't have much left," Olin groaned. His face was covered in a sheen of sweat as he struggled to keep the demon at bay. Maera stepped up beside him and put her hand on his shoulder.

"Stand down, Olin. Allow me."

The Head Master picked up Olin's spellcraft where he'd left off, and Olin collapsed to the ground beside Adamon. Maera's relatively fresh mind allowed her to extend the vines further up the beast, effectively locking it in place. As impressive as that was, however, it didn't solve the problem of getting the demon through the portal and closing it so that nothing else could sneak into their world.

"Son of a bitch!" Baris swore, and Volinette whirled to see what could have caused such an outburst.

What she saw made her take an involuntary step back. She nearly tripped over Olin, who looked over at Baris and said his own oath.

At the edge of the vortex, just coming into view, were the forms of three looming demons. Two-thirds as tall as the arch demon, they flew forward on stunted wings of black leather. Arms and legs were curled, like a predatory bird, each hand and foot tipped with a four-inch talon that was slick with blood. As horrifying as they were to behold, the faces were the worst. Volinette turned her head, determined not to be sick. Janessa gave an inarticulate cry.

The demons had twisted mockeries of the faces of Nixi, Halsie, and Syble. Their features were elongated and swollen, their eyes replaced by burning orange coals that smoldered with hatred. Shrill screams escaped them as they raced toward the gathered Masters.

"They're no longer human," Adamon said firmly, answering a question that Volinette hadn't wanted to ask. "Putting them down will be a mercy. Make it as quick and painless as you can."

What happened next was nothing less than chaos. The three demons dipped and spun in the air, swooping down to attack with deadly claws. Volinette watched a woman in Master's robes plucked from the earth. The Nixi-demon flew her up as high as the shield would allow and then ripped her in half, raining blood and entrails onto those below.

Magic missiles, balls of flame, bolts of lighting, and shards of ice flew through the air. Sometimes colliding with each other, sometimes connecting with one of the demons flitting here and there. More often than not, they missed altogether, glancing harmlessly off the dome that protected the city from the demons running rampant within the Academy grounds.

Adamon reloaded his cannon and got unsteadily to his feet. Syble's demon swooped down on him, screeching so loudly that Volinette clapped her hands over her ears to drown out the sound. The Inquisitor didn't move. Ever closer the demon flew, throwing its feet forward, claws extended, intending to impale the impertinent Inquisitor. The cannon roared. The shell hit Syble between the eyes, splitting the head in half and spraying ichor and gore out behind it. The demon dropped like a stone, collapsing to the ground in a crumpled heap.

The two remaining demons continued to harry the Masters, dodging in and out of their lines of fire, trying to draw the Masters into hitting each other rather than their intended targets. Instead of evoking a missile of some sort, one of the older Masters summoned a jet of thick webbing and shot it from his hands, entangling Nixi and dropping her to the earth. Another fighter, a stout older woman with a pink, pig-like face, swung her staff over her head with two hands, bringing it down on the demon's head with a sickening crack. Nixi was still.

"I'm nearly spent," Maera gasped. She, too, had taken on the sickened look of a Quintessentialist pushing herself far past the limit of her endurance. "This isn't working. We need to do something else."

A gentle breeze caressed Volinette's cheek, and she thought she heard the faint sound of a wind chime. She shook her head, trying to clear the fog of fatigue and battle that dulled her senses. Something nagged at her, something that she should understand. Something that could help them, but she couldn't coax it out into the open. No matter how she tried to focus, the pandemonium around her seemed to drag her back into its turbulent seas.

Focus, she thought to herself savagely. Focus, focus, focus! Focus! That was it! Volinette slapped herself in the forehead with the palm of her hand. How could she be so blind? She dashed over to Adamon. The Transcendental Prism lay discarded at his feet. Snatching it up, she rounded on the Grand Inquisitor.

"I can close the portal," she said, ducking as Halsie made another pass through the assembled Masters, her wings barely clearing their heads. "I know I can."

"You don't know the proper rituals," Adamon snapped back. "This isn't a game. You can't just wing it and hope for the best."

"I'm not," she insisted. "I'm a conduit for the Quintessential Sphere."

"You're insane," Adamon said. "You're going to get us all killed."

"I believe in her," Olin said slowly. "Let her try."

"Volinette is special," Baris chimed in from behind Adamon.

"Everyone deserves a chance," Janessa added, flashing Volinette a small smile.

"Let her try," Maera grunted, driven to her knees by fatigue. Even so, she maintained the spell holding the demon away from the group.

"Masters!" Volinette shouted, holding up the Prism. "Masters! Summon forth memories of light and love and life, all the things that drive the darkness out of your heart. Call on the power of the Quintessential

Sphere and focus all your energies on the Prism. Concentrate!"

One by one, the Masters began to bow their heads, their mouths moving silently with the words they were using to invoke the power of the Ethereal Realm and draw it into their world. The Transcendal Prism began to hum in her hands, a subliminal sound that seemed to crawl out of the crystal and down her arms, into her body, and up her spine. It was like taking a warm bath from the inside out. The gentle, pulsing glow that enveloped her grew and grew, shrouding her in a cocoon of light that expanded steadily outward, fed by the will of the mages. Adamon, Olin, Baris, and Janessa took hands, forming a circle around Volinette as she felt the crystal's power grow.

The other Masters followed suit, moving inward, still chanting, locking hands with one another and forming an outer circle around the inner circle. Still, the light and humming grew from the Prism. It was getting harder to hold now, and Volinette crushed it to her chest, protecting it, nurturing it, encouraging it to take the memories it had received and use them for protection.

Seeing an opportunity for attack, Halsie screeched from high above, diving toward Volinette and the crystal. As she crossed over Volinette's head, a tendril of white whipped out from inside the Prism, a lash of pure light. It struck the demon on the top of her head, slicing down effortlessly through the body, bisecting it as if it had been cut with a blade. There was a brilliant flash, and it was gone. No body. No ash. No indication that it had ever existed at all.

Volinette barely noticed. The Prism was singing to her. She clutched it to her breast, cradling it like a child. She was vibrating with the harnessed power of the crystal now, every part of her alive with the light. Closing her eyes, she listened to the siren's song of the Prism, a hundred thousand voices from a hundred thousand memories of life and love and happiness, of the brightest things in life that chase away the monsters in the dark.

She sucked a breath, and the Quintessential Sphere whispered in her ear, complex words she would never understand, but didn't need to. The sweet melody burst from her lips as if it had been dammed up inside her for eons. She felt each breath, each fresh inhalation, and the air that carried the sound out from her lungs, entwining her song with the power of the Ethereal Realm. The words came unbidden to her mind, and she sang them dutifully, echoing the voice in her head that wasn't quite a voice.

The song was endless, eternal, touching every corner of time and space, of memory and thought. It flowed through her like a flood, infusing her with the power of the Sphere and the power that had permeated the Prism. For a bright, shining moment, she was the Quintessential Sphere, and it was her. She was all things. She felt. She knew. She mourned. The blight on the surface of Solendrea was a disease that threatened all. It must be excised and destroyed.

Volinette held the last note of the song for what seemed like forever. She knew it had to end but didn't want to let it go. As soon as she released it, it would be gone forever. It wasn't something she could keep. It was hers in this moment, but never again. She struggled to hold the note, to draw it out until she had nothing left. Until she had become part of the song that was moving through her with the accord of the Eternals.

Blinding light exploded from the Prism, setting them awash in its conflagration. There was a screaming howl. The arch demon was set ablaze from the inside out. Cracks, massive fissures, in the black demonflesh opened, showing rays of light that sought escape from inside. The cracks ran along every surface of its body until it could no longer hold. It exploded in a shower of silver sparks.

The light fought back the writhing blackness of the portal. It snaked forward, darting toward the black tendrils that crept out from the edges of the doorway to the Deep Void. Where the light and the darkness met, there was a hissing sound, like ice thrown on a hot stove, and the darkness evaporated, as if it were steam. Wailing screams went off from every corner of the Academy grounds as the light pressed ever inward, toward the center of the portal. Demons streamed from almost every building, racing toward the portal as if they could stop the assault on the link to their native realm.

Every demon that got near the portal was lashed by whips of pure light, torn asunder by the same forces that had destroyed the monster that Halsie had become. The Masters turned on the others, destroying them with what magic they had left after dedicating nearly all their resources to the Prism.

At long last, the searching light reached the center of the vortex of darkness. It blossomed like a firework, reaching out and touching everything in its path. The shield around the Academy collapsed and living air rushed through the grounds, fresh, with just a hint of fish and sea.

Her long struggle over, Volinette let the last note fade away. There was silence. Somewhere, in the distance, she heard a chime singing in the wind.

It was the last thing she heard.

Chapter Twenty-Five

Volinette woke to the sound of splashing water. Everything ached. Even her hair was sore. It felt as if someone had stuffed her in a barrel and rolled her down a long and rocky hill. There wasn't a single muscle in her body that didn't protest. She tried to wiggle her toes and found that they, too, were painful to move. She groaned. At least if she hurt, that meant she was alive.

"Ah, good, she awakens."

The voice was soft and gentle, and somehow familiar. Volinette had heard it before, she was certain. A moment later, she was sighing with relief as a cool cloth was laid across her forehead. Fingers, cool and still damp from wringing out the cloth, traced the curve of Volinette's neck and felt for the lifebeat there. Volinette tried to ignore the shock that coursed through her at the touch, but she couldn't help but whimper. It was like a hundred needles being pressed into tender flesh at once.

She opened her eyes, but saw nothing. Panic flashed through her. She tried to raise a hand to see if she could see it in front of her face, but the smooth hands of her caretaker forced her to lie still.

"Rest easy, Volinette. We didn't want to risk damaging your eyes. There's a bandage there. A moment of patience, and I'll remove it and we'll see how you are recovering."

"Who are you?" Volinette asked meekly. She couldn't place the woman's voice no matter how hard she tried, and at least knowing who was with her would stem some of the fear.

"Qadira, from the infirmary."

"The elf," Volinette blurted without tact of any kind. She blushed. "I'm sorry."

"Don't apologize, dear girl. It's true enough. Besides, a certain amount of leeway is always accorded to heroes and heroines."

"Who's a hero?"

"You are." Qadira's voice was light and musical, like the chiming voice of the Sphere. "You should prepare yourself for fame, if not fortune."

"I'm going to kill Baris when I can see again."

"I'm afraid that Apprentice Jendrek had little to do with the rumors. They were mostly perpetuated by the Head Master, Olin Oldwell, and the Chief Archivist."

"Oh, only them, then?" Volinette tried to sound nonchalant, but her voice broke. Her head swam. What had she missed? "How long was I asleep?"

"You've been unconscious for three days. Sleep is somewhat inaccurate. You've been suffering from a prolonged bout of overextension. Your body needed time to recover from that rather astounding piece of spellcraft you performed."

"It wasn't me."

"Yes, so I've been told." Qadira chuckled. "Baris is quite incensed that you won't take credit for your unique set of skills."

"It really isn't me," Volinette protested. "I'm just a…a…," She faltered. *She* didn't even understand it. How could she expect anyone else to understand?

Volinette felt Qadira's weight on the edge of the bed. The elf's fingers moved behind her head, loosening the gauzy bandage. With each layer of bandage she removed, the room got lighter and lighter. Eventually, Volinette could see the single candle that burned on the table beside the bed, and the blonde elf with the amethyst eyes who was looking at her inquisitively.

"Any spots in your vision? Any strange lights or patterns?" Qadira asked, her slender fingers blocking most of the light from Volinette's eyes.

"No."

"Good" The cleric lowered her hand, her eyes scanned Volinette's face before she continued. "It seems that you're over the worst of it. As for the other part of our discussion…my people have a word: *cinzaret*. Literally translated into your tongue, it means conduit…but it's so much more than that. Conduit is a cold word. It's a utilitarian thing.

"Cinzaret is the beauty of the Sphere itself, channeled through a willing soul. But it isn't merely transference. The soul molds the power of the Sphere, imprints upon it, and makes it unique. While it may be true that you're not doing anything *consciously* to influence the powers of the Ethereal Realm that flow through you, I assure you that you *are* doing something.

"You listen to the words the Sphere sings to you and then you make them your own. Magic is subtle and wondrous, tone and inflection matter. You've been chosen to sing for the Quintessential Sphere. Do you think anyone else could sing in exactly the same way, with the same notes and inflection that you do?"

Volinette turned that over in her mind, like tumbling a smooth rock between her hands. She'd always been told that she had to try harder. That to be a good singer, she needed to be more like her sisters or more like her brother. Sing this note just so. Hold this phrase this long. It had never occurred to her that the Quintessential Sphere had chosen her because she was the perfect conduit, no, the perfect *cinzaret* for the living memory that resided in the Ethereal Realm.

"I never thought of it that way," she finally said, a wide smile curving her lips. "I guess I *can* do something right."

"The Eternals work in mysterious ways," Qadira said solemnly. "We mere mortals can only guess at their intentions, but I suspect that their hands are at play in the skills you've come to exhibit." The elf was quiet for a moment, looking so deeply into Volinette's eyes that she started to squirm with discomfort. Qadira laid a hand on top of hers, link-shock dancing between them. Even so, the contact settled Volinette. There was nothing to fear from this woman. She was an emissary of the light. Volinette could feel it. "Just be careful which voices you choose to hear, Volinette. There are those whose intentions can't been seen until light is shown into the darkest crevices of their soul. That goes for beings of this mortal plane, and those beyond."

"I will," Volinette promised, though she doubted that too many beings beyond their plane would be interested in a singer turned Quintessentialist.

Qadira cocked her head to the side, then stood and smoothed down her white frock. "You have a visitor. I'll leave you now, but I'll be back to check on you later."

The elf glided from the room as if she weren't touching the floor. Volinette envied her grace and poise. She wondered if she'd ever be that comfortable in her own skin, or if it was a trait that was part of the elven state of being. Qadira seemed to know exactly what she was meant for and whom she needed to be. Volinette would have killed for a cheat sheet to answer just one of those questions. She sighed. There was time enough for that, she supposed. Her grandfather had always told her that wisdom came unexpected, when you needed it the most. She guessed she'd just have to wait.

The pale green curtain over the cubicle door was brushed aside and Janessa slipped inside. Her long blonde hair was pulled back in a braid. The circles under her eyes were gone, as was the redness. She smiled at Volinette as she entered, making her sharp features much less severe. Janessa was a girl who was prettier when she smiled, Volinette decided, and it was nice to see her doing so. Especially after so much anger and hatred had nearly destroyed the girl.

"How are you feeling?" Janessa asked solicitously, pulling a stool over beside the bed and plopping down on it so hard that the wood creaked.

"Like I got beaten up by a giant," Volinette groaned, then laughed. "But I guess it's better than the alternative, right?"

"Absolutely."

Janessa glanced up at the high slit window in the little cubicle. Her gaze was fixed somewhere beyond the infirmary, probably beyond the edges of Blackbeach. They sat in silence for a long while before she spoke again.

"I wanted to thank you, Volinette. I hope I can do it right. Gratitude isn't something that comes easily to my family. It isn't something we're taught. You gave me a second chance when no one else would. Not even my parents. They were furious when the Head Master brought them in. Disappointed that I would reflect badly on them. That I'd cause problems for them.

"I think that's all I've been to anyone in a long time…a problem. You saw something more than that. Something that I couldn't even see. Something I hadn't seen for a long time. Between that and sitting in that cell, I had a lot of time to think. So I wanted to say thank you."

Volinette stared at the girl. It wasn't that she didn't believe her. Janessa was the picture of sincerity. The earnestness in her voice would take a master stage player to pull off, and frankly, Volinette didn't think Janessa was that talented. It was just the oddness of the admission that set her off balance. Janessa's pale skin took on a deep flush and she looked at her feet.

"Please, say something. You don't have to accept my apology, but say anything."

"You're welcome? That sounds so pompous and ungracious." Volinette sighed. "Can't we just be friends? Or try it? See how it goes?"

When Janessa looked up, Volinette saw the sparkle of tears in her eyes.

"You'd want to be friends? After everything I've put you through?"

Volinette smiled.

"Second chances, right? Besides, it wasn't *entirely* your fault. You did some pretty awful things, don't get me wrong, but you were mourning, and grief does strange things to people." Volinette paused, not sure if she wanted to say the rest of what was running through her head. She decided to go on with it. If they were going to be friends, Janessa needed to hear everything. There wasn't any point in trying to spare her feelings or coddle her. "I'm sorry about Tenika. I really am…but there wasn't anything I could do to save her. You're right when you say that I thought of myself first…but that was just the way things played out. There wasn't anything I could do."

Tears welled in Janessa's eyes and slipped silently down her cheeks. She brushed them away with the back of her hands and nodded.

"I know. I was so angry with myself for not being there for her. For not being able to protect her. It was easier to put it on you than to deal with the fact that I failed her. We'd practiced it for so long. We *needed* to get in. We lost sight of everything else."

"Well," Volinette said, blustering through the discomfort of the moment. "From now on, you can talk to me about the things that make you feel bad. So there's that."

Janessa smiled. "I'd like that."

There was a crash from the hallway outside the cubicle. It sounded like someone had taken an entire tray of metal pans and shoved them to the floor. There was a muted argument, then the curtain was shoved aside as Baris burst into the room. He looked from Volinette to Janessa and back again.

"You're awake!"

"I am. Who did you knock over to get in here?" Volinette asked wryly.

"Just an orderly…and he shouldn't have been skulking about behind the corner where I couldn't see him. How are you feeling?"

"Getting better by the minute," Volinette replied, giving Janessa a little smile. Baris looked at the girl and quickly looked away, busying himself with finding threads out of place at the foot of Volinette's blanket.

"Don't tell me that you two are still at each other's throats?" Volinette asked him when he finally looked up.

Baris shifted from one foot to the other and then looked skyward, as if somehow the Eternals could help him. Finding no rescue there, he looked at his shoes and mumbled something.

"What?" Volinette asked, and watched as the color crept off the young man's cheeks and raced to the tips of his ears.

"I said," he grunted, "that she's alright."

"Baris has been very dutiful to you, Volinette," Janessa said with an impish grin. "He's come to see me every day to make sure that I knew how you were doing and if there were any changes."

Janessa winked at her, and Volinette knew that her condition wasn't the only reason Baris had been going to see the tall, pretty blonde. Volinette grinned back. She wouldn't have bet all the money in Dragonfell that Baris would find himself infatuated with Janessa Navita. She shook her head and laughed. The Eternals moved in mysterious ways, indeed.

"What are you laughing at?" Baris demanded.

"Nothing. It's just funny how things work out in the end."

Sudden silence descended over the room as the curtain was parted yet again and a lanky figure with dishwater brown hair stepped into the room. The temperature seemed to drop by ten degrees, and a shudder went up Volinette's spine.

Adamon was dressed in a simple brown tunic and breeches, his black traveling cloak cascading down his back like a shroud. The wide leather belt on which his hand cannon hung was slung low over his hip, laden with the weight of the weapon and its accessories. His gazed pierced each of them in turn, lingering longest on Volinette, before he addressed them all as one.

"I'm glad the three of you are together. It saves me the time of tracking you down individually. There are charges against you to be answered for. Theft." He eyed Janessa. "Unlawful entrance to private quarters." His gaze slid to Baris, who looked at the floor. "And countermanding the direct orders of a Master." His eyes were on Volinette now. "Among others both numerous and sundry. You will appear before the Head Master tomorrow morning at nine. Do not keep me, or her, waiting."

He quit the room, leaving them foundering in the sea of their own silence. Baris was the first one to break the tableau. Volinette expected no less.

"Well, a 'thanks for helping' wouldn't have been out of place," he groused.

The girls stared at him for a moment, then all three of them dissolved into laughter. No matter how much her muscles hurt, it felt good to laugh. Volinette knew that no matter what happened, no matter what charges were brought against her by the Grand Inquisitor of the

Orders, that as long as she had her friends with her, they'd be able to weather any storm.

"Do you think they'll kick us out?" Janessa asked.

Volinette thought about it. They'd managed to help the Masters defeat the menace of hundreds of demons swarming around the Academy grounds. They'd closed the portal to the Deep Void, and they'd returned (albeit in somewhat used condition) the Transcendental Prism. How much more could they want?

"No," Volinette answered at length. "I don't think so. I imagine that we'll have a lot of explaining to do, but Maera is nothing if not fair. She was there. She saw how we contributed to the battle with her own eyes.

"Adamon is powerful and he has a right to be angry about how things happened, but he's not a monster either. It'll work out in the end. Things usually do."

"Besides," Baris quipped, glancing sidelong at Volinette. "Maybe it's time for us to get our second chances."

Chapter Twenty-Six

Sunlight streamed into the courtyard from the east, illuminating motes of dust kicked up by the stonemasons who were working to repair the fountain. All around the Academy grounds, craftsmen scurried to and fro, often assisted by Quintessentialists who were recovering from wounds or had no other duties to attend to. Classes had been suspended until the repairs were complete, and knots of students were gathered under the trees. There was a fair amount of pointing and whispering as the trio passed, but Volinette, Baris, and Janessa kept their heads high, their eyes forward, and just kept walking.

Baris let out a low whistle as they approached the Great Tower of High Magic. Volinette followed his gaze and couldn't help but to let out a small sigh. Some Masters were working to repair the damage the arch demon had done to the tower, but it was a slow process to mend the magically infused obsidian that gave the tower its strength.

"That hole looks a lot bigger now than it did then," Volinette said quietly. "Did we really defeat something that came through there?"

"We? No," Janessa said, shaking her head. "You? Yes, absolutely. If I'd known what you were capable of from the beginning, I'd never have even thought about messing with you."

Volinette glanced at her, narrowing her eyes in mock anger. "Guess you better watch where you're stepping then, huh?"

Janessa nodded sagely. "Yes. Definitely." She rummaged around in the pocket of her tunic. "Oh! Before we go inside, I have something for you."

A moment's wariness ran through Volinette, but she quashed it. Janessa hadn't given her any reason whatsoever to doubt the profound change that had reshaped the girl. Janessa took a fine silver chain out of her pocket. Hanging from it was the knotted twist of hair, the ring that Janessa had made for the Rite of Fealty. Janessa opened the chain and nodded at Volinette. Volinette leaned forward, allowing Janessa to put the chain around her neck. Once it was on, she traced its line with a fingertip and raised one eyebrow at Janessa.

"I wanted you to have it," Janessa explained. "It meant a lot to me that you trusted me without it…and I thought it would be a good reminder."

Volinette folded her new friend in a hug. "Thank you," she whispered in Janessa's ear.

Baris scuffed the cobblestones with the tip of his boot. "Oh, *brother!*" he groaned.

"Quiet, you," Volinette snapped at him. "You're just mad you won't get to use it to manipulate a kiss from Janessa."

His mouth worked silently, unable to form a retort of any kind. The girls laughed and resumed their way toward the tower. Baris caught up to them a moment later, still muttering under his breath about how cruel, evil, and unfair the female mind was.

The entrance hall was being put in order. Many of the displays and artworks had been replaced or repaired. The urns of ancient Quintessentialists had been removed for repair and special attention. Masters and visitors flitted from one corridor to the next, or waited for the brass cage that would lead them to the other parts of the tower. Volinette's eyes landed on the foot of the stairs leading up to the higher levels, and her heart gave a hard thump in her chest. A little gasp escaped her lips.

Baris's hand found hers and he squeezed it. The link-shock that jumped between them was a subtle but important reminder of what they'd been through together. It had been awful and horrifying. There would be nightmares every night about what they'd seen and what they'd done. Still, no matter how it weighed on her, she'd never been alone. That was something to hold onto.

Volinette looked at Janessa and saw the girl's eyes were locked on the stairs descending into the tower. While Volinette and Baris had been fighting for their lives on the third floor, Janessa had been left alone. Left to die. No one to help. No one to share her fear. She reached down and took Janessa's hand in hers, hoping that the link-shock between them would reassure her new friend, and let her know that she'd never be alone again.

Janessa looked over at her and smiled. It felt good. Better than Volinette would have expected. Things finally seemed to be right. No matter what happened today. No matter what sanctions were levied for their willful abuse of the rules, at least she knew that she'd made her dreams come true. She may not be a Master of the Order, but she'd used her magic to save her friends, the Academy, and possibly the city. There was no small sense of satisfaction in that.

They walked, hand in hand, to the brass lift that would take them up to the Head Master's office. They weren't late, but neither were they early. There was no longer any time to dawdle. They had to meet their destiny, and meet it head on. No place to run, even if they'd wanted to.

"Well met, heroes," the page operating the cage said as they approached. He opened the grate and motioned them in with a grandiose gesture.

"We're not heroes," Volinette protested, but the page just winked at her.

"We'll see."

There was no time to argue, as the massive granite counterweight slid past them in its channel, descending into the bowels of the tower and lifting the cage slowly toward Maera's quarters. The trip, which seemed to have taken so long when she first made it, was over in the blink of an eye. A bell chimed, the gate retracted, and the three of them found themselves standing in the antechamber outside the Head Master's office.

All the confidence that Volinette had about the end result of their actions against the arch demon and the portals evaporated as soon as she stepped out of the cage. She watched the cage retreat to the floors below, as if it, too, knew what was about to happen. A shiver went up her spine and she turned to Baris in a panic.

"What if I was wrong?" she blurted. "What if they end up censuring us and kicking us out of the Academy?"

"Fine time to be worrying about that!" Baris quipped with a little grin. She could tell he was nervous too, but he just shrugged. "If it happens, then it happens. Not much we can do about it now."

"Better to face it together than alone," Janessa added.

Janessa was right. No matter what happened, they'd be together. Volinette swallowed her fear, smoothed down her tunic with shaking hands, and walked toward the tapestry that separated Maera's office from the antechamber.

The Head Master was there, behind her desk. Olin and Adamon stood to one side. Fulgent Casto and a Quintessentialist Volinette had never met stood on the other. There was enough magical power in the room to level a fair portion of the city, yet Volinette knew in the back of her mind that it had been her power that ultimately saved them all. It wasn't an arrogant knowledge, just an understanding of fact.

"Thank you for joining us this morning," Maera said, standing. Her ornate cloak had been cleaned, but was still tattered around the edges from the damage it had received during the battle. She hadn't had time to have it mended yet, Volinette thought. Or she wanted to keep it as a souvenir.

"As if we had a choice," Baris whispered loud enough so that only Volinette and Janessa could hear. Janessa giggled, but quickly hid it behind her hand, concealing it in a cough.

Maera swept out from behind her desk, her robes flowing like a receding sea around her ankles.

"Janessa, Baris, and Volinette," the Head Master said in a tone that was far too serious for Volinette's liking. "You've been brought before this tribunal to answer to the accusations lain against you. Chiefly that you disobeyed the mandate of the Masters charged with your protection and interfered in a situation beyond your training and experience. Would you like to speak on your own behalf?"

Baris opened his mouth before Volinette could stop him. "You bet your a—"

She kicked him, hard, in the shin and he clamped his mouth closed over the rest of his sentence. Volinette glanced at Janessa, seeking unspoken permission to speak for the group and receiving it by way of an almost imperceptible nod.

"Head Master, none of us dispute the validity of the charges. Grand Inquisitor Vendur was kind enough to enlighten us as to the number and variety of the complaints against us. He's right. We disobeyed a direct order, we took things without permission, and we interfered in a situation beyond our training and experience.

"None of that is in question, but I feel I would be remiss if I didn't point out several facts that may have escaped the notice of the Grand Inquisitor, or at least weren't given the weight that they should be given.

"We disobeyed a direct order to stay inside the admin building with the other refugees during the crisis. That's true. However, staying inside with the others meant that a fellow student and friend would have been left to die in the dungeon below the tower. Isn't the mandate of the Order of Ivory Flame to protect the Imperium and *all* its people? What kind of lesson would we have learnt if we had left one of our own to die, caged like an animal?"

Maera nodded and rolled her hand. Volinette continued.

"We also took things without permission. The Seer's Cube we took from Master Vendur's office. Although we didn't have permission, the cube was essential for our survival, and it allowed us to help rescue the other students who were trapped on the third floor with us. It was also instrumental in helping us to rescue Janessa. We took it, but that was the only thing we took, and we took it without entering his office."

"Aren't you forgetting something?" Adamon asked, his voice cool. Volinette glanced at him. He was fingering the ring of keys hanging from a lanyard on his belt. She felt herself flush, but nodded.

"I never said mistakes weren't made." She shrugged. "Time was of the essence and we needed to get Janessa out of the dungeon. I'm sorry we went into your office for the keys, Master Vendur. It was necessary."

"Was it also necessary to shatter my door? And scatter the contents of my desk all over the floor?"

Volinette shot a sharp look at Baris, who found it a good time to inspect the toes of his boots for any scuffs or scrapes. Volinette planned to give him a good scuffing of her own as soon as they were alone.

"No, probably not. For that, we apologize. Don't we, Baris?"

"Uh, yes," the boy mumbled. "Sorry about that."

"And your interference in the battle against the arch demon?" Maera asked, her voice no warmer than Adamon's had been.

"With all due respect, Head Master, I felt that I had an advantage and I exploited that advantage before anyone else could die. I think we can all agree that what happened to Nixi, Halsie, and Syble shouldn't happen to anyone. They were perverted by magic they didn't understand, and they paid for it in the worst way imaginable. It was my duty, to the Order, to the Imperium, and to myself, to make sure that no one else was hurt or killed by what they unleashed."

There was a long silence, which was finally broken by the rumbling laughter of the Quintessentialist standing off to Maera's left. His flowing brown hair and beard were shot with gray, but his hazel eyes were lively and full. He folded his arms across his chest and looked down at the Head Master with a smile.

"What's so funny, Master Indra?"

"Say what you want about their methods, Maera, but they got the job done when the rest of you couldn't. I remember a time not so long ago when you were standing in this very office between Tanglar and myself, explaining to Head Master Jotun why we shouldn't be censured and thrown out on our collective ears."

The Head Master sighed, running her hands through her silver hair. She glanced at the trio of students, her amber eyes flashing. She looked to Olin, who shrugged. Fulgent Casto spread his palms as if he were helpless against the logic that had been presented. Finally, she looked at Adamon.

"What is your recommendation, Grand Inquisitor?"

Volinette had never been subjected to such intense scrutiny in her life. The look that Adamon turned on her felt as if it had burrowed into the essence of her soul. Janessa and Baris each had a turn under that icy regard and fidgeted in much the same way Volinette had. They waited, and waited, and waited.

"I think, Head Master, that in this case, the ends were justification for the means. Since no *irreparable* harm was done during their foolhardy quest, and the Prism has been returned to its rightful place, I would say that their misadventures be considered time served."

"Why, Adamon," Faxon Indra said in a sly drawl. "I didn't know you had a heart."

"Everyone deserves a second chance, Faxon."

Volinette jerked upright as if she'd been shocked. She stared at the Grand Inquisitor, and he stared back.

"Just remember," Adamon said as he swept toward Maera's antechamber. "There are very few things that escape the notice of the Inquisitors. Come along, Olin."

Adamon disappeared and Olin followed with a sigh. He paused as he passed the trio. "Good job, you three. I look forward to seeing what you can do when you're actually working at it." Then he followed Adamon from the room.

Fulgent Casto looked at the trio, then to the Head Master. "I trust I'll have my students back when repairs have been completed?"

"All but one of them, I'm afraid," Maera replied.

Volinette's blood went cold. Were they still planning to punish Janessa for the theft of the Prism? Why hadn't Adamon stayed?

Faxon stepped forward, casting an appraising eye on Baris, who involuntarily took a step back, away from the towering Quintessentialist.

"Olin tells me that he thinks you'd make a good Inquisitor," Faxon said. "What do you think, young

Baris? Want to learn the mysteries of the realms and become a defender of what's good and pure?"

Maera snorted and Faxon shot her a sideways glance. "Alright, she's probably right. Forget good and pure. Want to learn to hunt down rogue mages and put them in their place?"

"Really?" Baris bounced from one foot to the other. "Who's going to train me?"

Faxon feigned shock. "I am, you foolish boy."

"You?"

"Of course." Faxon grinned. "Who do you think taught Adamon everything he knows?"

Faxon declared that he wanted to return to King's Reach, but there was time enough for a quick goodbye. Baris promised Volinette and Janessa that he'd be back as soon and as often as his training would allow. As they made their way through the curtain, Baris was peppering Faxon with questions as fast as he could think of them. Their conversation was lost beyond the partition.

"So I get these two back?" Fulgent asked, his tone dubious.

"It would appear that way," Maera said, ignoring the sigh of long suffering that Fulgent heaved in reply.

"Very well," the old Master said. "Return to class on Monday morning. We have much to discuss." He offered his arm to Janessa. "Come along, dear girl. I believe the Head Master has some words for Volinette's ears alone."

Janessa glanced at her, as if for permission, and Volinette nodded with a smile. Whatever was to come next, she could handle it. The past few days had been a study in treachery, death, and destruction. She had little to fear from Maera or the other Quintessentialists who lived and worked around the Academy. As Fulgent and Janessa left the Head Master's chambers, Maera walked out on the balcony, beckoning for Volinette to follow.

They looked out over the grounds. From above, the workers looked like industrious ants, scurrying back and forth to complete their varied assignments. It wouldn't take long for them to return the Academy of Arcane Arts and Sciences to the condition it deserved, and that made Volinette smile.

"How do you feel?" the Head Master asked, her eyes never leaving the bustle below.

"I'm good," Volinette said. "For the first time, it feels like I belong somewhere."

Maera nodded. "There's no other place you *could* belong, but here, Volinette. You are a uniquely skilled and talented individual. Master Jotun believes you will go far in the Academy."

"What do you think?" Volinette asked earnestly. The Head Master's opinion meant more to her than probably anyone else's that she'd ever met.

"I think you'll excel at anything you put your mind to. If your interest is in academics, you'll go far within these walls."

Volinette thought that over. She'd come a long way in just a few short weeks. "I'd like that. I think I'd like to spend some time with Master Jotun in the library. I'm sure he has amazing stories to tell."

"I'm sure you're right," Maera said with a tolerant smile.

Volinette took the lift down from the Head Master's office. She walked across the entrance hall and out through the wide doors that had seemed so imposing when she'd arrived. Her feet carried her into the sandstone courtyard beyond, where her journey had begun.

Turning in a slow circle, she took in the Academy grounds, the blue sky, and the city beyond. A happy sigh escaped her lips.

Her life had just begun.

ACKNOWLEDGEMENTS

Thank you to every single reader and fan who has made the Solendrea stories a success. Your interest and support means more to me than you will ever know. From the bottom of my heart, thank you.

Special thanks to my alpha readers for helping to keep me on the right path. Thank you Barbara, Jr., and Maisha.

Thanks to those who volunteered their time to beta read: Laura, Amy, Eric, Faith, and Ann.

Thanks to my editor, Amber Bungo, for all her hard work.

ABOUT THE AUTHOR

Martin F. Hengst resides in South Central Pennsylvania with his wife and two children.

An avid reader since childhood, he attributes his love for fantasy and science fiction to his father. Martin's passion is creating intricate stories with intimate details set in worlds that exist only in his readers' dreams.

For news and information on upcoming titles and promotional events, please visit:

http://martinfhengst.com

The author can be reached via email at:

mfh@martinfhengst.com

If you enjoyed this book, please take a moment to review it favorably on Goodreads, Amazon, or other social media sites you may frequent. Your favorable review is the best compliment an author can receive.